The Best Woman
Gracie Island Book Two
Leigh Fenty

Chapter One

"We have our own set of rules."

J asper was sitting on a two-by-four, with his feet on another, while pounding a nail into the supporting beam for the roof. With some help from Lewis and the guys in the volunteer fire department, the new house was almost completely framed. They'd had a long wet winter, but now that spring was almost there, it was coming together.

He took the day off so he could get some work done, since he'd be on duty tonight. St. Patrick's Day on the island could be crazy. Any holiday that encouraged drinking was popular on Gracie Island. Jasper would be in uniform, without his gun, making his presence known, but not be intimidating. It was an easy duty. He'd hang out with his friends, play some music, and be the only one celebrating without drinking. He'd done it every year since he'd become a deputy sheriff.

The chief would be the one dealing with the aftermath. Tomorrow, when half the town was hungover, is when the trouble would start.

Though trouble on Gracie Island usually consisted of drunk and disorderly, reckless driving, minor disputes, and trivial acts of revenge by jealous partners. There had only been two murders on Gracie Island. One fifty years ago, and one ten months ago.

Jasper rubbed his shoulder. It hurt occasionally when the weather was bad, or when he overdid, such as pounding nails for a couple of hours. But it was okay. It reminded him of last summer, which wasn't all bad. Along with dealing with his first murder case, he met Poppie.

When Jasper saw Lewis' truck pull into the driveway, he stopped hammering. He wasn't expecting his friend to show up today.

The truck stopped, and the door opened, but Lewis didn't get out. Instead, Lewis' petite, blonde sister stepped out of the vehicle and gave Jasper a smile and a wave.

Speak of the devil. Jasper waved back. "What the hell are you doing here?"

Poppie put her hands on her hips. "What kind of greeting is that?"

"Just answer the question."

Poppie closed the truck door and took a few steps toward the framed house. "Are you going to come down from there and give me a proper welcome? Or should I go find my brother? He'll probably be glad to see me."

"You borrowed Lewis' truck without telling him?"

Poppie shrugged. "He was busy at the marina. He'll never know it was missing. So, I'll ask again. Are you coming down from there?"

Jasper tossed the hammer onto a folded tarp on the plywood flooring, then slipped down between parallel two-by-fours After hanging from one for a moment, he dropped the two feet to the ground, then made his way through the wooden framework, and went out the front door.

She smiled. "You don't believe in ladders?"

"Only to go up." He wiped his hands on his pants as he approached, then stopped a foot in front of her. "You're a week early." She held her arms out, and he gave her a quick hug, then stepped back and grinned. "It's really good to see you."

"You too, Deputy Goodspeed." She nodded toward his right shoulder. "You must be fully recovered."

"Good as new, except when it rains."

"Which is how many days a year?"

"Why didn't you tell me you were coming?"

"And miss that look on your face?"

"What look is that?"

She studied his face for a moment. "Surprise. Maybe even shock. But I do believe you're genuinely happy to see me."

He put a hand on her cheek. "You could be right."

She looked past him at the house. "Look what you've done."

He glanced at the house. "I had some help."

"Will you give me a tour?"

"Yeah. Come on." She followed him to the four-by-four platform in front of the door. "This is the porch."

She looked at the small space. "You might consider making it bigger. At least big enough for a couple of chairs."

"It'll be plenty big. In fact, it's going to wrap around the house. So you can put your chair anywhere you want to."

"I get my own chair?"

"You can have a chair, a chaise, anything you want." He went through the doorway and she stepped in after him. "This is the foyer."

"Whoa, aren't you fancy? A foyer? Very impressive."

He moved to a big open space with the rock fireplace that had survived the fire last summer on one end. "Living room." He pointed to the front of the room. "A row of floor to ceiling windows there. They'll catch the afternoon sun and warm the place up." He turned. "And French doors here opening to the back porch. The morning sun will come through them."

"I love it. Lots of light. Natural solar power when the sun is shining. Perfect."

"Around here, you need to let in as much light as you can." He headed for a framed in arch and went through it. "This is the kitchen. My mom insisted on designing it. It'll be the best equipped kitchen that never gets used on the island."

"You'll use it someday."

"More windows here, and a pantry and mud room."

"Well, that'll certainly get used."

He left the kitchen and went through another door frame. "This is the guest bedroom."

"Hold on. *Guest* bedroom? Does this mean you've changed your stance on visitors?"

"Anything's possible. Actually, my mom insisted on that too." He went to a wall. "Another set of doors here going to the porch, which will be covered and protected on three sides, making it enjoyable most of the year."

"Very nice."

He left that room, crossed through the living room, and entered another larger room. "This is the master bedroom. Has its own bath with a custom shower I can't wait to use. And doors to the porch, with windows on the wall facing the ocean. I can watch the sunrise from bed if I should so desire."

"Sounds wonderful. I love it, Jasper. I'm so happy for you."

"It's going to be great."

She looked at the trailer visible through the framework of the house. "And in the meantime, you're still in the trailer?"

"Yeah. I'll be glad to move out of that." He headed for the front door and stepped through it to the gravel in front of the house. "It was a long, cold, noisy winter."

She walked past him a few feet and looked back at the house. "So you've had some help with the building?"

"Yes. Just not today. Everyone's resting up for tonight."

"Tonight?"

"St. Patrick's Day." He pointed at her. "And Poppie Jensen's day. Happy birthday."

"You remembered."

"Only because it happens to be on St. Patrick's Day. It if wasn't I'm not sure I would've."

"Hmm. Well, I remember yours. October fifteenth. Which means..." She lowered her voice. "You've turned thirty."

He smiled. "Now I feel like a jerk. But thirty's not too bad. You'll get there in a few years."

"Don't remind me." She took his arm. "Will you buy me a 'not thirty yet,' birthday lunch?"

"Of course. Just let me change my shirt." Poppie followed him to the trailer. "Um, you'll need to wait outside. It's pretty scary in there."

Poppie laughed. "Fine. Are Penny and Pepper inside? Can I see them?"

"Penny is. Pepper's been staying with my mom. He was having trouble navigating through the small space. He's a little physically challenged since the fire."

"I'm sorry."

"He's fine. He's a trooper. Just happier at my mom's." He opened the door and Penny stuck her head out. Poppie squealed and Jasper picked the dog up.

"Let me see that sweet puppy."

Jasper handed Penny to her. "Don't slobber all over her. I just gave her a bath."

Poppie kissed the tiny chihuahua on the nose. "Kisses aren't slobbering."

"Depends on who's doing the kissing." He went inside the trailer. "I'll be right out."

When Jasper came out a few minutes later, Poppie looked at his shirt. "I thought you were changing your shirt."

"I was. I did." He glanced at the blue plaid cotton shirt under his jacket.

"It's identical to the one you had on."

"No it's not. This one... Why do you care?"

"I don't. Just curious."

"I like blue."

"Okay."

After putting Penny inside the trailer, they both headed for their respective vehicles and Jasper stopped and frowned at Poppie. "Are we taking both trucks?"

Poppie laughed. "No. I just wanted to mess with you. *You* may drive. Since you're the man and all."

"Wow. You can drive if you want."

"No. I wouldn't want to upset the natural order of things. I'm pretty sure the first cave woman never got a chance to drive."

"Cave woman?"

"You know what I mean." She opened the passenger door of the Jeep and got in.

Jasper got in beside her. "You actually drove the Jeep, sort of, last summer."

"That's true. But only because you were...incapacitated."

He started the engine. "You were going to say useless."

Jasper drove them to The Sailor's Loft, which had gotten a new coat of light blue paint since last summer, and they parked across the street. They got out and crossed over, then Jasper rang the bell on the mast three times before heading for the door.

Poppie glanced at him. "Three times?"

"I figured since I was with Roger when he went overboard, I should at least honor his memory. Even if he wasn't a very nice person."

"You are very sweet."

He opened the door for her.

She smiled. "Thank you, sir."

They went into the nearly empty dining room and found Jasper's Aunt Peg and the bartender, Deidre, putting up green streamers and St. Patrick's Day decorations. The women stopped what they were doing and went to greet Poppie.

Peg gave her a hug. "Welcome back. So good to see you."

Deidre hugged her next. "Lewis said you weren't coming until next week."

"Don't tell him I said so, but my brother's getting a little nervous about the wedding. So I thought I'd come early for moral support." She nudged Jasper. "Besides, I didn't want to give this guy a chance to skip town before I got here."

Jasper put a hand on his chest. "I'd never run out on Lewis' big day. Even though he didn't choose me to be his best man."

Poppie smiled. "Family first."

Peg put a hand on Jasper's arm. "Are you here to eat?"

"Yes, ma'am."

She started walking, bringing Jasper with her. "Come on then. I'll sit you at the best table in the house." She led them to a table by a big window with a view of the ocean breaking on the rocky shore. They sat, and she asked, "Coffee?"

"You have to ask?"

Peg looked at Poppie. "You too, dear?"

"I'll have an iced tea please. And a water."

Jasper raised a finger. "Water here, too."

"Okay. I'll be right back. And I'll tell your mother you're here."

When she left, Jasper said, "Great. You don't mind another person fawning over you, I hope."

"Not at all. They're very sweet."

Jasper unfolded his napkin and put it on his lap. "So, did you get an extra week off work?"

"Actually, I left my job."

"Willingly?"

"Yes. I didn't get fired. I put in my notice the end of last month."

"I thought it was your dream job."

She sighed. "I thought so too. But it wasn't what I thought it was."

"So, what are you going to do now?"

"I'll find something."

Jasper glanced toward the bar where Deidre was sticking green shamrocks to the mirror behind it. "Do you know how to tend bar?"

"No. Why?"

"Deidre's leaving us."

"Really? What's she going to do?"

"Believe it or not, she's leaving town. She met someone online. Started going to see him. And is leaving us for him."

"Well, good for her. I mean, if she's happy, right?"

"Yeah. So her job's open."

"Two problems with that. I don't know how to tend bar. And I'd have to move here."

"I don't see either of those things as a problem. I can teach you to pour drinks. I manned the bar for two years before I left for...sheriff school."

"I thought you went to Augusta when you were twenty."

"I did."

"So, you were tending bar when you were eighteen?"

Jasper shrugged. "This is Gracie Island. We have our own set of rules. Besides, I wasn't drinking the alcohol. I was just serving it."

"You didn't drink at all before you were twenty-one?"

"I didn't say that. I just didn't drink in the family-owned restaurant. Aside from your lack of bartending skills, I'm sure Lewis would love to have you in town."

She studied him for a moment. "Only Lewis?"

Jasper smiled. "I guess I wouldn't mind it too much either."

Peg returned with their drinks on a tray and set them on the table. "Do you need some time? Or are you ready to order?"

Jasper looked at Poppie.

She smiled. "What's good?"

"We have some fresh salmon."

"Mmm. Sounds good."

"How do you want it?"

"Surprise me. Whatever you think is best."

"Baked potato and steamed vegetables?"

"Perfect."

Peg turned to Jasper. "You too, honey?"

"How's the shrimp?"

"Just came in this morning."

"How about shrimp scampi? Extra garlic."

"Coming right up. Soup? Salad?

Jasper took a drink of coffee. "Clam chowder here."

Poppie glanced at him, then smiled at Peg. "Salad please. No dressing."

Peg left and Poppie returned her attention to Jasper. "Not a fan of salmon?"

"I used to be. But I've been force-fed it for so long, I can't stand it now. But they never stop trying."

"You could tell them you don't like it anymore."

He shook his head. "They'd take that as a challenge. 'Well, you haven't tried it this way. Here, Son, try it.'"

Poppie laughed. "Force-fed salmon. What a tragedy." She glanced around the room. "Gearing up for St. Paddy's, huh?"

"Yeah. It's a pretty big deal here. Any holiday that involves drinking goes over big."

"Are you going to be drinking tonight?"

"No. I'm actually on duty tonight."

"So, you're going to miss out on all the fun?"

"I'll be here. But I'll be in uniform and not drinking."

"Awe. That's no fun."

He shrugged. "It's fine. I haven't been drinking much lately. And I haven't gotten drunk for a while."

She tilted her head. "Not even on the fifth?"

"Not since November. I went to The Rusty Pelican in December—the two-year anniversary—and I left after one drink. I guess I figured out I don't need to forget anymore. I just want to remember the good times. Of which there were a lot."

Poppie smiled and reached for his hand. "I'm so happy to hear that. I'm glad you were able to turn that corner."

He nodded, then pulled his hand away and put it on his lap when he saw his mother approaching.

Kat pulled up a chair and sat down. She patted Poppie's hand. "So glad to see you."

"It's good to be back."

"Are you excited about the wedding?"

"Yes. Can't wait. Actually, I can't believe my brother's getting married. He had his first date with Sarah when I was here last. And now...they're getting married."

Kat smiled. "Well, I guess when you know, you know." She looked at Jasper. "Did Peg get your order?"

"Yes."

"And you're ready for tonight?"

"Ready as I'll ever be. The token show of force to keep the hooligans in line."

She smiled at Poppie. "It gets pretty crazy, but nothing Jasper can't handle. You're coming, of course."

"Wouldn't miss it."

Kat stood and kissed Jasper on the cheek before rushing off. Jasper wiped his cheek, then watched his mother until she disappeared into the kitchen.

Poppie laughed. "What?"

"My mom. She's been extra cheerful lately."

"I've never seen her not cheerful."

"No. This is beyond her normal, 'I love everyone, let me help with that,' persona. Something's up."

"Maybe she's in love."

The notion astounded Jasper. "Don't be ridiculous."

"Why? You think she's too old?"

"No."

"Because she's your mother?"

"Of course not. It's just not possible. I know everyone in town. There's no one here—"

"Worthy of her?"

Jasper looked at Poppie. "After the chief, no. It's something else."

"Whatever. But it happens to the best of us."

Jasper took a sip of coffee, then grumbled. "Not possible. She'd tell me."

"Right. Because you'd be so understanding and supportive."

Chapter Two

"This town is so weird."

Lewis leaned on the bathroom door frame and watched Poppie brush her hair. "How much longer is this going to take?"

Poppie looked at him through the mirror and smiled. "Almost ready."

"Who are you trying to impress?"

"Um, seems to me, the last time I was here, you wanted me to look good for the town meeting. I imagine the St. Patrick's Day celebration is even more important."

Lewis sighed. "I'm leaving in five minutes, with or without you." He walked away.

Poppie called after him. "I'll be ready."

She and Lewis had always been close. They were fifteen months apart in age, putting him a year ahead of her in school. Even in high school, when it wasn't cool to be friends with your brother, she preferred his company over anyone else's. And when she had a problem, she'd turn to him.

Now he was getting married, and their relationship would change, But if things went the way she hoped they would with Jasper, maybe, someday, they'd be raising their children together.

Poppie studied her reflection. "Don't get ahead of yourself. You've only been in town a few hours."

She was ready in seven minutes and was putting on her jacket as Lewis opened the front door. She picked up her purse from the table next to the door and followed him to the truck. It had cooled off considerably since the sun went down, and she wished she'd worn a sweater under her jacket. She considered asking Lewis to wait while she went to fetch it, but knew he'd throw a fit if she did.

Lewis opened the door for her, then went around and got in behind the wheel. He glanced at her as he started the engine. "You look presentable."

"Gee, thanks, brother. So do you."

He ran a hand down the front of his shirt. "I look okay, right? I'm being serious."

Poppie put a hand on his arm. "Lewis, you already won the girl. But yes, you look very handsome."

"Thanks. You too."

Poppie buckled her seatbelt. "That's what I was going for."

"You know what I mean."

They arrived at The Sailor's Loft and parked a couple blocks down the street, since the lot was full and cars were parked on both sides of the street. The only other business in town open for the festivities was the Rusty Pelican. It would draw its own crowd, smaller and rowdier. The two bars in town had very different clientele.

She'd only been to the Pelican once on the night she met Jasper. And he only went there once a month to mourn his wife. But on December fifth, that had changed for him and she hoped she was part of the reason for it.

Poppie got out of the truck. It seemed all three hundred residents of Gracie Island were celebrating. "Wow. This has to be everyone in town."

"Pretty much, yeah." They started walking along the raised wooden sidewalk. "Actually, it's probably only half. Everyone under seventy and over twenty-one."

When they got within a block of the restaurant, they started running into groups of people, all happy and most of them with a drink in their hands. There were a lot of green shirts, sparkly paper bowlers, and sequined bowties. Poppie recognized a few people from her brief visit last summer. Lewis, who'd been there for almost seven years, seemed to know most of them.

Poppie leaned in toward Lewis' ear. "So, drinking on the streets is legal around here?"

"If you can see the restaurant, it's all good."

"Okay."

"You're not in Boston anymore."

"How's Jasper going to keep an eye on all these people?"

"Everyone is pretty mellow. No one wants to ruin the festivities."

She looked at the people as they passed them. Mellow wasn't really a word she'd use to describe them. But they did seem to be behaving, at least up to this point. And six-foot-three, Deputy Goodspeed in his uniform, was definitely impressive.

Lewis and Poppie arrived at the Loft and went inside the packed room. The restaurant was closed for the night, and the door between the dining room and the bar area was propped open. Both areas were full of people, sitting at tables, standing in groups, and leaning against the walls.

Again, Poppie had to lean in for Lewis to hear her. "Where's Jasper?"

Lewis glanced around, then pointed at the bar. "Looks like he's helping Deidre."

Poppie looked toward the bar. Jasper was there, along with Deidre and two other men. They were all pouring shots and handing out beers. A sign on the bar stated they were only serving five dollar beers and shots of Irish whiskey. It was so busy, they were keeping a tally on a pad of paper, and the money was going right into their pockets to be sorted out later. They made change as best they could and the rest was considered a tip. Nobody seemed to care one way or the other.

Lewis and Poppie made their way to the bar, then waited at the least crowded end, until Jasper saw them.

After a few moments, he noticed them and nodded as he held up a finger, then finished pouring two drafts. He delivered them to two women with bright green hair, then went to Poppie and Lewis.

"What do you think?"

Poppie leaned over the bar. "This is crazy."

He smiled. "It's only eight. It gets crazier."

"How are you keeping the peace from behind the bar?"

"The guys from the fire department are my eyes and ears. They'll let me know if something comes up." He tapped the bar. "Rum and Coke?"

"The sign says beer and whiskey only."

"Do you want one or not?"

She smiled. "Yes, please."

Lewis yelled over the ruckus. "I'll follow the rules and take a beer."

Jasper got their drinks and a glass of water for himself, then came around the bar as three seats became available. They all sat, putting Poppie in the middle.

Jasper leaned in front of her to talk to Lewis. "Where's Sarah?"

"She'll be here soon. She wanted to wait until right before we go on. She's not a fan of wall to wall people."

Jasper nodded, then turned his attention to Poppie. She smiled at him. "Are you guys playing tonight?"

"About nine-thirty."

"Can't wait. I haven't heard a good sea shanty in months."

Jasper motioned to Deidre as he dug a wad of money out of his pocket, then handed it to her when she came to him.

She took it from him. "You should keep some of this."

He waved her off. "You keep it. Put it toward your moving expenses."

She smiled. "Thanks."

"Can you get that thing I left back there?"

She winked at him. "Sure thing, Deputy."

She opened a cupboard and retrieved a brown paper bag folded over at the top, and handed it to him. He set it in front of Poppie.

"Happy Birthday."

"You got me a present?"

"Of course. It's your birthday."

"You shouldn't have." She unfolded the bag and peered inside, then shook her head. "You *really* shouldn't have." She pulled out a bottle of gin and a sixpack of grapefruit flavored carbonated soda.

Lewis looked at Jasper. "What am I missing?"

Jasper leaned in to Poppie's ear. "For our next game."

"Thank you. Just remember, I get the first question." She returned the items to the bag and asked Deidre to hold on to it for her, then she turned in her seat toward Jasper. "You're very cute."

"I am, aren't I."

Lewis got to his feet. "Okay. Feeling a bit like a third wheel now. I'm going to go mingle."

Jasper waved at him. "See ya." He smiled at Poppie. "Want to get some air?"

"Sure." She took a sip of her drink, then stood.

Jasper nodded toward her glass. "You can bring that with you."

"This town is so weird."

Jasper reached over the bar and grabbed his coat. "Let's go." He slipped it on as they headed through the crowd for the door. At one point, several people got in between them, and when they were clear, he took her hand until they made it to the door.

Before they went outside, he stopped to talk to a stocky man posted at the door. "I'll be on the pier if you need me." The man was taller and heavier than Jasper, which made him someone not to mess with.

Once they got outside, Poppie glanced back at the man. "One of your sets of eyes and ears?"

"Yeah. Not too many guys in town want to mess with Lance."

They continued along the sidewalk toward the waterfront and the crowds slowly disappeared until Jasper and Poppie were alone. They headed down a pier extending fifty feet over the water, passing a couple of boats tied to cleats, and went to the end. It was a cloudless night, and the moon was nearly full.

Poppie looked at the stars. "My goodness. It's beautiful."

"You don't see stars like that in Boston."

"No. You sure don't." She took a sip of her rum and Coke.

"Honestly, we don't often see them here, either."

"It's a present from Mother Nature."

Jasper reached into his pocket. "Speaking of presents, I have another one for you."

"Really?"

"Yeah." He showed her a small seashell in the palm of his hand. "I found this shell when I was ten years old."

"You did?"

He started laughing. "No. I found it this morning on the beach."

She punched him in the shoulder. "Oh my gosh. You're such a brat." She took the shell from his hand. "Just for that, I'm going to keep this forever and pretend it's special."

"You do that." He glanced at her light jacket. "Are you warm enough?"

"Yes. It feels good. It's a bit stuffy inside with all those people."

He took another moment before saying, "I do actually have another gift for you."

She tilted her head. "What now?"

"No, I'm serious. I've been wanting to give this to you for a while."

She took a breath, not knowing quite what to expect. "Okay."

He turned toward her and then leaned in, hesitated a moment, then kissed her lightly.

She touched her lips. "I believe that's the best birthday present I've ever gotten."

He took her hands. "Wait, I can improve on that." He leaned in again, but stopped when he heard someone calling his name.

They both looked toward the beginning of the pier and saw Lewis jogging toward them. He took a moment to catch his breath before saying, "The Murphy brothers."

Jasper checked his watch. "Already? It's not even nine."

"They're threatening to beat the hell out of each other."

"Dammit." He looked at Poppie. "I need to take care of this. I'll see you back at the bar." He then looked at Lewis. "Can you take her inside?"

Lewis nodded and gave him a thumbs up.

Poppie watched Jasper run down the pier, then turned toward Lewis. "The Murphy brothers?"

"Doyle and Reece. They own the Blue Dolphin fishing boat. They work together every day and get along fine. But every holiday, they get drunk and all the little daily annoyances come to the surface."

"Jasper's going to stop them?"

"Yeah. It's not the first time. He'll be fine." He looked closely at Poppie. "Did I interrupt something here?"

Poppie gave him a small smile. "He was giving me another birthday present."

"Hmm. I don't think I want to know what that means." He took her arm. "Come on. We might be able to catch the action."

"So drunk holidays include what? New Years, St. Patrick's Day..."

"Fourth of July. Halloween."

"Halloween?"

"Sure. What else are we going to do on Halloween?"

She shook her head. "Well, I hope you at least wear costumes while getting drunk."

"Of course. It's Halloween."

They arrived in front of the restaurant to a crowd of people, and Lewis pushed through them and cleared a path for Poppie. Jasper was in the middle with his arms spread out, and his hands on the broad chests of Doyle and Reece Murphy. They were big guys, identical in appearance, and both of them outweighed Jasper by quite a bit.

"Okay guys. Let's take a breath." The two men struggled to get past Jasper. "I mean it. I'll throw both your asses in the same jail cell. Then I'll leave you there to tear each other apart. Won't really care if you do at that point."

The men seemed to relax and took a step back from Jasper's hands. "Okay. Are we done now?" The men nodded, and Jasper lowered his arms.

Doyle suddenly rushed past Jasper to get to Reece. As he threw a punch, Jasper stepped in to intervene and Doyle's fist landed on Jasper's left eye.

Jasper dropped to one knee and Doyle stepped away from his brother and put a hand on Jasper's back. "I'm sorry, man. I didn't mean to hit you."

Jasper got to his feet. "I know." He put a hand over his eye. "Now are we done?"

Both men nodded.

"Get out of here and stay away from each other."

The men left in two different directions, and Lewis and Poppie went to Jasper.

She put her hand on his wrist. "Let me see."

He lowered his hand. There was a welt on his cheekbone and his eye was already starting to bruise.

"Oh my. He got you good."

Lewis took a close look. "Yeah. You're going to have a shiner tomorrow."

Sarah suddenly appeared at Lewis' side. "No. Not for the wedding."

Jasper frowned at her. "It should be gone by the twenty-sixth. And I'm fine, by the way."

She patted his arm. "Sorry. I just want everything to be perfect. You know?"

Jasper nodded, and Lewis took Sarah's hand. "We'll see you inside."

Poppie cocked her head. "*One* day. I'm here *one day* and you're injured again."

Jasper grinned. "I told you. You're a jinx. I've been injury free for ten months."

She took his right arm. "Come on, let's get some ice for your eye."

He pulled his arm away and moved to her other side. "Just in case."

"You said your shoulder was fine."

"It has been. But now that *you're* here—"

They made their way through the crowd to the bar, and word of what happened seemed to beat them there. Two men stood and offered their seats. As Jasper and Poppie sat, Deidre handed him a small bag filled with ice, then set a shot in front of him.

He put the ice on his eye, then looked at the shot. "I'm still on duty."

Deidre pushed it closer. "Just drink it."

He picked it up and drank it, then handed her the glass and she went to tend to her customers.

Poppie lowered his hand to check his eye again. "Ouch. Does it hurt?"

"Not as much as a dislocated shoulder." He put the ice back on his eye.

"So, is Doyle or Reece, whichever one hit you, in trouble?"

"No. It was an accident."

"Still."

Jasper shook his head. "What good would it do?"

Lewis came up behind them and put a hand on Jasper's shoulder. "We're supposed to go on in a few minutes. You up for it?"

"Sure. I'm good."

"Take a few more minutes. We'll start in fifteen."

Jasper nodded, and Lewis walked away.

Poppie put a hand on Jasper's arm and leaned in to his ear. "So, about that present?"

He smiled. "I owe you one."

Chapter Three

"Stand down, Mellie."

Jasper and the band played mainly Irish folk songs in honor of the holiday, and were on stage for an hour and a half, which was longer than their usual sixty minutes. But the crowd was receptive, and as long as they were listening to the band, they weren't getting into trouble somewhere else.

Jasper's voice was better than Poppie remembered. He was relaxed and charming, and the crowd loved him. *That smile. How could I not fall in love with that smile?*

When they finished, Jasper went to the bar to get some water, then moved down to Poppie, who was still where he left her at the end of the bar.

She smiled and clapped her hands. "That was so good. I didn't want it to stop."

Jasper put the cold glass on his cheek below his eye, which was now a deep shade of blue. Poppie leaned in and looked closely at it.

"That must really hurt."

He shrugged. "It's fine."

"Right, your standard answer. 'I'm fine. It's just a dislocated shoulder. Or a broken cheekbone.'"

"My cheekbone isn't broken." He drank some of the water. "I need to make the rounds. Do you want to take a drive?"

"Definitely." She glanced around the room. "Just let me tell Lewis."

"He's on the front porch. We'll tell him on the way out." He helped her into her coat, then took her hand and led her through the crowd. Once they got outside, he let go of it as they approached Lewis and Sarah.

Sarah put her hand on Jasper's arm. "I'm really sorry about before." She touched his cheek. "I didn't mean to be inconsiderate."

"You're getting married in a week. You're allowed to be a little...self-absorbed." He looked at Lewis. "I'm going to take a drive around, and Poppie's coming with me. I'll drop her off at home in a bit."

"Okay. Sounds good." Lewis glanced at Poppie. "I'll see you at home."

Jasper and Poppie went down the steps, then headed for the Jeep, which was parked a block down the street. She took Jasper's arm. "That's brother for, 'I'll be waiting up for you.'"

Jasper laughed. "I figured."

They arrived at the Jeep and he opened the door for her. When she got in, he smiled at her. "I know. You don't like chivalry. But I can't help it. I was raised by my mother."

"You may be chivalrous all you want. I don't mind."

"Hmm. Really?"

"Yes. I'm beginning to like it, actually."

"Being coddled?"

"Being respected."

He walked around the vehicle and got in behind the wheel. "We need to make a couple of runs around the town to let people know I'm still watching." He started to turn the ignition, then stopped and turned in his seat toward Poppie. "I almost forgot. I owe you that birthday gift."

She smiled. "Right. I've been waiting all night."

He leaned in and kissed her. As he put his hand on her face and kissed her again, there was a knock on his window. "God dammit." He turned to see who it was.

The man who'd been watching the door all night stepped back and gave him a small wave.

Jasper rolled down his window. "What's up, Lance?"

"A couple of guys reported a truck in the ditch near Harper's Fork."

"Thanks. I'll go check it out."

Lance nodded. "I'll keep an eye out here."

"If you need me, call dispatch." Jasper checked his watch. "Stan's off tonight. You'll get the chief."

"Okay."

Jasper rolled his window up and started the Jeep, then glanced at Poppie. "Sorry."

"No problem. Duty calls."

"Do you want to stay here?"

"No. I want to come with you."

They drove out of town, past two streets of houses, then into a grassy area interspersed with stands of trees. There were still houses, but they were farther apart and set back from the road. At night, only the lights in the windows gave them away. As they approached the fork, Jasper slowed down and turned on his mounted spotlight. There was no sign of a truck, so they drove down the road toward the neighborhood where Lewis lived. The road ended at the rocky shore. Jasper went a mile, then made a U-turn.

"Must be on Lighthouse Road." Jasper returned to the fork and turned left. A half-mile down the road, they spotted a truck on its side on the edge of the road. He pulled in behind it, left the spotlight shining on the wreck, and took a flashlight out of the glove box.

He glanced at Poppie. "I don't suppose you're going to listen to me and stay put?"

She opened her door. "Not a chance."

He got out of the Jeep and walked to the truck with Poppie behind him. "It's Tom Everson's truck." He went to the roof and peered into the window, then stepped back. "It's empty." He felt the hood and found it still warm. "Happened not too long ago."

Jasper shone his light around the truck and into the brush behind them. Then he checked across the road. "Looks like he took off."

"Do you think he was drunk?"

"Probably. He'll show up tomorrow. Sober. Claiming he—" Jasper stopped and shone his light in front of the truck. "Did you hear that?"

A soft whimper came from the bushes next to the bed of the truck. Jasper followed the sound, then knelt.

Poppie came up behind him, then gasped. "Oh my gosh."

Jasper put a hand on the black dog lying under a bush. "It's okay boy." He looked up at Poppie. "This is Blackjack, Tom's dog."

"He left him here?" She knelt next to Jasper. "Is he hurt bad?"

"I don't know. Can't tell. We need to get him to town." He handed her the flashlight, then picked up the dog. Blackjack let out a whine, but seemed to realize Jasper was there to help him. "Tom drives around with

Blackjack in the truck bed. I've told him so many times it's not safe." They arrived at the Jeep and Jasper put the dog in the backseat.

Poppie got in with him. "I'll keep him quiet."

Jasper began driving for town, but before they got there, the radio went off.

"What's up, Chief?"

"Lance called and said Tom Everson showed up in town, bloody, drunk, and obnoxious."

"Okay. I just found his truck on the side of the road. Maybe we can finally get him on a DUI."

"Do what you can."

Jasper glanced at Poppie. "Do you mind if I drop you and Blackjack off at Doc Hannigan's while I go take care of Tom?"

"No, of course not."

"How's he doing?"

"He's shivering. But he licked my hand. So, that's good, right?"

"I hope so." Jasper drove to the doctor's house, which was right next to the clinic. Dr. Hannigan was on call twenty-four hours a day, and his patients were typically human ones. But he was the only doctor in town, so he'd take non-human patients as well.

Jasper parked in front of the house, then took Blackjack out of the Jeep and carried him up to the porch. Poppie came up beside him and rang the bell under a small sign that read, *Ring For Emergencies.*

A few moments later, Davis Hannigan opened the door. "Jasper? Who do we have here? Is that Blackjack?"

"Yeah."

"Bring him in. What happened?"

Jasper laid the dog on the table in the small room Davis led them to. "Tom ran his truck off the road and flipped it. We found the dog in the brush. Must've fallen out when it went over."

"Is Tom okay?"

"Apparently. I got a call from the chief. Tom's causing trouble at the Pelican."

"Do you need to go tend to that?" He nodded toward Jasper's black eye. "And what happened there?"

"I got in the way of Doyle Murphy's fist. He and Reece were going at it."

Davis shook his head. "Every holiday." He reached into a small refrigerated cupboard and took out an icepack. "Put this on it to bring down the swelling."

Jasper took it from him. "Thanks. Poppie will stay here with the dog. I'll be back as soon as I can."

"You go. I've got it from here."

Jasper nodded, then put a hand on Poppie's arm. "Thanks."

"Of course."

While Jasper drove the two blocks to the Rusty Pelican, he held the icepack on his eye. When he arrived, he checked the damage in the rearview mirror. It looked worse than it felt. He'd only had one other black eye, and it was in high school. The one fight he got into his senior year. He still couldn't quite remember why he was compelled to defend his father's honor. The chief had never been a part of Jasper's life, and at that point, he'd moved out of the house. But Pete Morrison had made a comment about the chief's drinking, and Jasper had shoved the boy to the ground. Pete, who'd been in plenty of fights, jumped up quickly and punched Jasper in the nose. It wasn't broken, but he had two black eyes for the next week.

Jasper tossed the icepack in the passenger seat, then got out of the Jeep and retrieved his pistol from the gun safe in the back. The crowd at the Rusty Pelican was different from the one at The Sailor's Loft. The Pelican drew the loners, habitual drunks, and those looking for a quick hookup. The Sailor's Loft, being owned by the chief's ex-wife and deputy's mother, drew a much more respectable group. They could be boisterous on the holidays, but they rarely got out of hand.

It was nearing midnight, and the party was still going on inside the bar. Jasper clipped his holstered pistol onto his belt before going inside. Lance met him at the door.

"He's at the bar. I didn't want to approach him without you."

"Okay. Let's go talk to him."

They went to the bar and found Tom arguing with two other men. Mellie, the bartender, had a small baseball bat in her hands. It wasn't just for show. Mellie was more than capable of using it if she needed to.

Jasper nodded at her. "Stand down, Mellie. I got this."

She hesitated a moment, then dropped the bat to her side, but didn't put it down.

Jasper stepped in between the three men. "Let's break this up, guys."

One of the men started to argue, but stopped when Lance took his arm and said, "Walk away."

The man took a few steps back, then turned and headed for the door. Lance looked at the other one. "Time to go."

The man sighed, then also left.

Tom took a step toward Jasper, but stopped when Jasper rested his hand on his gun and put the other on Tom's chest.

"Take a seat."

Tom, in an obvious state of intoxication, dropped onto the stool and glared at Jasper.

"I haven't done anything."

"Except roll your truck and leave your dog to die in the brush."

Tom stood. "Blackjack's dead?"

"Sit down." Jasper waited until Tom sat again. "He's at Doc Hannigan's. You better hope he doesn't die."

Tom seemed to return to defiant mode. "Is it illegal to wreck my truck?"

"Only if you were drunk when you wrecked it."

"Maybe it happened a long time ago. Like this afternoon."

"It didn't. The motor was still warm." Jasper took Tom's arm. "Stand up."

Tom stood.

Jasper took his cuffs out. "Turn around, you know the drill."

"Why are you arresting me?"

"Drunk and disorderly. Suspicion of driving under the influence. Take your pick. If you pass the test, then I'll apologize."

Tom allowed Jasper to put on the cuffs without any trouble. Then Jasper looked at Mellie. "Are you okay?"

She leaned the bat against the counter and shrugged. "You know it."

Jasper smiled. "I should deputize you."

"Cumberland County couldn't pay me what I make here."

"I'm sure that's true."

"You take care, Mel." Jasper took Tom's arm and led him out of the bar. Lance followed them to the Jeep.

Jasper put Tom in the backseat, then closed the door and turned to Lance. "Thanks for all your help tonight. Consider yourself off-duty. Go have a beer or two."

Lance grinned. "Yes, sir. I'll see you around." He started to walk away, then turned back. "Sorry about interrupting you earlier."

Jasper smiled. "You weren't the first this evening."

"Well, put that asshole in the cage and go finish what you started."

"I just might do that."

Jasper drove Tom to the station and took him inside the dark building. Once Maisy went home at five, the station was closed. Jasper was usually gone soon after Maisy, but the chief would often stay later. Jasper wasn't exactly sure what the chief did after hours, but he assumed it had something to do with all the stuff he himself wasn't looking forward to doing once he became Chief Deputy. Jasper becoming chief someday wasn't something he and his father talked about, but it was the natural order of things. Someday, Jasper would become the fourth Chief Goodspeed on Gracie Island.

He sat Tom in a chair, then tested him for alcohol. It registered well above the legal limit, as expected.

"Looks like you're staying here tonight."

Jasper pulled Tom to his feet, then took him downstairs to the four jail cells. They were rarely occupied, but they were there, if they were needed. Along with the cells was a small kitchen, which Jasper doesn't remember ever getting used, and a bathroom with three toilets and two shower stalls. The showers he'd taken advantage of since he'd been living in the chief's camp trailer. It was either there, or his mother's house, since the plumbing in the trailer wasn't hooked up. There was also a small collection of exercise equipment and some free weights. Jasper took advantage of that, as well, working out several days a week.

Jasper put Tom in one of the cells, then removed the cuffs. "Get some rest. The chief will be here in the morning."

"You're going to leave me here tonight?"

"Yep." Jasper headed for the stairs and flipped off the light before going up them. "Have a good night, Tom."

Tom yelled after him. "Screw you!"

Chapter Four

"There's always tomorrow."

Poppie was lounging on the couch in the small waiting room next to the examination room. Dr. Hannigan had put Blackjack in a crate and brought it into the room. The dog had broken his hip when he fell out of the truck, but with a little love and care, the prognosis was good. Blackjack would make a full recovery, though he may have a slight limp that would slow him down a bit.

Blackjack was sleeping, still under the effects of the sedative, but Poppie wanted to stay with him. Jasper had been gone for over an hour, and she hoped he'd be there soon. Even though the doctor and his wife were upstairs asleep, she still felt a little spooked in the quiet house.

She tried to distract herself by thinking about Jasper. He'd kissed her. Twice. She hadn't really expected it. Not on her first day in town. They'd barely kept in contact over the last ten months. She'd talked to him several times when she'd called Lewis and Jasper happened to be with him. Over the last couple of months, it seemed he was with Lewis every time she made her Sunday night call. She hoped it was planned, but he never said and she didn't ask.

It was strange. She never felt it was weird that they didn't directly communicate while she was gone. Somehow she knew when she came back, they'd go right back to how they'd left it. But actually, it was a few steps above how they'd left things. He'd said he'd be ready at some point. Apparently, he's at that point.

She smiled. "Jasper Goodspeed, you're so darn cute."

Jasper left the station and drove to Dr. Hannigan's house. He parked out front of the house, which was dark except for a light on the porch. He was afraid the dark house was bad news. Maybe Blackjack didn't make it. Not sure what to do, he went to the porch and found a note hanging on the door.

Poppie and Blackjack are in the waiting room. Go on inside. D. Hannigan.

Jasper opened the door and stepped into the foyer, which was lit by a dim light on an entryway table. The only other light was coming from the partially open door of the waiting room. Jasper went to the door and opened it to find Poppie dozing on the couch and Blackjack in the crate.

Jasper stepped into the room. "Poppie?" She stirred, and he stepped closer. "Poppie?"

She opened her eyes and smiled at him. "Hey."

He went to the couch and sat next to her. "How's Blackjack?"

"He'll be fine. Broken hip. But it'll heal."

"Dammit. And how are you?"

"I'm good. Especially now." She took his hand. "How'd it go with Tom?"

"He's sleeping it off in a cell. Blew way past the legal limit."

"What about Blackjack? Will he get him back?"

"Not if I can help it. I'll charge him with animal cruelty if I have to."

Poppie gently touched Jasper's cheekbone. "How's this?"

"Doesn't hurt much. Vision's a little blurry, but probably because it's so swollen."

"I told Dr. Hannigan I'd stay with Blackjack tonight."

Jasper took off his gun and laid it on the table. "I'll stay, too."

"Thank you. I know I'm perfectly safe here. But it's still a little scary in this big house."

He settled down next to her and checked his watch. "It's not your birthday anymore."

"That's okay. Because it was a perfect day."

He smiled. "It was pretty perfect, wasn't it?" He put his arm around her and she laid her head on his shoulder. "I never got to finish giving you your birthday present. I guess you'll have to wait until next year."

She put a hand on his cheek. "I don't think so, Deputy."

"Do you want it now?" He didn't wait for her answer as he leaned in and gave her the birthday kiss he'd been trying to give her all night.

When he moved back a few inches, she opened her eyes. "Wow. Can I have another one of those?"

Jasper grinned. "If we weren't in the Hannigan's house, I'd... Well, we need to keep an eye on Blackjack."

"Right." She sighed. "There's always tomorrow."

"And the day after that."

"And so on. And so on."

Jasper kissed her on the forehead. "We should get some sleep."

Poppie glanced at the couch. "I think there's room on here for both of us."

Jasper took off his boots and remove his uniform shirt and belt, leaving him in his green cargo pants and a white t-shirt. He looked at her. "How come I'm the one always taking off my clothes?"

"I'm just lucky, I guess."

He stretched out on the couch and she laid next to him. It was a bit of a tight fit, but she didn't seem to mind. He put his arm around her and put the other one behind his head.

"You told Lewis what was going on, right? I don't want him to think you're out somewhere with me."

"I am with you."

"You know what I mean."

She laughed. "Yes. I called him and told him I was staying here with Blackjack." She put a hand on his chest. "He's not going to worry about me with you. He trusts you. You're his best friend."

"Still. Sister trumps best friend."

Jasper was tired, and he expected Poppie was too. It'd been a long day, but a good one. When he'd awoken that morning, he never imagined he'd be ending the day with Poppie in his arms. She smelled good, and she felt great lying next to him. He wanted to give her another kiss and a lot more, but it wasn't the time or place. He'd know when the time was right. He'd know when to give himself completely to her.

Jasper woke to the sun coming in the windows and Poppie sitting on the floor next to Blackjack's crate. She was talking quietly to him and petting him through the opened door. Jasper watched her for a few minutes before she turned and saw he was awake.

She smiled. "Good morning." She got to her feet and went to the couch.

As she sat next to him, Jasper took her hand. "Good morning. How's Blackjack?"

"He seems to be okay. He wagged his tail."

"That's a good sign." Jasper looked at her for a moment. "And how are you?"

"I'm perfect."

"Yes. You are."

"No, no, not that kind of perfect. There's only one being in this room who's perfect and it isn't me."

Jasper grinned. "Blackjack?"

"Yes."

When the door to the waiting room opened and Dr. Hannigan came in, Poppie got to her feet and Jasper sat up.

The doctor glanced at them, then went to Blackjack's crate. "Looks like Blackjack had lots of company last night. He knelt by the crate and opened it up, then tapped the floor. "Come on, boy. Let's see how you're moving this morning."

Blackjack wagged his tail, and let out a whine, then belly-crawled out of the crate and nudged the doctor's hand.

"That's a good boy." Hannigan looked at Jasper. "He's going to be fine. Just needs a little time to mend." He got to his feet. "You're not giving him back to Tom, are you?"

"No. I'll keep him until he's better, then find a good home for him."

"Good. I want to keep an eye on him a little longer, but you can come and get him this afternoon around four. If that works for you."

"Yeah. I'll come back then."

"You two don't need to rush off. I'm headed to the clinic, and the Missus is taking the ferry to the mainland. So take your time. There's coffee in the kitchen."

"Thanks, Doc."

Dr. Hannigan left the room and Poppie sat next to Jasper.

"He's a very nice man."

"He's the best."

"Do you want me to go get you a cup of coffee?"

Jasper put his arm around her and pulled her in close. "After you give me a good morning kiss." She kissed him lightly on the lips. "You call that a kiss?"

Poppie glanced toward the door. "They're still here. It's a little weird."

"Alright. Then go get me some coffee, woman."

She pointed a finger at him. "Don't even."

He laughed. "Sorry, ma'am. I lost my head."

"You'll lose your head if you ever call me *woman* again."

When Poppie returned with the coffee, Jasper was dressed and was clipping his gun to his belt. He took the cup from her and sat on the couch.

"So, I have time to take you to breakfast."

She sat next to him. "I'd love that. But I really should go check in with Lewis and I'm meeting Sarah this morning to talk to Randy about the cake. Can you drop me off?"

"Of course."

"I can definitely do dinner if you're free."

"I need to work this afternoon, but dinner sounds good." After taking a moment, Jasper asked, "How do you feel about games?"

"Games? Like emotional games?"

He grinned. "No. Jesus. Board games."

"Oh. Sorry. That was an accidental peek into my past world of dating." She looked up at him. "Board games are...great. Other than you beating me at Monopoly and embarrassing me at Twister, I haven't played any for quite some time. But Lewis and I used to play when we were kids. Why?"

"We still have game night every Wednesday. And tonight is Wednesday."

She sat on the coffee table in front of him. "It's amazing what people do to fill the time when they don't have cell phones, or internet, or absolutely no social life."

He frowned. "Excuse me. We have a social life. We have not one, but two bars to choose from depending on your...mood. Two restaurants, three if you count the deli."

"I don't think you can count the grocery store deli as a restaurant."

"We celebrate every holiday with lots of music and alcohol."

"And you have game night. You're right. This place is hopping."

He set his cup down next to her. "I'll skip it if you don't want to go. I haven't missed one in years, but, for you—"

"Stop. Of course I'll go to game night. But I won't play Monopoly with you."

"That's fine. I stopped playing Monopoly a few months ago. No challenge when you win all the time."

"Wow. I forgot how modest you are."

"I'll pick you up at six."

Jasper was halfway through his biscuits and gravy when Lewis came up to his table.

"Hey. What's up?"

"I need to talk to you."

Jasper motioned toward the chair across the table. "Sit. Have some coffee."

"I'd rather stand."

Jasper put his fork down. "What's going on?"

"I need to know what your intentions are with Poppie."

"My intentions?"

"Yeah. If this is just an experiment to see if you're ready to move on—"

"Hold on. What are you talking about? And I'm offended by the accusation."

Lewis took a moment to regroup. "I want to make sure you genuinely like her. I don't want to see her hurt."

Jasper leaned back in his chair. "Where's this coming from? I thought we were friends. I *thought* you trusted me."

"You are. And I do. I'm just not sure I trust you with Poppie. Or at least your instincts."

Jasper studied Lewis for a long moment. "Please sit down." Lewis took a breath, then pulled out the chair and sat. Jasper leaned forward on the table. "If I was experimenting...testing out how I felt about moving on from Ivy, I would've done it with Deidre or Mellie, or any one of several other women in town who see me as the lonely widower." He took a sip of his coffee. "Poppie doesn't see me like that. She never knew me as Ivy's husband. For some reason I don't really understand, she likes spending time with her. She challenges me. And I frustrate her. Somehow that works for us. I never would've made any kind of move if I wasn't sure we had a shot of creating a weird, wonderful, exasperating, damn interesting relationship."

Lewis saw Katie, the waitress, coming toward the table with a pot of coffee and he turned his cup over and sat it on the edge of the table.

Katie filled it. "Hey, Lewis. Can I get you something to eat?"

"No. Just coffee, thanks." She topped off Jasper's cup, then left, and Lewis turned his attention back to Jasper. "I'm sorry. My only excuse is I'm getting married in a week."

Jasper picked up his fork and took another bite of his breakfast. "I was about to call off the bachelor party."

"You're throwing the bachelor party?"

"Yeah. Poppie didn't tell you? She thought it'd be more appropriate than your female best man."

"Awesome. What do you have planned?"

"I'm not telling you."

"Come on. A hint. Give me a tiny hint."

"It's on Sunday after the game."

"And?"

"That's all you get."

"Damn. It's going to be great though, right?"

"Hell yeah."

Chapter Five

"So, second base is...?"

Poppie and Sarah came out of Buns of Steele and walked down the street.

Sarah took Poppie's hand. "It's perfect. I really wanted Kat to do it. But she said Randy was much better at decorating cakes than she was. I guess she was right."

Poppie laughed. "Who knew?" She touched Sarah's arm. "It's going to be a beautiful cake."

"Thanks for coming with me. Since my sisters have gone to the mainland to get their dresses fitted, it's nice to have some help."

"Well, Jasper is more suited to the best man duties. So helping you gives me something to contribute."

Sarah nudged Poppie. "So, yeah. Jasper. How's that going?"

"It's going fine. Even though I'm technically leaving after the wedding."

"Technically? Does that mean you might stay longer?"

"I'm thinking about it. Haven't really discussed it with him."

"Of course he wants you to stay."

They went into the café and sat at a table by the window. After Katie brought them each water, coffee for Sarah, and iced tea for Poppie, she left them with menus.

Poppie set hers aside. "So, how well do you know Jasper? How long have you known him?"

Sarah smiled. "All my life. We grew up together."

"So you knew Ivy, too?"

"Yes, but I don't know if I should discuss her with you."

"Why not? Did they date in high school?"

Sarah put cream and sugar in her cup and stirred it before taking a sip. "This didn't come from me. They, of course, knew each other. We all did. And he dated quite a few girls in high school...including me."

"What? You dated Jasper?"

"Sophomore year. And no to your next question. We never got beyond second base."

"Who else did he date?"

Sarah took another sip of coffee. "Teri and Janice Lawrence. But they left for college and never came back."

"Sisters?"

Sarah shrugged. "Jasper was very popular. Lisa, cashier at the grocery store."

"The tall brunette?"

"Yes. Um. Mellie..." She glanced at Katie. "And Katie."

Poppie watched Katie deliver food to another table. "Mellie, the bartender? Was she as...edgy in high school?"

Sarah smiled. "Mellie has always been her own person. But she came back from college with the tattoos and piercings. And in high school, her hair was black and short."

Poppie shook her head. She couldn't quite picture Jasper with Mellie. Or maybe she didn't want to. "Seems like an odd pairing."

"It was. I think they bonded over absent fathers. They've always been good friends and still are."

Poppie thought about it for a moment. Jasper and Mellie. She certainly didn't see that coming. *The boy scout and the wild child. Interesting.* "It must be so weird to be around all the people you ever dated."

"We're all in the same boat, so when it's weird for everyone, it's not so weird."

She watched Katie for a moment. She was tall too, as was Mellie. She wondered if her being five-six was a first for him.

"And when did he start dating Ivy?"

"Senior year. We were all so jealous when it became obvious she was the one."

The wedding picture on Kat's mantle came to Poppie's mind. "They were really in love, huh?"

"Yes. And the whole thing was tragic. But he's ready to move on. And it seems he wants to do it with you. So, I'd say you'd be crazy to leave after the wedding."

"So second base is...?"

"Kissing and a little exploring, but the clothes stayed on."

Poppie touched her lips. "He's a really good kisser."

"I'm glad you know that. So how can you walk away? I mean, aren't you curious about what else he's good at?"

Poppie blushed. "I think I need to stay and find out."

"Perfect. It'd be very nice to have my sister-in-law married to my husband's best friend."

"And her ex-boyfriend?"

Sarah smiled. "Just a tiny blip. Nothing worth thinking about."

"Does Lewis know?"

"Playing in the band together, it came up a few years ago. No big deal. High school was a long time ago."

"This is a very weird town."

Jasper spent the morning filling out paperwork about the previous night's activities. The chief had released Tom, who'd get his day in court in a few weeks. James then went out to take care of the aftermath of half the town partying. So, other than Maisy, Jasper had the office to himself.

He was half-way through his third cup of coffee for the day when Tom tapped on his open door and stepped through it.

Jasper studied him for a moment. He looked pretty good, considering how drunk he was last night. "What's up, Tom?"

"Where's my dog?"

"Blackjack is at Dr. Hannigan's, recovering from a broken hip. He's going to stay with me until he's better."

"You're keeping my dog?"

Jasper leaned back in his chair. "You left him to die, Tom."

Tom took off his ball cap and held it with both hands. "I thought he ran off."

"I don't think so." Jasper leaned forward on the desk. "You're not getting him back. If you want to fight me on it, then take it to court. I'm pretty sure I'd win, though."

Tom put his hat back on. "Fine. You can have him." He turned then and walked out.

Jasper grumbled. "Bastard." But when Maisy appeared in the doorway, he put on a smile.

She stepped in. "What did he want?"

"His dog."

"You didn't—"

"Of course not. Blackjack is going home with me tonight. Penny will gladly share the bed with him."

"Are you going to keep him?"

"Nah. I'll find him a good home."

She smiled at him. "He already has a good home with you."

He nodded. "I'll think about it."

"Good boy."

She left and Jasper mumbled. "She still thinks I'm twelve."

When Jasper was done with his paperwork, he picked up a sandwich from the deli and drove to the east end of town. He pulled through the iron archway at the entrance to the cemetery and drove slowly to the back side. The cemetery had been around as long as there had been people to bury in it, including the first Gracie's, Alma and Henry. A two foot high white metal fence separated the Gracie family plots from the rest of the graves. There were currently fifteen graves inside the fence, with two of Alma and Henry's grandchildren, six great-grandchildren, and five great-great-grandchildren still living on the island.

When Jasper got to the far end of the cemetery, he pulled over and turned off his engine. He rolled down his windows while he ate his sandwich and washed it down with a bottle of Coke. When he was done, he left the car and walked across the damp grass to a headstone under a large oak. There were fresh flowers on Ivy's grave, which Jasper knew came from his mother's garden. Kat was a regular visitor, as were Ivy's sister and her family. He sat on the bench Ivy's father had built a year after she died and read the inscription on the headstone.

Ivy Goodspeed and Child. You are a song in our hearts forever.

The word child bothered Jasper. But when Ivy died taking their unborn child with her, he was too grief-stricken to give the baby, who he didn't even know was a boy or a girl, a name. So, her family had settled on child.

Jasper sighed. He didn't come here as often as he should and he felt guilty about it. But he didn't need to sit at their grave to remember his wife and their baby. Today, however, he needed to talk to her.

"I want to talk to you about Poppie. Penelope. She's nothing like you. But she keeps me on my toes and she makes me happy. Something I never thought I'd feel again. Happiness. I'd been sad for so long, I'd forgotten what it felt like. Then she shows up last summer, and I was smiling again. Laughing. Of course, she also makes me want to pull my hair out."

He looked at the grass for a moment. "Which you'd probably find extremely satisfying. I think you'd like her. Anyway, I think she might be my next chapter. I just want you to know that it doesn't diminish what we had in any way. I'll always love you, Ivy. And that little peanut we never got a chance to know."

At three-forty-five, Jasper left the office and headed to the pier. Poppie had called and told him she was there keeping Lewis company while he worked on a boat. He parked in the lot and walked to the end of the pier, finding Poppie and Lewis sitting in the back of the boat talking.

Jasper walked up to the boat. "Working hard, I see."

"Always, Deputy. Almost as hard as you work."

Jasper smiled. "I'll have you know I spent hours doing paperwork today. And if you don't think that's hard work, then you've never filled out forms in triplicate before."

"You win. I'd rather sand down a boat."

Poppie stood. "Are you ready to go get Blackjack?"

"Yes, ma'am."

She shook her head. "Okay, we're going to have to break you of that little habit."

Jasper took her hand and helped her off the boat. "Can't help it. I grew up with two strong women who insisted I called them ma'am."

She patted his chest. "Well, I'm not your aunt or your mother."

Lewis stepped off after Poppie. "So I'll see you guys at game night?"

Jasper nodded. "We'll be there."

Poppie pointed at Lewis. "But no Monopoly and no Twister."

Lewis laughed. "But you were so close to winning... Oh wait. No you weren't."

She took Jasper's arm. "I'm not even going to respond to that. Let's go get Blackjack."

Jasper waved at Lewis. "See you in a bit."

They made their way down the pier to the parking lot, then drove to Dr. Hannigan's house. Mrs. Hannigan greeted them at the door with her usual welcoming smile.

"Come on in. Davis is busy at the clinic, but he said Blackjack is ready to go."

Jasper and Poppie went inside and followed her to the waiting room. Blackjack was lying by the couch and wagged his tail when they came in.

Jasper went to him and gave him a pet. "Hey buddy, how you feeling?" Blackjack thumped his tail on the carpeted floor. "That's a good boy. Do you want to come stay with me for a while? It's nothing fancy, and it's a bit crowded. But I think you'll be happy there."

Mrs. Hannigan handed Poppie a folded piece of paper. "Here are the instructions for his care. Basically, keep him quiet. Let him eat and drink when he feels like it. And, of course, the directions for his pain medication." She looked at Jasper. "How's your eye, honey?"

"It's fine. Doesn't hurt."

She looked closely at it. "I think you're just saying that to make both me and Poppie feel better."

"Maybe a little."

She patted his hand. "You take care now. Davis wants to see Blackjack early next week."

"Thank you. Hopefully, I won't see you before then." He picked up Blackjack, carried him to the Jeep, and put him in the backseat. "There you go, boy."

Poppie looked in at him. "Should I sit back there with him?"

"I think he'll be fine."

They both got in the front of the Jeep and Jasper drove the two miles to his house. When they arrived, Jasper picked up Blackjack and carried him to the grass in front of the framed house and set him down. "I know all these two-by-fours are tempting, but you need to go pee in the grass."

Blackjack looked at him, as though he understood, then limped a few feet away and did his business.

"Good boy." Jasper picked him back up and carried him to the trailer. He glanced at Poppie. "I'm going to get him settled inside. I'll be right out."

"You're still not going to let me inside the trailer?"

"I haven't had a chance to clean, yet. I haven't been home since we left for lunch yesterday."

"Okay. I'll be down by the water."

As Poppie walked down the dirt path to the beach, she once again couldn't help but picture herself living on the property with Jasper. It was beautiful, with wild grass around the house, trees shielding it from the two close neighbors, and a lovely section of sandy beach. A lot of the coastline around the island seemed to be rocky, so a large section of sand was rare.

Lewis' house was right on the beach as well, but he only had a small section of sand nestled between rocky outcroppings. And when the tide came in, the water surrounded three sides of his house, which was built on pilings. It was a little unnerving and Poppie much preferred Jasper's house, solidly on the ground and far enough away from the high tide line to stay dry.

She sat on a worn wooden bench and waited for Jasper, entertaining herself by watching the seagulls flying overhead. Once in a while, one would dip down and snatch something from the water.

After about fifteen minutes, Jasper came to join her, and he sat next to her on the bench and took her hand.

Poppie glanced at him. "What did Penny think?"

"She took right to him. I think she knows he's hurt."

"Of course she does." She squeezed his hand. "I think you should keep him."

"So I've been told."

"It'd give Penny someone to hang out with while you're at work. She probably misses Pepper."

"Yeah. She does. I take her to Mom's every couple of days to spend time with him."

Poppie kissed him on the cheek. "You're such a sweetie."

Jasper frowned at her.

"You are." She turned in her seat toward him. "Now, if I remember correctly, you criticized me this morning for giving you a wimpy kiss."

"I sure did."

"Well, I'd like to make up for that now."

Jasper grinned. "Let's see what you got."

Chapter Six

"Who's the child here?"

J asper and Poppie stayed on the beach until it was time to go into town for game night. Once a month the gathering was also a potluck, so they stopped at The Sailor's Loft to pick up some food Aunt Peg had prepared for them to take along.

As they carried out a platter of shrimp tacos, a pan of carrot cake, and two loaves of freshly baked bread, Poppie shook her head.

"This seems so unfair. It makes the homemade casseroles seem pretty inadequate."

"It's all good food."

"Except for Eunice's brownies?"

"Yes. Though Eunice's been a little under the weather, so she might not be there tonight."

"Is she going to be okay?"

"Sure. I checked on her yesterday. Brought her some lunch." He stashed the food in the back of the Jeep, then looked at Poppie, who was smiling at him. "What?"

"Can you be any sweeter?"

"Get in the Jeep. I was just doing my job."

"I'm pretty sure there isn't a rule in the Deputy Handbook that says you must be nice to little old ladies."

He glanced at her. "There isn't a Deputy Handbook."

"Well, if there was, the first rule would be, 'Do what Deputy Goodspeed would do. He's a sweetie.'"

They drove to the Ice House, which was the gathering place for town meetings, game night, and various other events during the year. It had once been an actual ice house where the daily catch was stored when the fishing was still profitable. But it'd been twenty years since the harbor was filled with fishing boats. Most of them had now moved on to better water, leaving the remaining Gracie Island citizens to make do with other various ways to make a living. But if you didn't own a business in town, or had money from some other source, it could be difficult. The three hundred residents left in town had figured out how to remain, and they were a close bunch.

Jasper parked on the street and retrieved the food from the back of the Jeep. Poppie took the bread from him and they went inside. There were about forty people, some at tables midway through various games, and some standing around and visiting. The food table was full and Poppie checked it out after setting down the tray of bread.

Jasper put down the tacos and the carrot cake and joined her as she walked the length of the table.

She glanced at him. "Anything I should stay away from?"

"I'd say it's all safe to eat tonight. Looks like Eunice didn't make it."

Poppie spotted something she couldn't identify. "What about that?"

"Hmm. Avoid anything you don't recognize."

When a woman came up to Jasper, Poppie recognized her as his sister-in-law. Last summer he was barely polite to her. Tonight, however, he seemed genuinely glad to see her.

"Hey, Cami."

She kissed him on the cheek, then frowned at his black eye. "What happened here?"

"The Murphy brothers."

"Ahh. Every holiday." She smiled at Poppie. "I'm Cami, Jasper's sister-in-law. We sort of met last summer."

"I remember. Nice to see you again."

Cami turned back to Jasper. "We're about to start a game of Uno. Would you like to join us?"

Jasper glanced at Poppie. "Sure. Just let us get some food. We'll be right over." She left, and he turned to Poppie. "I know. Things have changed."

"I'm glad."

"It's been a very transformative winter."

She kissed him on the cheek. "I hope I had something to do with that."

He shook his head. "Not a thing. You popped into my life last summer, nearly got me killed in a hurricane, then disappeared for ten months."

"Well, I'm here now."

He put his arm around her waist. "For how long?"

She sighed. "We'll have to talk about that."

"What are you going to eat?"

"Would it be wrong of me to eat what we brought?"

He headed for the platter of tacos. "Not at all. That's what I'm eating."

He took four tacos and Poppie took two, then they cut three slices of bread. After picking up a bottle of beer and a can of Coke, they went to find Cami.

On the way, Poppie leaned toward Jasper. "Uno, huh?"

He sighed. "It's the kids' favorite game."

"But not yours?"

"No." He grinned. "But I can still beat you at it."

"You think so? I happen to be pretty good at Uno."

"Hmm. We'll see."

They found Cami at a table with a man and two young girls. Poppie smiled as she set her food down.

Cami put a hand on the man's arm. "This is my husband, Matt, and our daughters, Summer and Skye."

"Nice to meet you. I'm Poppie." She took her seat as Jasper sat beside her.

He winked at the girls. "You girls ready to get beat?"

Summer, who appeared to be around ten, laughed. "No. You always lose at this game. Even Skye beat you the last time."

Jasper glanced at Poppie, then shook his head. "Hmm. I don't remember that."

Skye was younger than Summer, and she smiled at Poppie. "I like your name."

"Thank you. I like yours, too."

Jasper picked up a taco and took a bite. "Let's get this game going."

Matt shuffled the cards, then dealt them out.

Jasper set his taco down and picked up his cards, then frowned at them. He glanced at Skye, then winked at her when he caught her watching him. He rearranged his cards, then picked up his taco and took another bite. When some of the beef fell out and dropped onto his lap, the girls giggled.

He picked it up and put it in his mouth, then licked his fingers. "It's good with or without the shell."

Cami shook her head. "Jasper, you're a bad influence."

"That's what I've been trying to tell you." He finished his taco with a large last bite.

Poppie nudged him. "Who's the child here?"

He pointed at the girls while they pointed back at him.

Matt cleared his throat. "Alright. Let's get this game started."

They played for thirty minutes, with everyone staying pretty even. Jasper leaned in toward Poppie's ear. "This could take all night."

She nudged him. "I think Uncle Jasper needs some dessert."

The girls were instantly onboard with the dessert idea, and Cami looked at Matt. "How about you, honey? What do you want?"

Matt set his cards down. "Anything but Eunice's brownies."

Cami stood. "I believe Eunice didn't come tonight." She smiled at Poppie. "Do you want to come help?"

"Sure." Poppie got to her feet and put a hand on Jasper's shoulder. "Carrot cake?"

"Yep."

Poppie and Cami headed for the food table, and when they got there, Cami stopped and took Poppie's hand.

"I don't know where you guys are in your relationship, but it's obvious there's something going on."

"Yes. We're working on it."

"Well, I think it's wonderful. Jasper has been like a brother to me. In fact, he and I were friends before he started dating Ivy."

"Seems like everyone who grew up here are still friends."

"Pretty much, yeah." Cami squeezed Poppie's hand. "Ivy wouldn't have wanted him to be alone. And for a while there, it seemed like he was set on that."

"I'm not sure what he sees in me. But I'm glad for it, whatever it is." She watched Jasper across the room, laughing with the girls. "He sure is good with your daughters."

"He loves kids. He and Ivy were so excited when they found out they were pregnant."

"What?" Poppie pulled her hand away and put it to her mouth. "Ivy was pregnant?"

A sadness passed over Cami's eyes. "Yes."

"When she...died?"

Cami nodded. "I'm sorry. I thought he would've told you."

Poppie shook her head and tried to fight back the tears in her eyes. "No. I had no idea."

"Honey. I'm so sorry. I didn't mean to upset you."

Poppie couldn't control her tears and she wiped her eyes. When she glanced at Jasper again, she saw that he was watching her and she turned her back to him. "Darn." She wiped her eyes again. "I'm sorry. Not sure why that upsets me so much."

When Jasper came up behind her, he put his arm around her and looked at Cami. "What's going on? What happened?"

Poppie shook her head. "It's fine. I'm okay." She wiped her eyes again, which seemed to be leaking uncontrollably.

Cami gave him a small smile. "I'm sorry, I—"

Poppie touched her arm, then looked at Jasper. "Can we go outside for a moment? I just need some air."

"Of course." He took her hand, and they headed for the door. Once they got outside, he kept walking around the building and down the pier they'd gone down last summer the night of the town meeting. It was colder tonight than it'd been that night, and Poppie shivered when they got to the end.

Jasper took off his coat and hung it around her shoulders, then wiped the tears from her face. "What's all this about? What did she say to you?"

"Nothing. I mean nothing inappropriate. She just mentioned something she thought I already knew."

"What?"

Poppie shook her head and looked away from him. He put his hand on her chin and turned her head to face him.

She sighed. "She told me about...the baby."

"Baby?" He took a moment. "My baby?"

Poppie nodded. "I don't know why I'm crying. It's just so, so sad. Don't be mad at her. She thought I knew."

He took a deep breath and blew it out slowly. "I should've told you. I just don't like to think about it."

"I know. And I understand."

She wiped her face and put her arms around his neck. "I don't know how you came back from that."

"I almost didn't. And I might not have if you hadn't blown into town last summer."

She snuggled into the collar of his shirt. "We don't ever need to talk about it. But if you want to, I'll listen."

He stepped away from her and took her hand. "Let's sit." He went to the end of the dock and they sat, hanging their legs over the water, a foot below their feet.

"I have two regrets that I struggle with. The first is that I didn't marry Ivy sooner. And secondly, that we didn't have kids right away. There was always a reason why I thought we should wait. I wanted to be financially secure. When I bought the house, I wanted to fix it up first. Then we got married, and I wanted to add a bedroom."

"You just wanted to provide for her."

"I wasted so much time. Time we could've been together. If we'd had kids right away, I'd have more than an ultrasound picture of my child."

She laid her head on his shoulder.

"Actually, I lost it in the fire. But that's okay, because the image is burned into my memory. I couldn't really tell what I was looking at, but the Doc tried to explain it."

"Do you know if it was a boy or a girl?"

Jasper shook his head. "No. It was too soon."

She was quiet for a few moments. "Thank you."

"For what?"

"For sharing this with me." She felt a few raindrops and looked up at the sky, then smiled at him. "No warning, Rainman?"

"Sorry. I guess I was distracted." He stood and pulled her to her feet. "Not really feeling game night anymore."

"Me either."

They started walking toward the Ice House. "I'll take you home."

She let go of his hand and took his arm. "Okay."

They reached the Jeep, and he opened the door for her. "How do you feel about ice cream?"

"I love ice cream." She got into the Jeep and he closed her door, then went in and got in behind the wheel. "The Loft?"

"No. The café. They make it there. Mom gets her ice cream from them, so we might as well go to the source."

"Do they have a lot of flavors?"

"Chocolate and vanilla. But the toppings are where it's at. Chocolate, of course. Caramel, butterscotch, pretty much any berry you can think of, pineapple, bananas, peanuts, and so much more."

"Oh my gosh. Let's go."

By the time they got to the café, the rain was coming down harder, and they made a run for the door and ducked inside. There was a coat rack by the door and Poppie hung Jasper's coat and her jacket, before they went to find a table.

Jasper steered her toward the window. "I like to watch it coming down."

"Of course you do." She watched the waitress talking to some customers, and the cook through the window to the kitchen. "Is your great uncle still alive?"

"No. His grandson runs it now."

"Is that him cooking?"

"No, Aaron works the day shift. Big guy, beard, friendly. Fifteen years older than me."

"Are there any Gracie's left on the island?"

"Yeah. Several. Including my mom and Aunt Peg."

"You're related to the Gracies?"

"Yeah. Alma and Henry were my mom's great-grandparents."

"And when did the Goodspeeds get here?"

"The original Jasper Goodspeed became the first sheriff in the forties."

"So basically, you *are* Gracie Island."

He laughed. "Yeah. I guess I am."

The waitress came to their table and Jasper smiled at her.

"Hi, Shar."

"Jasper." She nodded at Poppie. "What can I get you?"

Poppie smiled. "Ice cream. Do you have boysenberries?"

"Yes. And they're good."

"Vanilla with boysenberries, please."

Jasper nodded his approval. "I'll take chocolate with chocolate, bananas, and peanuts."

"Coming right up."

Poppie grinned. "Look at you, going all out."

"When it comes to ice cream, it's the only way to go."

Chapter Seven

"There you go again, trying to get me naked."

Jasper sat at his desk with every intention of getting some work done, but when his eyes kept glazing over, and he couldn't concentrate, he moved to the couch and laid down. He just needed a little nap. He smiled. At least he had a good reason for being tired. He and Poppie had stayed at the café until they closed, then went to The Sailor's Loft. It was also closed, but Jasper had the key, and they sat in the kitchen while he ate some clam chowder he'd found in the walk-in and warmed up. He didn't get home until after two.

When someone shook him awake, he opened his eyes to find the chief leaning over him. Jasper sat up as James took a step back.

"Sorry. Do you need me?"

"Are you okay? Are you hungover?"

Jasper rubbed his eyes. "No. Just sleep deprived."

James looked like he was going to ask why, but then seemed to change his mind. "I need you to go check on Sam. Bo went by yesterday and Sam wouldn't open the door. Said he was sick."

"Okay. I'll pick up a few groceries for him and drive out there."

"I'll be out for a couple of hours this afternoon, but I'll check in with you later when you get back."

Jasper refrained from asking what that meant. The chief spent the majority of his time in his office. And when he left the station, he always let Jasper or Maisy know where he was going. The only time he was out of contact was when he was binge drinking. But James had seemed fine for a while. This was something else.

He watched the chief leave the office, then stood, stretched, and clipped his gun to his belt. He could hear rain hitting the roof, so on the way out, he took his hat and coat from the rack by the door. When Maisy smiled at him from behind her counter, he went to her.

"I'm headed to Sam's, so I'll be out of range for an hour or so."

"Okay, honey. Check in when you're back in town."

"I will." Jasper glanced toward the chief's closed office door. "So, where's the chief headed to today?"

Maisy shook her head. "I wasn't aware he was going anywhere."

"Hmm. Okay." Jasper smiled. "I thought you knew everything that went on in this office."

"Apparently not."

"I'll see you in a bit, Maisy."

Jasper walked to the grocery store and bought a few essentials for Sam, along with a carton of cigarettes and a bottle of whiskey. He was the only person Sam would talk to, mostly because he brought him smokes and a bottle every Saturday when he made his rounds to visit the few homes on

Lighthouse Road. So Jasper had seen Sam five days ago, and he was his usual ornery self.

Along with the groceries, Jasper bought himself a sandwich, then he went to his Jeep, which was parked in front of the station, and put the groceries in the back. He brought his sandwich up front and set it on the passenger seat, then pulled onto the road and headed for Harper's Fork.

The fork was a three-way split, with one road going to town, another went to a small neighborhood where Lewis lived. And the third crossed the island and ended on the east side at the lighthouse.

He'd taken Poppie to the lighthouse last summer, and it ended up being the start of their week of hell. He rubbed his shoulder. Somehow, despite injuring his shoulder repeatedly, capturing and losing the bad guy twice, and riding out a hurricane on a boat, everything turned out alright. He'd fought it at the time, but now he knew he was falling in love through it all. How could he not? Poppie was amazingly resilient. She was stubborn and frustrating, but brave when she needed to be.

Jasper turned onto Lighthouse Road and picked up his sandwich. It was his favorite thing to order from the deli. Built on sourdough bread, the sandwich was filled with smoked turkey, pepperjack cheese, lettuce, onion, and chilis. As he took a bite, he thought about the ride back from the lighthouse last summer on Bo's horses.

"Damn horses. Damn Poppie. What am I going to do with you?" He took another bite of his sandwich while he contemplated the question, then posed another. "What am I going to do without you?" He glanced at his reflection in the rearview mirror. "You need to convince her to stay."

After two miles he turned onto the road to Sam Jeffer's property, and in another half-mile he pulled in front of the house. The first thing Jasper noticed was that the gate to the goat shed was open, and the goats weren't in their pen. The fenced in run attached to the chicken coop was open as well, and the chickens were in search of food in the high grass in front of Sam's rundown house.

Jasper turned off the engine and studied the house. "Well, this can't be good."

He got out of the Jeep and went up the steps to the small porch, avoiding the middle one, which was missing a board. The screen door was propped open by a stack of old newspapers, so Jasper knocked on the door that had once been painted blue, but was now mostly bare wood.

"Sam? It's Jasper. I brought you some groceries." He waited a few moments, then knocked again. "Sam, open up."

When Sam still didn't respond, Jasper tried the knob. Finding it unlocked, he opened the door a few inches. "Sam?" The house smelled like mold and old food and Jasper wrinkled his nose and took a step back. He'd never been inside. Sam, a very reclusive man, had always come out to the porch and closed the door behind him.

Jasper opened the door wider. "Sam, I'm coming in." He stepped inside the door and frowned at the mess and the smell, which was worse inside. Sam wasn't a hoarder, but it seemed like he never threw anything away. The room was dim, but Jasper could see the old furniture and stacks of books, newspapers, and magazines. There was an old padded dress form in the corner, which Jasper found odd. And on a table with three legs—the fourth was a pile of books—was a Victrola and a stack of records.

Jasper walked across the creaky floor to the closed door across the room. When he opened it, the blackout blinds covering the windows made it dark. He went to one and rolled it up, letting in enough light to see with.

Jasper turned back to the room. "Shit." Sam was lying on the bed and Jasper didn't need to get any closer to him to see that the man was dead. "Oh, Sam."

Even though he was sure beyond a doubt, and it was the last thing he wanted to do, Jasper went to the bed and felt for a pulse. There wasn't one, and Sam's skin was cold to the touch. Jasper didn't think he'd been dead for too long, and had most likely died during the night.

Jasper left the room and went through the front door to the porch. The rain had stopped for the time being, and he took a few deep breaths of the damp air. He'd seen a few dead bodies during his years as a deputy. But when it was someone you knew, it was different. He and Sam weren't friends by any means, but he'd spent time with him. Jasper and the closest neighbor, Bo Redford, were Sam's only contact with civilization, and had been for quite some time.

"Okay, first things, first." He went to the small shed next to the goat pen and got a bucket of grain and some hay. He spread the hay in the pen, then shook the bucket of grain. "Come on guys, I know you didn't go far."

After a moment, one goat came out of the brush and ran toward the pen. She was followed by another, then a few moments later, the other two showed up. They all went into the pen and Jasper poured the grain into a feeder for them before closing them in.

The chickens had heard Jasper shaking the grain and were all headed back for their fenced-in coop. He filled the bucket with chicken feed, then tossed it to the chickens before closing the gate to their run.

He took the bucket back to the shed and picked up a shovel. Sam was a recluse. He didn't like people. The last thing he would want would be for Jasper to haul him into town and bury him in the cemetery.

Even though he might get in trouble for doing it, Jasper went to the edge of the trees near the house and started digging. He got warm with the effort and by the time he was half-way done, he'd removed his coat and uniform shirt, leaving him in a t-shirt.

He leaned on the shovel for a moment to catch his breath and give his muscles a rest. This was his first time digging a grave, other than burying his mother's cat a year ago. Not really the same, though. Burying a human was very different. He set down the shovel and went to the Jeep and drank a bottle of water, then retrieved the bottle of whiskey.

He opened it and held it toward the house. "Rest in peace, Sam." He took a few swallows. Then left it in the Jeep and returned to the grave as it started raining again.

Jasper looked at the sky. "You couldn't wait another hour?" With a sigh, he continued digging.

Forty-five minutes later, he figured the hole was deep enough. There were no predators on the island, except for a few feral dogs and cats. But the depth of the grave was sufficient to keep them away.

He scowled at the house. Digging the hole was actually the easy part. He headed for the door and went inside. After wrapping the body in the blanket from the bed, Jasper carried Sam outside and laid him next to the grave. When he heard something in the brush, he turned to see a black Lab sitting ten feet away.

Jasper knew Sam had a dog, but he was usually off running around. Jasper knelt on one knee and held out his hand. "Hey, boy. It's okay."

The dog stood and walked to Jasper. He smelled his hand, then sniffed the blanket around Sam. With a little whine, the dog laid down next to the body.

Jasper petted the dog's head. "I'm sorry, buddy. He's gone." Sam didn't like people, but he loved his animals and took good care of them. The dog appeared healthy and seemed to know his master was gone.

Jasper dropped into the hole, then pulled Sam gently into it and laid him down. The dog stood and peered over the edge. Jasper pointed at him. "Stay." The dog laid down again.

Jasper hoisted himself out of the hole, then retrieved the shovel. He started to fill it in, then stopped and stabbed the blade of the shovel into the pile of dirt. He went to the Jeep and retrieved the whiskey and the cigarettes, then brought them back to the grave. He climbed back in and put the cigarettes next to Sam's body. After taking another drink from the bottle, he put it on Sam's other side. "Sorry I couldn't do more for you, Sam."

After climbing out of the hole again, Jasper picked up the shovel, but stopped once more when he heard a vehicle approaching. The truck pulling in next to the Jeep belonged to Bo, Sam's neighbor. He sat for a moment, then got out and walked to Jasper.

Bo glanced into the grave. "I was afraid of what I might find today."

"He was gone when I got here a couple of hours ago."

Bo put a hand on Jasper's shoulder, then went to his truck and took a shovel from the bed. He returned to Jasper, and without further conversation, the two men filled in the grave leaving a small mound of dirt on top of it. After placing a few stones at the head of it, they went to the porch and sat on two mismatched wooden chairs. The rain had stopped again, but both men, wet and muddy, were beyond caring.

Bo looked at the goats and chickens.

Jasper followed his gaze. "I fed them. Can you take them on, or should I get someone out here to haul them into town?"

"I can take them. The wife and I will come get them in the morning."

Jasper nodded. "Good. Thanks." He looked at the dog.

Bo smiled. "The dog I can't take. He and my shepherd don't get along."

"Okay. I'll take him with me."

Bo glanced over his shoulder at the house. "Is there anything in there worth saving?"

"No. It needs to be cleaned and aired out. I'll check the county records and see if Sam had any relatives. I doubt he had a will."

"Okay. If you need me to do anything, just let me know."

"I brought some groceries. You can take them if you want."

"Sure, thanks."

They both stood and went to the vehicles. Jasper handed Bo the groceries, then watched him get into his truck. There was really nothing to say, and as Bo drove away, Jasper gave him a small wave.

When the dog sat at Jasper's feet, then whined, Jasper frowned at him. "I don't even know your damn name. Knowing Sam, he probably never gave you one." He studied the dog for a moment. "How about I call you Sam?" The dog wagged his tail. "Okay. Sam it is."

Jasper opened the passenger seat and Sam jumped in. When Jasper got in behind the wheel, he glanced at the dog. "I already have one dog too many." He shook his head. "What the hell. What's one more dog?"

When Poppie heard a knock on the door, she peered through the window before going to open it. Jasper, looking tired, wet, and disheveled, was muddy up to his knees.

"Oh my gosh. What happened?"

Jasper sighed. "Can I come in?"

"Of course." She opened the door all the way and took a step back.

Jasper took off his muddy boots, then stepped inside. "Thank you."

Poppie put her arms around his neck. He held her tight and didn't seem to want to let her go. She whispered in his ear. "What can I do?"

After another moment, he released his grip on her and took a step back. "Is Lewis here?"

She shook her head. "He's staying at Sarah's tonight."

Jasper took a breath. "I need a shower."

She looked at his muddy pants. "Of course. Let's get you out of these clothes."

He gave her a small smile. "There you go again, trying to get me naked."

He headed for the bathroom and she followed him. "Take a long hot shower, and when you're done, I'll throw these things into the washer."

He nodded. "And then, we'll talk."

Poppie closed the door and went to the kitchen to check the cupboards for groceries. Lewis didn't keep much food, but she'd bought a few things since she arrived. She had the ingredients to make spaghetti, and a half-loaf of bread from The Sailor's Loft. She could make Jasper dinner if he so desired.

When she heard the shower running, she went to Lewis' room and took a pair of pajama bottoms and a t-shirt from his dresser, then went to the bathroom door and tapped. She opened the door a few inches. "Can I come in and get your clothes?"

"Sure."

"And I'll leave something for you to put on. I know how much you love wearing borrowed clothing."

He peeked around the edge of the shower curtain. "Thank you."

"Do you have everything you need?"

He held up a bottle of lilac and jasmine shampoo and raised an eyebrow.

Poppie smiled. "Ever since last summer, I've been attracted to the scent of that shampoo."

"Hmm."

"I can get you Lewis' shampoo."

"No. This will do." He closed the curtain.

"Okay. Are you hungry?"

"Maybe in a while."

She gathered his muddy clothes and left the bathroom. She wasn't sure what had happened to him, but she was glad he came to her to talk about it.

She took his clothes to the laundry room and rinsed off as much mud as she could from his olive cargo pants, before dropping them into the washer with his t-shirt. When she heard the shower water turn off, she started the washer, then went to wait for him in the living room.

She sat on the couch and picked up a pillow with 'Get comfortable in Santa Cruz, California,' written on it. It was something Lewis had bought several years ago when he traveled the states and visited the west coast. She set it in her lap as Jasper came out of the bathroom looking better and adorable in PJs and a t-shirt.

He sat next to her, then laid down and put his head in her lap.

She stroked his damp hair. "Are you ready to talk now?"

He was quiet so long she figured he wasn't, but then he sighed and asked, "Do you remember Sam Jeffers? We went to his house last summer."

"With whiskey and cigarettes. He wasn't too happy you brought me with you."

"He died today. Or last night. Not sure when."

"Oh, Jasper. I'm so sorry. Did you have to go deal with it?"

"I was checking on him and found him."

"How awful."

Jasper took a breath. "I'm going to catch hell tomorrow from the chief for not following protocol, but I buried Sam on his property."

Poppie didn't know how to respond. No wonder he looked like he did. He buried a man today.

He looked at her. "I couldn't bring him in to be buried with a bunch of people. He hated people."

"Of course not. You did the right thing. What will happen to his property? And his animals."

"Bo Redford will take the goats and chickens. I brought the dog with me."

"He had a dog?"

"Yeah. A Lab." He glanced at her again. "Seems like I now have three dogs."

She smiled. "What's his name?"

"I don't know what Sam called him. Probably Dog. But I named him, Sam."

"I like that. Can't wait to meet him."

He rolled onto his back. "Thank you."

"For what?"

"This wasn't a good day. But having someone to come home to and talk with makes it so much easier."

She touched his cheek. "I'm here for you for as long as you want me to be."

He smiled. "How about forever?"

"Don't say that unless you really mean it."

He sat up and put his arm around her. "I never say anything I don't mean."

Chapter Eight

"Wish me luck."

W hen Jasper opened his eyes, it took a moment to remember where he was. He rolled onto his back and rearranged Lewis' Santa Cruz pillow behind his head. When he heard a noise in the kitchen, he raised up enough to look over the back of the couch.

"Poppie?"

She peeked around the corner. "Good morning, Deputy." She disappeared for a moment, then came out of the kitchen with a cup in her hand. "I made you coffee."

Jasper sat and stretched. "I take it, I fell asleep on you last night."

"Yes. And you were too exhausted and too cute to wake up." She set the cup on the coffee table and sat next to him.

"Did we eat last night?"

"No."

"No wonder I'm so hungry."

"I've got eggs and bacon."

"Great."

"And your clothes are clean."

Jasper put his arm around her. "You're an angel."

"Hmm. You didn't think that last summer."

He laughed. "Well, last summer you were...annoying and—" He smiled at her. "And I'm sure you still are." He picked up his cup and took a sip. "What time is it?"

"Nine, I think."

"Oh, shit. I've got to go."

"No breakfast?"

"I'll order something from the Loft. I never checked in with the chief last night. He has no idea Sam's dead. And I need to walk the dogs." He set his cup down and stood.

Poppie got to her feet as well. "I can go walk the dogs."

"You sure?"

"I'd love to. I miss Penny and Blackjack, and I'd like to meet Sam."

Jasper kissed her. "Thank you." He picked up his clean clothes and headed for the bathroom. "Maybe we can do lunch. Or dinner. I'll call you."

"Okay."

When he came out of the bathroom, Poppie handed him a travel coffee mug. "Take this with you."

"Thank you."

Poppie followed him to the door. "Good luck with the chief."

"Thanks." He opened his door and found the mud had been cleaned off of his boots. He shook his head at her. "Aren't you something."

"Don't get used to it. I'm just reeling you in."

"And then you're going to bite the hell out of me?"

"Something like that."

He leaned in and kissed her. "Actually, that wouldn't necessarily be a bad thing."

Poppie laughed. "I'll see you later, Deputy Goodspeed."

"You certainly will."

Jasper drove through the fog into town and parked in front of the sheriff's station. James' Bronco was there, along with Maisy's SUV. Jasper picked up his coffee mug, his uniform shirt, and his gun, then went inside.

Maisy waved him to the counter. "He seems a little upset this morning."

"He's mad at me. I was supposed to check in last night."

"How's Sam?"

Jasper shook his head. "He...has passed."

Maisy sucked in a breath and made the sign of the cross. "Oh heavens. The chief doesn't know?"

"He will in a few minutes." Jasper set his cup and gun on the counter, then put on his shirt and tucked it in. After securing his holster to his belt, he picked up his cup and gave Maisy a small smile. "Wish me luck."

She nodded.

With a sigh, Jasper went to James' door and knocked. After hearing a gruff, "Come in," Jasper opened the door and stepped into the office.

James studied him for a moment. "You look unharmed. No broken bones, dislocated shoulder, head injury. I don't see anything that would've kept you from coming into the office, or at the very least, calling me last night. I tried your home phone and even checked to see if you were at your mothers."

"So, she's worried about me, too?"

"Of course not. I wouldn't worry her unnecessarily."

"Right." Jasper sat in the metal chair in front of the desk. "Sorry. I got back late, and honestly, I was exhausted. I crashed at Lewis'."

James leaned back in his chair. "What happened? How's Sam?"

"Sam's dead."

James leaned forward and rested his forearms on the desk. "The hell you say?"

"He was dead when I got there. Near as I can tell, he died during the night. And I think he was expecting it, because he let the goats and chickens out so they'd find food if nobody showed up right away."

James leaned back again and stared at the desk for a moment before looking at Jasper. "Did you take care of him?"

Jasper nodded. "I know it wasn't protocol, but yes. I buried him at the edge of the trees."

The chief was quiet for a moment. "I would've done the same. It's what he would've wanted."

Jasper was surprised and relieved at the chief's response. "Bo is taking the goats and chickens. And I brought the dog to my place."

James nodded. "You'll need to check the county records to see if you can track down his relatives. I know he had a son who left here years ago." He glanced at Jasper. "They were never close."

"He was married?"

"Once upon a time, yes. Sam wasn't always the man you knew. Your mother and I... Well, we knew them quite well."

That was news to Jasper. He couldn't remember James ever going to check on Sam. "You were friends?"

"Not friends exactly, but we grew up together. Went to school. You know how that is. Technically, you know everyone in town, but they're not all your friends."

"Right." Jasper got to his feet. "I'll go get on the computer. What about the...paperwork. Death certificate and such?"

"I'll take care of it. It won't be the first time Hannigan and I side-stepped the medical red tape."

Jasper nodded, then retrieved his coffee cup from James' desk. "Okay. I'll be in my office."

Jasper left and gave Maisy a thumbs up as he passed her and went into his office. He switched on the computer. City Hall, which housed the sheriff's office, the jail, and the Registrar's office, was the only building in town with internet service via a satellite dish on the roof of the two-story building. The internet was slow, and highly affected by the weather, so doing anything online could be a long process.

It was only partly cloudy today, and the fog was lifting, so it might not be too bad. While he waited for the computer to go through its powering up process, Jasper emptied the coffee from the travel mug into his favorite coffee cup, then topped it off with hot coffee from the pot Maisy kept going in his office.

The handmade ceramic mug was one he and Ivy had bought from a craft fair in Augusta. She'd come to visit him when he was at the police academy. Her visits were the only thing that kept him from going insane in the big city and far away from Gracie Island.

He drank his coffee and frowned at the spinning loading circle. After several minutes, he sighed, then got to his feet. He was going to have to do it the hard way.

He left his office and went to the reception desk. Maisy was on the phone, so he waited until she hung up, then smiled at her.

She cocked her head. "What do you want?"

Jasper laughed. "You know me too well, Maisy."

"Yes, I do. I still remember you locking yourself in one of the jail cells when you were twelve."

Jasper leaned on the counter. "Right. The chief left me in there all afternoon to teach me a lesson."

"It was only a couple of hours."

"Are you defending his actions?"

She patted his hand. "No. But you never did it again." She topped off his coffee. "What do you need?"

"Sam's records. If he has any. The internet is being its usual non-existent self.'

"Honey, I know. I've been trying to get on all morning."

"So, you probably can't get much done until it starts working." He smiled at her again.

"Would you like help going through the records in the Registrar's office?"

"Yes, please."

Jasper and Maisy spent two hours going through boxes of records and finally determined Sam's son Evan was the only heir. Unfortunately, as Jasper feared, Sam never wrote a will.

The last information they had on Evan was fifteen years old when he left Gracie Island to go to college. Apparently, he never returned. Jasper took the file with the information and returned the box to the metal shelving unit along the wall of the records room.

He smiled at Maisy. "I'll see if I can track him online, though I'm not expecting to find much."

Maisy held out her hand. "Let me."

"Really?"

"Yes. It's what I do, Jasper. There's a good chance he's on social media."

Jasper grinned at her. "Well, look who's all social media savvy."

"I've found it's the best way to find people these days. Unless they live on Gracie Island, of course."

He handed her the folder. "Okay. Please, do your thing. I'm going to head to his house and see if there's anything there. If they stayed in touch, maybe there's an address or phone number."

"Okay, honey. Good luck."

Jasper picked up some chicken nuggets from the deli before heading to Sam's house. The fog had long since burned off and the clouds were mostly gone. It was a beautiful day, and he wished he was spending it with Poppie instead of digging through Sam's smelly house.

When he arrived at the house, he noticed the animals were gone. Bo had come and collected them, as promised. Jasper went into the house and opened all the windows to air the place out and let some light in. The sunny day helped and he could see well enough without having to turn on the generator.

He stood in the middle of the living room and looked around, not sure where to start. Spotting a cluttered desk, he went to it and sat in the chair. It seemed like the most logical place to begin.

Jasper spent an hour going through the desk and came up empty. There wasn't one thing even indicating Sam had a child, much less information on how to find him.

He checked the kitchen next and avoided the bedroom. He didn't want to go back in there if he didn't have to. But the kitchen was a dead end, so with a sigh, Jasper opened the bedroom door and went inside.

He checked the dresser and the closet, then finally the pictures on the wall. There was one photo that drew Jasper's attention, and he looked at it before removing it from the frame. It was a picture of a young man in a cap and gown. It had to be Evan. On the back was written.

Thought you might like to see this. Wish you could've attended.

Jasper looked at the picture again. The young man was standing in front of a Northeastern University sign. He tucked it in his pocket.

"There's a place to start."

He closed the windows, leaving them open an inch to continue airing, but not let in the rain, then left the house. There wasn't much else to do. The house would sit until they either found Evan or gave up trying. If they didn't find him, then the property would be auctioned off.

On the way back to town, Jasper realized he hadn't called Poppie. He went straight to the station and went into his office. He sat, turned on the computer, then dialed Lewis' number.

Poppie answered with a cheery, "Hello?"

"Hey."

"Deputy Goodspeed. I thought maybe you lost the number."

"Sorry. I was stuck at Sam's most of the afternoon."

"Oh, how was that?"

"Not fun."

"Are you free now?"

Jasper watched the computer come to life and connect to the internet. "How much do you know about searching online for people?"

"Like on social media?"

"Yeah."

"Who are you looking for?"

"Sam's son. And the internet in the office seems to be working at the moment."

"Would you like some help?"

"Can you bring food?"

"I'll be there in thirty."

Poppie showed up thirty minutes later with two Styrofoam boxes and a six pack of beer. Jasper smiled at the beer.

"Um. I'd like to remember what we find today."

"You don't need to drink it all. I just couldn't buy one beer at the grocery store."

"What did you bring to eat?"

"Aunt Peg's Cobb salad. For old times' sake."

"Perfect. Did you try it in Boston?"

"I did." She dragged a chair over to sit next to Jasper. "And you were right. None of them compared to Aunt Peg's."

"No brownies from Buns of Steele?"

"I thought about that. But he was closed."

Jasper checked his watch. "Oh right, school just got out. He picks his kids up every day. I guess this will have to do. And the beer helps make up for it."

Poppie looked around his office. "Oh my gosh. You're at work. We're at the sheriff's station and I brought you beer."

"The chief is in no position to say anything about me drinking on the job. Besides, it's just beer."

"Okay, if you say so." Poppie took a can out of the holder and handed it to him, then opened one of the salads and set it in front of him with a napkin and a fork.

"So, Sam had a son?"

After an hour of digging, they found Evan on Facebook. He hadn't been on recently, but they took a chance and left him a message. They also left one with the administrator of the Northeastern alumni page on the off chance someone there would know how to get in touch with him.

Jasper leaned back in his chair and took a sip from his second beer. "Not bad, Penelope."

She smiled at him. "You know, you're the only person in the world who calls me that. Even my parents have called me Poppie since I was two."

"Do you want me to stop?"

She shook her head. "No."

He grinned. "Good. Because I wasn't about to." As he turned off the computer, he stifled a yawn. "Oh, sorry."

"You look tired."

"Yeah. It's been a rough couple of days."

"Go home and get some sleep."

He took her hand. "I owe you a dinner."

"We just had dinner."

"The sky is clear. Sunset is in about two hours. How about some dessert while we watch the sun go down?"

"At the park? On the beach?"

"I was thinking from my living room. Without walls, we have a clear view until the sun drops behind the trees."

"Sounds perfect. I need to give Lewis his truck back. He and Sarah have plans tonight."

"I'll wrap things up here and pick you up in thirty."

"Can't wait."

Chapter Nine

"It's only been four days."

When Jasper pulled in front of Lewis' house, Poppie was sitting on the old couch next to Lewis' dog, Hank. She gave him a wave, kissed Hank on the head, then came down the porch steps with the paper bag holding her birthday present. Jasper reached across the seat and opened the door for her.

"Are we playing our game tonight?"

"I thought it might be fun." She got in the Jeep and put the bag in the backseat. "If you're up for it."

"We just need a bottle of whiskey and I'm ready."

She buckled her seatbelt. "And some dessert. Food first, so we don't get too silly."

"God, no. Wouldn't want that to happen."

They drove to The Sailor's Loft and parked in the lot, which only had a few other cars. Since Jasper knew who each car belonged to, he knew who was inside the restaurant. The mayor and his wife, and the Stuarts, who owned the mercantile, would be eating. The other patrons would be in the bar.

As usual, Peg greeted them when they came through the door. She kissed Jasper on the cheek and took Poppie's hand. "Are you here for an early dinner?"

Jasper returned Mayor Haskell's wave, then smiled at Peg. "We'd like a couple slices of apple pie to go."

Peg let go of Poppie's hand. "Coming right up. Something to drink?"

Jasper glanced toward the bar. "No, we've got that covered."

"Okay. Give me ten minutes."

Peg left and Jasper and Poppie went into the bar. Deidre was serving one of the four customers in the room, but smiled when she saw Jasper.

"Hey. What are you doing here? Kind of early for a drink." She nodded a hello to Poppie.

Jasper sat on a barstool. "Waiting for some food to take home. I don't suppose you have a bottle of whiskey back there you could sell me."

Deidre went to the glass shelf behind the bar and picked up a bottle of whiskey, then set it in front of Jasper. "My treat! We made a ton of money in tips Tuesday night and you didn't take any of it. So it's on me."

"Thank you."

"Are you two planning on drinking this tonight?"

Jasper grinned. "Not all of it."

"Okay. Whatever. I'm a discreet bartender. I'm not going to tell anyone."

Jasper touched her hand briefly. "I'm going to miss you, Deidre."

She winked at him. "I'll be back to visit."

"Yeah. That's what they all say."

Deidre turned to Poppie. "How long are you in town?"

"Um. Until after the wedding." She glanced at Jasper. "It's kind of up in the air at the moment."

When a customer came to the bar and Deidre left to serve him, Jasper turned in his seat and put a hand on Poppie's waist. "Up in the air, huh?"

She shrugged. "I'm unemployed at the moment, so I don't need to rush back. That is, if you don't mind me hanging around a little while longer."

"It seems we had a brief conversation about forever last night."

"Yes, we did. But you were also exhausted and fell asleep about five minutes later."

"You think I'm just fooling around here? I want you to stay at least until we figure out what..." He moved his hand to her cheek. "Where this is going."

She moved closer to him. "Where do you think it's going?"

He shook his head. "Somewhere crazy." He brushed some hair from her face. "And interesting." He leaned in and kissed her. "And a bit terrifying."

"Oh my. Well, I certainly need to stick around for that."

They took their bottle of whiskey and sat on the couch inside the front entrance to wait for Peg. She approached them with two Styrofoam boxes in her hands. "This is fresh cornbread. Your mother just pulled it out of the oven."

Jasper took the containers and smelled the one with the cornbread. "Mmm. Thank you."

Peg patted his arm. "You two enjoy, now." She glanced at the bottle of whiskey. "You're not planning on drinking all of that, are you?"

Jasper kissed Peg on the cheek. "Not tonight."

They took the pie, cornbread, and whiskey and put it in the Jeep, then drove to Jasper's house. They retrieved the food and Poppie's birthday present, then set it all near the rock fireplace. With the plywood on the roof, they were protected from the rain if it came. But without walls, the wind blew right through the house. Currently, there was only a light breeze, but when the sun went down, it could get chilly.

Jasper gave her a quick kiss. "I'm going to go get some blankets to sit on and I need to walk the gang.

"Can they come have dinner with us?"

"Sure."

While he was gone, Poppie walked through the house again. It was going to be a beautiful house, and she was very impressed Jasper was building it himself. Or at least mostly by himself. She tried to imagine living there. *Don't get ahead of yourself. Maybe the guest room would someday be a nursery. Wow, now you're really jumping ahead.* She remembered him saying last summer he didn't plan on being a father. Was that his grief talking? Or was it how he really felt? The fact Ivy was pregnant when she died most likely had something to do with the statement. The way he was with animals and his nieces, she knew he'd be a wonderful father. She watched Jasper with the three dogs at the edge of the trees. "What am I going to do about you, Deputy Goodspeed?"

When Jasper returned, he had his arms full with blankets, pillows, a lantern, and a propane heater. Perched on top of it all was Penny. Poppie took Penny and the heater. She set the heater near the fireplace as Penny wiggled and licked her face.

"How's my Princess Penny? Look how happy you are to see me." She glanced at Jasper, who was watching her. "I think someone's jealous. I think you like me more."

Jasper reached for the dog. "Don't go putting ideas in her head." He took Penny, then patted his thigh. "Come on, Sam. It's okay." The Lab hesitated a moment, then jumped onto the foundation and came to him. Blackjack, who couldn't yet jump, whined.

Jasper set Penny down, then went to Blackjack and picked him up. "There now, we're all together." He looked at the three dogs. "One big happy family."

Poppie put her arm through Jasper's. "A very cute family."

"Hmm."

They watched the dogs settle for a few moments, then Jasper went to the blankets and pillows. "Let's get comfortable and eat." He pulled a bottle of water and a beer out of his back pockets and handed the water to Poppie. "Sorry, that's all I have."

"It's perfect, thanks."

They arranged the blankets near the fireplace, rested the pillows along the rock hearth, and sat down to eat. Poppie handed a piece of pie and the cornbread to Jasper.

Jasper looked at her. "You need to have cornbread."

"Not really a fan."

He set his pie down. "Have you ever had real homemade cornbread?"

"I've had cornbread from a box."

He shook his head. "That's not cornbread." He took a knife out of his pocket, wiped it off on a napkin, then sliced a piece of cornbread in half. He then added some butter and honey, which Peg had provided, and held it out to her. "Take a bite."

She took a bite. "Oh my. That's—"

"Cornbread."

She took the slice from him and finished it. "Okay. I love cornbread. Peg makes this?"

"My mom's the baker. The pastries, bread, cakes, pie, all her."

"How do you not weigh three hundred pounds?"

Jasper laughed. "I work it off in the weight room in the basement of the station."

"I'd like to see that sometime."

"The basement?"

"No, you working out in the basement."

"Only if you work out with me."

"I'm afraid that'd just be embarrassing."

"Even better."

They continued eating and when Jasper was done, he set his plate aside, and leaned back on the pillow with a groan. He stretched his legs out and crossed his ankles as he rubbed his stomach. "I ate too much."

There was one small piece of cornbread left, and Poppie looked at Jasper. "Can I give this to the dogs?"

"Sure. Just remember, Penny's stomach is about the size of a grape."

"Really?"

He shrugged. "I don't know. But it's small. Doesn't stop her from overeating, though."

Poppie ripped off small bites for Penny and bigger ones for Sam and Blackjack, who seemed to have his appetite back. When she glanced at Jasper, she saw something in his eyes she couldn't quite identify. She gave the dogs each one more bite, then went to him.

She sat beside him and put a hand on his cheek. "What's wrong?"

He gave her a small smile. "Nothing. I'm good."

"No you're not. You had a moment." He looked away from her, but she turned his face back toward hers. "It's okay. Penny was your and Ivy's dog. And it's okay to remember that. I want you to think about her. And if you ever want to talk about her, I'm here for that, too." She kissed him lightly on the lips. "Okay?"

He nodded. "Okay." He sat up a little. "It's about an hour until sunset. Do you want to take the dogs to the water and watch it from there?"

"Sure." She started to get up, but he pulled her back down and kissed her. When Penny barked, they both looked at her.

"What's up, girl?" Jasper kissed Poppie again and got another bark from Penny.

Poppie laughed. "Somebody's jealous."

"Yeah. But jealous of who?" He patted the ground. "Come here, Penny." The dog ran to him and he put her in his lap, kissed Poppie again, then he looked at Penny, who wagged her tail.

Poppie laughed again. "This could be a problem."

"You think?" He put Penny on the ground before standing and helping Poppie to her feet. He stretched and groaned. "I need to walk off some of this cornbread. Although, I believe you ate more than I did."

"No way."

He picked up Blackjack. "There were four pieces, and I only had one and a half."

"You're such a liar."

"I'm a deputy."

"So? Are you saying all law enforcement officers only tell the truth?"

He thought for a moment. "Well, not all of them. I'm sure there are some that don't. Probably quite a few. But me? Always."

"You're so full of it." She picked up Penny, and they headed for the beach.

"Full of what?"

"You know what."

"One and a half pieces of cornbread?"

"Two and a half pieces of cornbread. And you *know* what."

"Just say it, Penelope. Say the word. You can even say crap. Crap is a very tame word. Jasper Goodspeed is full of crap."

Poppie nudged him with her shoulder. "Yes, he is."

He set Blackjack on the sand. "Why don't you swear? I want to know."

"I just don't feel the need."

He took Penny and set her in the sand next to Blackjack. "But it feels so good. You've no idea how satisfying it is to yell out—"

"Stop." She put her hands over her ears. "Don't say that word. That's the worst. And I've never heard you use it. Not even in the middle of a hurricane."

Jasper laughed. "I was going to say crap."

"No you weren't." She took his arm, and they started walking slowly down the beach.

"I'll remove that word from my vocabulary."

"So you do use it on occasion?"

"I've been known to utter it a time or two."

They continued in silence for a few minutes before she said, "Hmm. So it's been quite a week."

"It's only been four days."

"Really? With all the social activities, it seems like so much more."

He took her arm and turned her, reversing their direction. "You're jaded."

"I am not jaded. I'm beginning to appreciate the simplicity of Gracie Island."

"Oh yeah?"

"Yeah. And I'm really starting to appreciate the locals."

"All the locals?"

"Well, I haven't met all of them."

"Anyone in particular?"

"Hmm. There is this tall, sexy deputy in town."

"I heard about him. They say he's a great guy."

"They do, huh?"

"No. Actually, they say he's full of crap."

"From what I've seen. He has just the right amount of...it."

"Dammit. So close. You thought about saying it, didn't you?"

"No."

"And you say I'm a liar."

Chapter Ten

"This is a big bottle of gin."

Jasper and Poppie stayed on the beach and watched the sun drop down behind the trees before heading back to the house. While Poppie settled the dogs down, Jasper lit the lantern and the propane heater.

When Poppie came to join him on the blankets, he was frowning at the fireplace. "Why didn't I think of using the fireplace?"

"That would've been quite romantic."

"Yeah. Too romantic. Probably a good thing I didn't bring firewood."

"How is being too romantic a problem?"

"I don't want things to be too easy. I like a bit of a challenge." He laughed. "I know. 'Shut up, Jasper'."

She reached for the paper bag with her birthday present in it. "I think it's about time we played our game."

"Yes. Perfect way to change the subject."

She took out the gin and the sixpack of grapefruit drink. "Did you want to get a couple of glasses from your trailer?"

Jasper peered into the dark in the direction of the trailer. "No. We'll rough it."

"Okay." She opened the gin and one of the cans while Jasper opened the bottle of whiskey. "I get the first question, right?"

He nodded and took a drink from the bottle. "Go for it."

She took a moment. "Let me see."

He shook his head. "Like you haven't been thinking about this question for the last ten months."

She laughed. "All right, fine. What was Jasper like in high school?"

"Seriously? That's the question you ask after thinking about it all winter?"

"I'm just warming up." She held up the bottle of gin. "This is a big bottle of gin."

"Jasper was an average kid in a group of average kids. Nothing remarkable. Solid B student. Didn't skip class. Didn't pass notes. Didn't get into trouble."

"Boring."

"Would you rather I was the class troublemaker?"

"No. I figured with all those Boy Scout badges in your mom's display case, you were a good kid."

"You wasted a question on one you already knew the answer to. Drink."

Poppie took a sip of gin, followed by a sip of grapefruit drink, then moaned. "So gross."

"How old were you when you had your first kiss? And if it was in kindergarten, that doesn't count."

"Micky Saunders. Eighth grade dance. It was sloppy and disgusting, and we never talked about it again."

Jasper laughed. "Wow. What a great memory." He took a drink.

She looked at him for a moment, then asked, "What's your best all-time memory?"

"Hmm. Well, I really can't pick one. I've been pretty damn lucky in the good memory department. But this moment, right here, is moving up the list."

She moved to him and put her head on his shoulder. "Deputy Good-speed, I swear, you're beginning to live up to your name."

He kissed the top of her head. "I get another question. Sit up and take a drink." He waited until she did, then took another moment before saying, "This will be the last question no matter what your answer is, because either way, I don't want to be drunk."

"Well, now I'm intrigued."

He took a breath. "Would you consider staying here with me tonight and watching the sun come up in the morning?"

She smiled at him. "Are you sure Penny's not going to have a problem with that?"

"I'll put her in the damn trailer if I have to."

She sat up. "So, just to be clear. By staying the night, you mean…staying the night?"

"Um." He took her hand. "Well, we're not going to be playing Twister." He grinned. "Actually, that might be kind of interesting."

She pointed a finger at him. "Let's save Twister for another time." She moved close to him. "I'd love to stay here with you tonight."

He took another sip from the bottle before closing it and setting it on the fireplace. "Just so you know, this wasn't some elaborate plan."

"I know."

"How?"

"Because if it was, you would've thought about bringing the firewood."

He nodded. "I'm less of a planner and more of a let things happen and see where they lead, guy."

"I think I figured that out about you when you drove Duke's boat right up to the Dragonfly and let Roger take you aboard."

"But, see, *that* was stupid. This is...a very good idea."

She put her arms around his neck. "I'd have to agree." She kissed him, then they both looked toward Penny, who seemed oblivious.

"Okay. I guess she's over it."

Poppie woke to find that sometime during the night, Penny had left the other two dogs and was snuggled between her and Jasper. She watched Jasper sleep as she petted Penny's back.

"You're a sneaky little thing. But don't you worry, I'm not going to do anything to hurt your favorite human."

Jasper grumbled. "Don't believe her, Penny. She tried to kill me two, no three, times last night." He picked up Penny and moved her, then pulled Poppie into his side. "I should arrest you for... intent to do bodily harm. No. Illegal search? No wait. Breaking and entering."

Poppie laughed. "It think that last one would be on you."

"Oh right." He rolled on top of her. "I'd like to revisit the entering part." He kissed her neck and got a giggle out of her, then stopped when he heard something. "Oh, shit."

"What?"

He sat up. "It's Saturday."

"Yes. Why?" She heard what he'd heard. "Is that somebody coming down the road?"

"A few somebodies, yeah."

"Jasper!"

"It's the guys coming to work on the house."

"Oh my gosh."

"If ever you were going to swear. This would be it."

"Shut up. Get rid of them." She pulled the blanket over her head and curled into a ball.

"Okay. Not the morning I imagined." He pulled on his pants and went to the front door as Lewis' truck, along with two others, pulled up to the house. Lewis and four other men got out of the vehicles and Jasper raised a hand.

"Hey guys. Lewis, can I talk to you for a moment?"

Lewis joined Jasper as he walked a few feet away from the house. "What's up?" He spotted the pile of blankets. "Did we interrupt...something? Is that my sister under those blankets?"

Jasper put a hand on Lewis' shoulder. "I think your last question answered the first two. And you can get mad at me later, or whatever, but right now, I need you and the guys to go check out the surf for ten or fifteen minutes."

Lewis grinned. "She's pissed, isn't she? There's nothing I can say to top what she's got in store for you." He stepped away. "We'll give you twenty." He headed toward the other men. "Come on guys, let's go see how low the tide is this morning."

Jasper watched them go, then went back to Poppie, who was still under the blankets. "You can come out now."

"Are they gone?"

"They're down by the water."

"Jasper."

"They're here to work on the house."

She lowered the blanket and glared at him.

"It's not that bad."

"My brother just caught me in bed with his friend."

"It's not like I picked you up in the bar last night. Come on. He's not blind. He knows how we feel about each other."

"Hold the blanket up so I can get dressed." Jasper held up one of the blankets. "How could you forget they were coming?"

"Well, after about eight o'clock last night, I damn near forgot my name."

She almost smiled, but stopped herself. "Don't be cute. I'm mad at you."

"Okay."

She put on her shoes and then her jacket and Jasper dropped the blanket and picked up his shirt. "I'll take you home."

"No. I'll take Lewis' truck."

"Poppie." When she gave him a look, he said, "Okay. I'll drive Lewis home later."

She headed for the front door, then went to Lewis' truck and peered through the window. "He took his keys."

Jasper pulled his own keys from his pocket. "I'll drive you."

She held out her hand.

"What? You want to take my Jeep? The Jeep you said you'd never drive again?" When she didn't answer him, he put his keys in her hand.

She got into the Jeep, took a moment, then started the engine.

He watched her struggle to find reverse. "All the way to the right, then down."

She glared at him through the windshield, as she ground the Jeep into reverse and backed up twenty feet.

He mumbled to himself. "Okay. Good. You found it." He watched her stop, fumble into first, then move forward with a jerk. "Keep it under fifty."

He watched the back of the Jeep until it disappeared around a curve, then he went back to the house and picked up the blankets, pillows, heater, and lantern. As he headed for the trailer, he passed the guys returning.

"Hey, Jasper."

"Morning."

"We'll get started."

Jasper nodded. "I'll be right back."

He went inside and dropped everything, then sat at the table. "Good job, Jasper. You really screwed that up." When someone knocked on the door, he said, "Yeah?"

Lewis opened it and stepped inside, then sat across the table from Jasper. "She'll get over it."

Jasper looked at him. "I really like your sister, Lewis."

"Yeah. I got that. She fell for you about two days in last summer."

"No way."

"Truth. So don't you worry about this little setback. Like I said, she'll get over it."

"I asked her to stay awhile. Is that totally selfish of me?"

"No. You know Poppie won't do anything she doesn't want to do. She knew from the very beginning that getting close to you would include embracing Gracie Island. You and the island are inseparable."

"That's why it's selfish, because I'd never consider moving to Boston."

"And why is that?"

"Because I'd hate it and I'd begin to resent her for it. I'd be miserable and impossible to live with."

"And she knows that. So, not selfish, just a fact." He stood. "Come on. Let's go get some work done before it's time to freeze our asses off in the ocean."

"Shit. I forgot about that too. What's wrong with me?"

"You're in love, man. I know exactly how you feel."

"I haven't missed your wedding, have I?"

Lewis laughed. "Don't worry. I won't let you miss that." He opened the door. "So, how long do you think Poppie will last in the water?"

Jasper followed Lewis outside. "What do you mean?"

"She's taking the plunge today."

"What? How come I don't know about that?"

Lewis shrugged. "I assumed she told you. I guess you had other things to talk about. Or not talk at all." He shook his head. "Okay, not going there."

"There's not much to her. She'll have a rough time."

"Knowing my sister. I'd bet my last dollar on her succeeding."

"Me too. She's too damn stubborn to give up. Even if she gets hypothermia."

Chapter Eleven

"Sounds like loads of fun."

T he men worked on the house until noon, then called it a day so they could get ready for the polar bear plunge at two-thirty. Jasper caught a ride with Lewis to his house and, hopefully, the Jeep.

The Jeep was parked in front of the house in one piece and both men sighed with relief.

Lewis peered at it through the windshield. "I wasn't sure if she'd make it."

"You and me both, brother." Jasper got out of the truck, but Lewis remained inside.

"I'm going to go see if Jake needs any help setting up."

"Thanks."

"Good luck." Lewis backed onto the road, then, with a wave, drove away.

Jasper refrained from checking out the Jeep in case Poppie was watching him through the window. He went onto the porch, then knocked on the door.

Poppie opened it, blocking him from coming inside. "Deputy Goodspeed."

"Penelope."

She gave him a small smile. "I should still be very mad at you."

He smiled. "You can't do it. I'm too damn cute."

"Shut up."

"What's this I hear about you wanting to join the Polar Bear Club?"

"Right. I didn't want to tell you in case I chickened out."

"Have you?"

She shook her head. "Will you stay by me in the water? Keep me motivated? Cheer me on? Keep me warm?"

"Yes. All of that and more."

"Do you think I have a chance?"

He nodded. "You can do it. You *will* do it."

She let go of the door and hugged him. "I'm sorry."

He kissed her, then stepped away. "Enough of that. We need to get you ready."

"It's not for two more hours."

He went past her into the house and paced around the living room. "What are you going to wear?"

"Um. A swimsuit. One piece for extra warmth. A pair of board shorts. A parka."

He pointed at her. "All allowed except the parka. But you'll want one when you get out."

He stopped walking. "Go put on your suit and your shorts under your clothes. I'd come help you, but I don't know when Lewis is coming back."

She laughed. "I'll be right out."

He called after her. "Bring a wool sweater and a coat. Oh, and a beanie if you have one." He sat on the couch. "When you get out, you're going to be freezing."

She talked to him through the closed door. "Sounds like loads of fun." When she came out with a sweater, coat, and stocking cap in her arms, she said, "Why do you do this every year?"

He took her arm. "Come on. We need to go eat."

"Eat?"

"Yes. We're going to eat a lot. The digestion process will warm you from the inside."

Jasper took Poppie to The Sailor's Loft, and he ordered steak and lobster for them.

Poppie shook her head after Peg left the table. "I can't possibly eat this much food."

"What you can't eat, I'll finish."

She leaned back in her chair and smiled. "When did they start wearing swim suits? In the mural in front of the grocery store, the men are all naked."

"The naked butt, two guys from the left, is my great-grandfather Gracie."

"Wow."

"They started wearing suits in the eighties."

"That late? Goodness." She folded her arms across her chest. "So. If they were still jumping into the ocean in their birthday suits, would you be a member?"

He took a moment. "Probably."

"I guess it wouldn't be that big of a deal, since half the women in town have seen you naked."

Jasper laughed. "How do you figure that?"

"I heard you were quite popular in high school."

"From whom?" He pointed at her. "Sarah."

She took a sip of her iced tea and looked at him over the rim of the glass. "She gave me a brief rundown of your dating history."

"Just because I dated a few girls in high school. It doesn't mean they saw me naked. And I didn't date half the women in town. You've been misinformed."

"How many?"

"How many, what?"

"How many of them saw you naked?"

"Wow. Well, certainly not Sarah."

"I know. She told me."

Jasper took a sip of water and put his napkin on his lap. "Why do you want to know?"

"Since they're all still here. I just find it weird. And if a waitress or some woman ringing up our groceries, has been...close to you. I'd like to know."

He took a deep breath. "Well, aside from what you may think, I only got close to one other woman besides Ivy."

Poppie looked like she didn't quite believe him. "Hmm."

"And I'm not going to tell you who she is."

"Fine. Don't really care, anyway."

"Can we change the subject, then?"

"Sure."

Peg delivered the food to the table and put a hand on Jasper's shoulder. "Anything else, honey?"

"No. I think we're good."

"Mellie is helping at the bar today for the after-plunge party."

Jasper glanced at Poppie. "Great. It's Deidre's last day."

Peg left and Poppie smiled at Jasper. "It was Mellie."

He shook his head. "I told you I'm not telling you."

"You don't have to. I know I'm right."

Jasper picked up his fork and steak knife and cut a bite to eat. After he finished chewing, he said, "We dated for about eight months, figured out we wanted different things, and broke up amicably."

"What different things?"

"I didn't want to leave the island after I graduated and she did."

"For college?"

"Yes. And to travel the world and never look back."

"But she ended up coming back?"

He shrugged. "She's here."

"What happened?"

He took another bite of steak. "She had an affair with her professor. Got pregnant. Came home to raise her son."

"Mellie has a son?"

"Yes. He's ten."

"Wow."

"Can we stop talking about this now?"

"Yes. Unless you want to know anything about me. I mean, it's only fair."

He shook his head. "I don't want to know. Especially if your number is more than three." She laughed, and he studied her for a moment. "I assume you were close to Tiny Rum Bottle Guy. Otherwise, you wouldn't have carried it around in your purse for two years."

"You assume correctly."

"Okay. Let's talk about the plunge."

While they ate their lunch, Jasper filled Poppie in on everything she needed to do to stay in the water for the necessary ten minutes.

She pushed her plate aside with half of her steak still on it. "Easy."

"No. It's not. The shivering will start almost immediately, followed by an increase in your heart rate as it tries to pump more blood to your extremities. Next, you'll feel lightheaded and forget why the hell you're in the water. By the time you get sleepy and are about to lose consciousness, it's time to get out."

"Why are we doing this again?"

He grinned at her. "Tradition." He reached across the table and took her hand. "But, seriously, you don't have to do it."

"I'm not backing down now."

He squeezed her hand. "Of course you're not. But if at any time you want to call it quits. I'll go with you."

"You don't need to do that."

"I know. But I will. You say the word, and we're out of there."

She smiled. "Okay. And you won't call me a wimp? Or a quitter?"

"I promise." He pushed his plate aside and took hers. "At least not to your face."

Poppie threw her napkin at him.

He caught it and set it on the table. "Be nice to me. I'm the one who's going to be keeping you warm after you get out of the water."

After lunch, Jasper and Poppie went back to his house so he could get the things he needed for the plunge. Poppie took the dogs for a walk on the beach while he got ready. When he came out, he joined her.

There was a cool breeze coming off the ocean and the sky was partly cloudy. The temperature was lower than it had been the last few days.

Poppie shivered in her sweater. "So, how cold is the water?"

"About forty degrees."

"And what's the temperature out of the water?"

"Today? Probably fifty."

"It feels colder than that."

Jasper put his arms around her. "It's not too late to change your mind."

She sighed. "We were probably colder than that last summer during the hurricane, right?"

"Yes. But you didn't have a choice then. Today, you do."

"Ten minutes?"

"Ten minutes."

She snuggled into his side. "Let's do it."

"That's my girl."

They put the dogs inside, then drove to the marina, where a crowd had already started to gather. There was a small section of sandy beach next to the piers with a large fire pit. There was a roaring fire going, with wooden benches around it. Many of the onlookers brought their own beach chairs or blankets to sit on. There was also a food booth from the café with hot drinks and pastries.

Poppie took it all in. "This is quite the event. I didn't know I'd have a big audience to witness my humiliation."

"No judgement here. You're a star for even trying." He looked around. "I don't see any other women joining the group."

"That's because they're all too smart."

Jasper laughed. "That could be."

Lewis and Sarah came up to them and Sarah hugged Poppie. "Are you sure you want to do this? I don't want you catching pneumonia five days before the wedding. It's bad enough my groom is partaking in this nonsense."

Poppie glanced at Jasper. "How many opportunities am I going to get to be the first woman to do something?"

Jasper put his arm around her. "I told her we can walk away right now."

Sarah smiled. "That sounds like a good plan. I like that plan." She took Lewis' arm. "What do you think? We could all go get a drink somewhere nice and warm and dry."

Lewis kissed her. "Honey, I've survived the last six years. I think I'll be okay."

At the sound of a voice on a megaphone, they all turned toward Mayor Haskell, who was trying to get everyone's attention.

"Okay, folks. Ten minutes until the plunge. Polar Bears, get ready. Support teams, time to give that last minute pep talk."

Poppie took Jasper's hand. "Support team?"

He started walking. "Come on." They went to Kat and Peg, who had a table with towels, blankets, and two thermoses.

Kat shook her head at them. "Okay, you crazy kids. We'll be ready for you."

Jasper kissed her cheek. "Thanks, Mom."

She looked at Poppie. "Are you sure about this, honey?"

"Yes. I just need everyone to stop asking me that question. I'm...ready."

Peg took her hand. "I tried several years ago. Only lasted a couple minutes. But I wasn't nearly as...determined as you."

Jasper grinned. "I think she means stubborn."

Poppie looked at him. "Takes one to know one."

He put a hand on his chest. "Me? Stubborn?"

Kat checked her watch. "Okay, you two. Time to start taking things off."

Jasper grinned at Poppie. "You heard the woman."

Chapter Twelve

"If we get caught--"

As she stood on the beach next to Jasper and Lewis, along with fifteen other men, Poppie's resolve started to slip. *What am I doing?* She glanced at Jasper in his swim trunks, who seemed excited and totally committed to jumping into the forty degree ocean water.

He glanced at her. "You okay?"

She nodded and rubbed the goose bumps on her bare arms.

He leaned in to her ear. "By the way, that swimsuit is sexy as hell."

She nodded toward his bare chest. "You're not so bad yourself, Deputy." She smiled at Lewis. "And who knew my brother was...almost buff?"

Lewis frowned. "Thanks, Sis."

When the crowd started counting down from ten, Jasper took Poppie's hand. "Okay. Here we go."

"Don't let go."

"I won't."

When the count got to two, an airhorn went off, and Jasper started running. Poppie held on tight as he practically dragged her into the water. The shock of it didn't hit her until the water was at her waist. When it got to her chest, Jasper stopped.

She grabbed his arm. "Oh, my God. I'm going to die."

"Nonsense. That was the hard part."

She frowned at him. "It's not fair. The water is only at your waist."

He sunk down and went under the water.

She pulled him back up. "You crazy man."

He shook his head, spraying her with water, and she squealed. "Stop." He went behind her and put his arms around her. "How long has it been?"

"About two minutes."

Lewis came over to them. His hair was wet as well. He pointed at her. "Doesn't count until you go all the way under."

Poppie looked at Jasper. "Is that true?"

"Afraid so." He tightened his grip on her. "Ready?"

"No."

He started sinking slowly into the water until they were both under. Poppie felt like her head was going to crack open from the cold. She came up gasping. "Oh, my God. That was horrible."

Jasper laughed. "Isn't this fun?" He spotted a wave coming, and he turned Poppie to protect her with his body.

She turned and snuggled into his chest. "I can't feel my legs and arms."

The airhorn sounded again, and Jasper said, "Halfway there."

"Only halfway?"

"You can do it."

Lewis bounced in the water. "You got this, Poppie. Almost there."

"I'm wondering why I should want to?" She felt lightheaded and closed her eyes as Jasper continued to hug her to his chest. "Are you keeping me warm, or am I keeping you warm?"

"Both." He kissed her on the forehead. "I'm proud of you."

When the crowd started counting down again, Jasper let go of her and took her hand. When the airhorn sounded the third time, they headed for the shore. When the water was at her hips, her numb legs didn't want to hold her. Jasper picked her up and carried her the rest of the way.

He whispered in her ear. "You did it."

"Never again."

He laughed. "You'll do it again next year."

Kat and Peg met them at the water's edge and wrapped towels around them. Jasper continued to carry her until they got to the firepit. He set her in a chair and Kat put a blanket around her.

"Are you okay, honey?"

Poppie was shivering too much to speak, but she nodded her head. Jasper dried her hair with the edge of his towel, then knelt beside her. Peg handed Jasper their beanies, and he put Poppie's on, then put on his own. She also had the two thermoses, and he took one and opened it.

Poppie looked at him. "What is it?"

"Soup."

She stuck a hand out from under the blanket and took it from him. "Hot soup?"

"Take it slow."

She took a sip of the soup. She couldn't tell what kind it was, but it was hot and really good. She gave Kat a small smile. "Thank you."

Jasper opened the other thermos and took a drink. "It's not Burt's generic vegetable soup, but it'll do."

Poppie smiled. "Do you think being cute is going to stop me from being mad you talked me into this?"

"Me talk you into it? I didn't even know you were considering it until this morning."

"Hmm. Well you could've—"

"I gave you every opportunity to back out."

"Okay. I guess I only have myself to blame." Kat and Peg had wondered off, and she lowered her voice. "Would taking a hot shower be against the rules?"

"Only if you take it by yourself. The rules clearly state—"

She pulled him in and kissed him. "I need a hot shower right now."

"Yes, ma'am."

They both stood and Jasper called to Kat. "We'll see you at the Loft in a few."

"Okay, honey. Don't be too long."

Jasper and Poppie gathered their clothes, then headed for the Jeep. When he cranked up the heat, Poppie put her hands in front of the vent.

"How come you're not cold."

"I am." He pulled the blanket aside and pointed at his chest. "Goose bumps."

She felt his skin. "Aw, you *are* cold."

"Of course. I'm just not whining about it."

"Whining?"

He laughed. "Just kidding. You've been a trooper. And you'll be applauded when we get to the Loft."

"Really?"

"Yes."

She took stock of where they were. "Where are we going? You don't have a shower in your trailer."

He pulled in front of the sheriff's station and parked. "There's a shower in the basement."

She cocked her head. "Isn't the jail in the basement?"

"Yes."

"So, this is the shower your prisoners use?"

"Occasionally."

"Eww."

"We haven't had anyone in custody long enough to shower in eight months."

"Have you used the shower?"

"Yes. Quite a bit lately. It's here or my mom's."

She opened her door. "Okay."

She followed Jasper to the door and waited while he unlocked it. He glanced over his shoulder. "No one here today. We have the place to ourselves."

"Right. Like this morning?"

He laughed. "That was me forgetting the guys were coming over."

"Okay. So you haven't forgotten the chief was coming in to work out in the basement? Or it's the day Maisy cleans the cells?"

"No. All clear." He held the door open for her.

"If we get caught—"

He put his arms around her and kissed her neck as he closed the door with his foot. "It's all good."

They went to the basement and Jasper dropped his blankets and towel, then took off his trunks. Poppie blushed, then hesitated before removing her swimsuit.

Jasper grinned at her. "After last night, you're going to be shy now?"

"That's different."

"How so? Naked is naked."

She cocked her head. "Well, when you look like you do, there's no reason to be shy."

He stepped up to her and kissed her. "You can leave the suit on if you want."

She took a moment, then slid a strap down her shoulder.

He took the other one and pulled it down. "Here, let me help you with that."

They stayed in the shower longer than necessary and way past the point of getting warm. They finally got out when the hot water started cooling off. Jasper handed Poppie a dry towel, and she wrapped it around herself.

"Is this a prisoner towel?"

Jasper laughed. "No. It's my towel, and I washed it...recently."

"Okay, fine."

They dried off and got dressed, then Poppie went to Jasper and put her arms around his neck. "Other than the ten minutes in the water, and when Lewis and the guys showed up this morning, this has been a very good day."

"It's not over yet."

She sighed. "So plunge party at the Loft?"

"Yep."

"Do we have to go?"

"Of course. You're going to be officially inducted into The Polar Bear Club."

"Do I get a trophy or something?"

"You get a plaque. And a t-shirt, I think."

"Okay, cool." She slipped on her coat. "Do you have a plaque and a t-shirt?"

"I did. Lost them in the fire."

She hugged him. "Oh. I'm sorry. They should replace those for you."

"It's fine. I don't need them. I know what a stud I am for doing it for twelve years."

She patted his chest. "Stud, huh. Does that mean I'm a stud, too?"

"Not until you've done it eleven more times."

She smiled. "Challenge accepted."

"I knew you'd do it again next year."

When Jasper and Poppie walked into The Sailor's Loft, everyone got to their feet and congratulated her. Jasper stepped away from her and clapped as well, then whistled loudly. Kat came to hug her, then led her to a table.

Poppie sat down and Jasper sat across from her.

Kat smiled at them. "You two relax. I'll bring you some food. Jasper, do you want a beer?"

"Yes, please." He looked at Poppie. "Rum and Coke?"

She shook her head. "Hot tea, please."

Kat left, and Lewis and Sarah sat at the table. Sarah reached for Poppie's hand.

"You did it. Congratulations."

"When my arms and legs went numb, I wasn't sure if I was going to make it."

Sarah glanced at Jasper. "Well, good thing you had a big, strong deputy to carry you out of the water."

Jasper smiled. "Just doing my job. Never leave a man behind." He glanced at Poppie. "Or woman."

When Kat returned with Poppie's tea, she set it down and looked at Jasper. "Sorry, honey. I'll get your beer in a minute."

"Don't worry about it. I'll get it." He glanced at Lewis. "You want one?"

Lewis nodded, and both men stood. "We'll be right back."

As the men left, Sarah moved her chair closer to Poppie. "Okay, I want details."

"Details?"

"Lewis told me about this morning."

Poppie closed her eyes and shook her head. "So embarrassing."

"So you guys...obviously... Come on, spill."

"I'm not giving you any details. But it was...amazing."

Sarah squealed, then put a hand over her mouth and glanced at the tables near them. She lowered her voice. "Sorry. That's so exciting. So you're staying in town, right?"

"For a while, yes. We haven't really talked about it yet."

"Well, yeah. With all the sex, when was their time to talk?"

"Shh." Poppie giggled. "There *was* quite a bit of—" She stopped when she saw the men headed back.

Jasper eyed the two women. "You guys look like you're up to no good."

Sarah patted Poppie's hand, then moved her seat back next to Lewis'. "We're making plans for tomorrow night."

Lewis turned in his seat. "You have plans for tomorrow night?"

"Do you really think we're going to sit home while you guys are out doing whatever Jasper has planned for your bachelor party?"

"What are you going to do?"

"None of your business."

Lewis looked at Jasper. "Did you know about this?"

"Nope. News to me." He took Poppie's hand. "But have fun."

Sarah laughed. "Oh, we will."

Chapter Thirteen

"You've always been a good boy."

J asper walked into Kat's kitchen, then stopped when he saw James sitting at the counter.

"Oh. Hey."

"Good morning, Son."

James didn't often visit Kat's house, certainly not this early in the morning. "Is Mom okay?"

"Yes. We're just having a cup of coffee." He glanced at his watch. "Before I go into the office."

"Hmm." Like Jasper, James liked his coffee, but Maisy always had a pot going at the station. There was no reason for him to come get a cup from Kat. Jasper thought about what Poppie had said, but quickly dismissed it. *Impossible.*

Kat came in from the back door with an arm full of flowers from her garden. "Jasper. Good morning, honey."

"Mom."

"James and I were just having a cup of coffee."

"Right. So I heard." Pepper came up to the stool and rubbed his face on Jasper's boots. Jasper reached down and gave him a scratch behind the ear.

Kat went to the counter and took a vase from a cupboard. "Can you stay? There's plenty of coffee." She filled the vase, then began arranging the flowers, while humming quietly to herself.

Jasper watched her for a moment. "Um. I came to get some things from my room for the bachelor party. Might not have time after the game."

Kat poured a cup of coffee and brought it to him. "What are your plans for the party?"

Jasper took a sip. "We're throwing it at Lance's cottage. Bonfire on the beach, roasting hotdogs, beer." He smiled at her. "Lots of beer."

"I can imagine."

"Then we're going to have a marathon of the worst scary movies ever made."

James turned on his stool and looked at Jasper. "You're watching movies at a bachelor party?"

"Terrible movies. We make bets on them. Like who dies first. Who survives the movie. And we take a shot every time someone does something stupid or falls down while running away from the bad guy."

"What happened to strippers at bachelor parties?"

"We've evolved past strippers. Besides, most of the guys coming are married or in a relationship."

"Right. Of course. I was joking."

Jasper drank some more coffee then set the cup in the sink. "Okay, well, I'm going to go dig around in my room. You two do whatever it was you were doing." He picked up Pepper and cradled him in his arms.

"Just coffee, Son." James turned back toward the counter.

Kat smiled at Jasper. "Okay, honey." She looked at James. "Did you have strippers at your bachelor party?"

"Me? No. Of course not."

Jasper smiled as he headed out of the room with Pepper in his arms. "Not what I heard."

The Sharks and the Barracudas had been playing each other every Sunday, weather permitting, for the last fifty years. Team loyalty was generally inherited. Everyone related by blood or marriage to the Gracie's was a Shark. The original Barracudas were fishermen and dockworkers. If you were born into a family that had family members on both sides, you needed to choose your team. Jasper made the choice when he was a junior in high school. As a descendant of the Gracies on his mother's side, he went with the Sharks. The chief was a Barracuda, but had stopped playing by the time Jasper started.

Barracudas had taken over the infield, so the Sharks were warming up in the outfield. Jasper was standing in as catcher so Lewis could warm up. The Shark's catcher was late. Randy was still cleaning up after an unusually busy Sunday morning at the bakery. But he assured the team he'd be to the field before the game started. When Jasper was distracted by something and missed a ball, Lewis turned to see what had drawn his friend's attention.

He turned back to Jasper. "Is that...?"

"The chief."

"Is he playing?"

Jasper watched James catch a ball and pitch it to another player. "Son of a bitch. He still has a pretty good arm."

Lewis moved to Jasper's side. "Did you know he was playing today?"

"I had no idea. I even saw him this morning and he didn't say anything about it."

Lewis watched James for a moment. "Is he any good?"

"Yeah. He was real good. Back in the day, anyway."

"Anything I should know before I pitch to him?"

"He swings for the fences."

Lewis grinned and patted Jasper on the shoulder. "Just like his son."

When the referee, Davis Hannigan, whistled, the men all headed for their respective dugouts. From his seat on the red bench, James caught Jasper watching him and he gave him a nod. Jasper returned it, then took his seat.

Lewis sat next to him. "Word is, he's filling in for Jake who's out with the flu." He adjusted his ball cap. "How long has it been since he played?"

Jasper shrugged. "Fifteen years or so. I was barely in high school when he stopped pitching."

"Why start again now?"

Jasper glanced at the stands and spotted his mother. "I don't know." She gave him a wave and he tipped his hat.

The Barracudas took their places on the field with James stepping onto the pitching mound. The red section in the bleachers cheered and James took off his hat and waved, then slipped into game mode.

Childhood memories of Sunday afternoon games came back to Jasper. They were memories he'd conveniently tucked away. As a child with mixed feelings about his father, he wanted to be proud of him, but it was much easier not to be. So he sat among the Shark's fans, next to his mother, and grumbled along with the rest of them when James struck someone out or hit one into the trees. His mother, a Shark through family loyalty, would quietly cheer her husband on, and wait for the tip of the hat he always gave her when he crossed home plate.

The first Shark at bat got a hit off the initial pitch and made it to first base. James seemed to take a moment to gather himself, while the second batter stepped up to the plate. He hit a groundball and made it to first while his teammate proceeded to second. By the time the third batter stepped up, James found his rhythm and the man struck out. Lewis was up next.

Lewis was a great pitcher, but his batting was unpredictable. So, Jasper wasn't sure how he'd fair against the chief, who in his day, had a mean fastball. If James was still capable, and did his research on the Sharks, he might know Lewis had trouble with a fastball.

The first ball came in slow and low, and Lewis let it go by. The next ball, flew in fast and true, surprising Lewis, who swung and missed.

He glanced back at Jasper, who gave him a nod and said, "Kick his ass."

Lewis took a deep breath, then prepared himself for the next pitch. It came in fast, and Lewis hit it, sending it to leftfield. Unfortunately, Duke wasn't hungover today, which he often was, and he caught the ball and threw it to second, before the runner on first got there.

With two outs, Jasper was up with a man on third. He adjusted his hat, and dug his toe into the dirt, then moved the bat into position. When he looked James in the eye, he couldn't quite read what his father was thinking. As good as James was, he'd never played with Jasper. There wasn't any playing catch in the yard, or pointers on how to bat or catch. By the time Jasper started playing, his father had stopped. They'd never faced off on the field, until this moment, and Jasper wasn't about to let his father have the upper hand.

James wound-up and threw the first pitch. It was fast, but a little high, and at the last moment, Jasper stopped himself from taking a swing. He prepared himself again, and looked at James, who nodded and almost smiled.

James took a moment, then pitched the ball fast and right over the plate. Even though it was a fastball, time seemed to slow down for Jasper, and he kept his eye on the ball as it moved toward him. He stepped into the speeding ball and swung hard. At the sound of the bat hitting the ball, time returned to normal and Jasper could hear his teammates yelling. He dropped the bat and ran for first as the ball soared over the head of the shortstop and the centerfielder. There was a line of trees serving as the back fence, and the ball disappeared into their foliage as Jasper rounded first and headed for second. When the man on third made it home, Jasper slowed down, jogged past third and headed home. As he stepped on the base, he took off his hat and held it up in the air.

The blue section of the stands exploded with cheering, and the red side was on their feet. James left the mound and approached Jasper.

He offered his hand. "That was a hell of a hit, Son."

"Thank you."

As James turned and returned to the mound, Jasper looked toward the stands and spotted Poppie on her feet. She clapped and threw him a kiss, as he put his hat back on and headed for the dugout.

In the sixth inning, Jasper got one more hit off of James and made it to third. He was then brought home by the next batter. The game ended with the Sharks winning four runs to two. No one else got a homerun off the chief, and he struck out several Sharks. In the end, Jasper had to admit, the old man still had it.

As Jasper made his way through the crowd to Poppie, he was stopped several times and congratulated on his homerun. When he got to Poppie, she hugged him.

"Wow! You're really good."

"You're surprised?"

"No. I could tell last summer when everyone was disappointed that you couldn't play with your shoulder injury. It's nice to see for myself." She leaned into his ear. "You nailed the chief's fastball."

Jasper grinned. "I did, didn't I?"

He took her hand and moved her away from the crowd. He wanted to say hi to his mother, but when he saw her, she was talking to James and he decided against it. But when she motioned for him to join them, he sighed.

"Dammit."

Poppie took his arm. "Come on. You need to say hi and let him congratulate you on winning the game."

"I don't think that's going to happen."

They walked to Kat and James, and Jasper gave his mother a kiss on the cheek.

"Good game, honey."

Jasper glanced at James. "Thanks."

James nodded. "You're a decent player. Even with a bum shoulder."

Jasper frowned. "My shoulder's fine and has been for a while now." *You'd know that if you ever came to a game. Or asked about it. Or gave a damn.* "Are you going to keep playing?"

"I just might. It took some convincing from the team, but I enjoyed it." He glanced at Kat. "And of course your mother, pretty much insisted I do it."

Jasper looked at his mother. "Okay, well, we're going to go eat some lunch before tonight's festivities begin."

Kat took Poppie's hand. "I hope you have something planned for tonight."

Poppie smiled. "Sarah and I and some of the women are going to hang out."

"How fun." She looked at Jasper. "And you, don't get too crazy."

"Mom. Do you know me at all? When was the last time I did something crazy?"

She gave him a hug. "Never. You've always been a good boy."

Jasper stepped away from her. "I'm not twelve, Mom." He took Poppie's hand. "I'll see you tomorrow."

Kat waved and the chief nodded, then said, "I'll be on call tonight if things get out of hand."

"I told you what we're doing. Pretty sure you can rest easy. Ice your pitching arm and go to bed early. You'll probably be sore tomorrow."

Jasper and Poppie walked away and she glanced over her shoulder before saying, "You just had to get a jab in, didn't you?"

"He called me a *decent* player. *Decent.*" He sighed. "I know. I'm being—"

"Immature? A bit sensitive?"

"I hit the only homerun of the game. Off of his famous fastball. That's more than a decent effort."

"Okay." She put her arm around him. "Does it really matter what he thinks? Or that he can't bring himself to congratulate you?"

"No." But it did. Just once, it'd be nice to hear, 'Good job, Son.' They'd reached the parking lot and Jasper steered them toward the Jeep. "I asked Aunt Peg to put together a lunch for us. Thought we could take it to the gazebo."

"Sounds great."

Jasper retrieved a small ice chest and a paper bag from his Jeep. Poppie took the bag from him. "I'm sorry you don't have the father you deserve."

He shrugged. "I've learned to live with it."

They walked across the park to the gazebo, and when they got close, they saw Lewis and Sarah there with a picnic lunch of their own.

Jasper stopped at the bottom of the steps. "Is this a private lunch? Or would you like some company."

Lewis waved at them. "Come on up. The more the merrier."

Jasper and Poppie sat on the bench a few feet from Sarah and Lewis and Poppie dug into the ice chest.

Sarah smiled at Jasper. "So, you finally got to face off against the chief."

"Let's talk about something else. He was the oldest guy on the field and he damn near annihilated us."

Lewis pointed at Jasper. "Everyone had trouble with his pitching, except for you. You saved us."

"I wasn't about to let him get to me. And as good as he is, he's not better than you."

"Well, sure. I'm thirty years younger. But he's pretty damn good considering he hasn't played in fifteen years."

"Okay, enough adoration for the chief. Change of subject. The bachelor party."

"Yes. What are we going to do?"

Jasper grinned. "Not telling you. Just wanted to get your mind off the game."

Poppie handed him a beer. "Might as well get started with the drinking."

Chapter Fourteen

"Never have I ever."

While the men were at the bachelor party, the women decided to have a sleepover at Amanda's house. Her husband was at the bachelor party and planned to spend the night with one of the guys, so the women would have the place to themselves. Along with Sarah and her two sisters, Amanda and Portia, three other women joined them. They were Mandy, Anna, and Tina, all women who'd grown up on the island. Poppie only knew Sarah, and she felt a little overwhelmed and out of place. But it didn't take long for the other women to welcome her into the fold.

They drank margaritas and painted their nails, while gossiping and wondering what the men were up to. Poppie had never gone to a sleepover while in high school, but she imagined this was exactly what it was like.

Sarah blew on her newly polished nails, then confirmed Poppie's assumption. "This is just like high school." She picked up her margarita. "With the added bonus of alcohol."

Poppie laughed. "I was never one of the popular girls. I preferred to hang out with Lewis and his friends. So this is my first sleepover party."

"Lucky you. Of course my sweet Lewis let his little sister hang out with him."

"I think he was a little bit afraid of me."

Sarah raised her glass. "Cheers to that." She took a drink. "My poor baby."

"He's just a really good brother and his friends liked me."

Portia took a drink. "I'll bet they did."

Poppie shook her head. "No. Not like that. We kind of had an unwritten rule. Neither of us would date the other's friends."

Sarah moved from the floor to a beanbag chair. "How'd that work out for you?"

"Lewis broke the rule his senior year when he started dating my friend Allison. I didn't talk to either of them for a month."

"And now, you've broken the rule."

"I guess I have. Good thing my brother is more understanding than I was."

Portia dropped a fluffy pillow on the ground and sat on it. "If we want to give you the full sleepover experience, we should play Never Have I Ever."

They all agreed, and Sarah refilled all the glasses from the pitcher of margaritas. "Okay. I get to make the first statement, since I'm the bride and all." She thought for a moment. "Never have I ever...gone out on two dates, with two different guys, on the same day."

Amanda pointed a finger at Sarah. "That was meant for me, wasn't it?" She took a drink and the other women squealed. "Mike Sutton and Robbie."

Anna shook her head. "You cheated on Robbie with Mike?"

"No. I cheated on Mike with Robbie."

Portia laughed. "And six months later, they got married."

Amanda held up her hand. "I get the next one." She smiled. "Never have I ever kissed Jasper."

Poppie and Sarah glanced at each other, then took a drink. When Tina drank as well, they looked at her.

Tina shrugged. "One time. On the beach during the spring break bonfire."

Sarah leaned forward. "What year?"

"Sophomore."

"He and I broke up a month before that."

"I guess he was feeling lonely."

Portia nudged Tina. "And you were only too happy to oblige." Portia glanced at the other women. "So, three out of seven of us have kissed Jasper."

Mandy cleared her throat. "Make that four." She took a drink. "Eighth grade dance."

Sarah laughed. "You might've been his first."

"I don't know. He sure seemed to know what he was doing."

They all giggled and looked at Poppie, who blushed. "He is a very good kisser."

Sarah raised an eyebrow. "And?"

"And that's all I'm going to say."

Tina raised her hand. "I have one." She grinned at Poppie. "Never have I ever slept with Jasper."

Poppie shook her head, then held up her glass before taking a drink.

The men were on their second movie when the woman Jasper had bet on to make it through the movie alive, was brutally killed by a machete wielding half-man, half-wolf.

He leaned back on the couch. "Dammit. I was sure she was going to make it."

Lance handed him a beer. "The women never make it. Why do you keep betting on them?"

Jasper looked at the beer, then set it aside. He'd had way too much to drink. He'd told the chief he'd be in by ten in the morning, which was a big mistake. He'd be lucky to make it by noon. He sat forward and ran a hand through his hair.

"I need to call it, guys."

"Oh come on."

Jasper glanced at Lewis. "Sorry man. I'm on duty tomorrow."

Lance laughed. "Good luck with that."

Lewis stood, wavered for a moment, then pointed a finger at Jasper. "I understand. I'll call Mellie."

"Nah, I can walk. It's only a mile or so."

Lewis shook his head. "I'm not sending you into the dark to walk a mile...or so, while intoxicated. Mellie said she'd be our chauffeur tonight."

While Lewis called Mellie, Jasper got to his feet and took a deep breath. "Final bet." He picked up the DVD case of the third movie and studied the picture. He turned it toward the guys and pointed at a blond man with a mustache. "Mr. Porn Star here, will survive the movie." He took a five-dollar bill from his wallet and set it on the table. "I'll collect my winnings in the morning."

"You lost every bet, man."

"I know. But I've got this one. Porn Star 'Stache, for the win."

When Mellie arrived fifteen minutes later, she came in and surveyed the six drunk men in Lance's living room and the paused movie on the television.

"Wow. You guys are pathetic." Jasper went to her and she took his arm. "Why are you leaving so early? It's only one o'clock."

"I need to serve and protect tomorrow."

She laughed. "Good thing you live on Gracie Island. The land that crime forgot."

Jasper pointed at her. "Funny." He picked up his jacket and stared at it for a moment, temporarily forgetting how to put it on.

Mellie took it from him and helped him into it, then looked at the other guys. "I'll take the deputy home, then be back for whoever is next."

Jasper stood still while she buttoned his coat. "You should watch the last movie. I bet on the guy with the mustache."

"I'm not sure if I'd be welcome in this manly group."

Jasper put his arm around her shoulder. "Of course you'd be welcome. You're one of the guys, Mel."

"Gee, thanks, Jasper."

After a round of goodbyes that lasted way too long, Mellie closed Jasper into the passenger seat of her small SUV, then got in behind the wheel and looked at him.

"You haven't been this drunk in a while."

"Not my fault. There are too many stupid people in those movies."

"And you took a shot for every one of them?"

"Yep."

"Okay. I really don't think you'll be up to serving and protecting tomorrow."

"Well, fortunately, as you so cleverly said, nothing ever happens on Gracie Island. Unless, of course, another jealous mainlander visits and takes out his cheating brother."

"I don't imagine that's going to happen again. At least for a while."

"I hope not. One guy with a hole in his head is enough for me." He laid his head back and closed his eyes.

When they arrived at Jasper's trailer, Mellie pulled close and put the vehicle in park. "Do you need help getting inside?"

"Nah. I'm good." He tugged on his seatbelt, then cursed when he couldn't get it off.

"Let me." Mellie released the belt. "There you go."

Jasper smiled at her. "Thank you. And thanks for the ride."

"Anytime."

He got out of the SUV, then gave Mellie a wave as she drove away. He could hear the dogs at the door, and when he opened it, they rushed out to greet him.

"Okay guys. I know. I missed you, too." He petted each one. "Now go on and do your thing."

The dogs ran off and after Jasper did *his* thing next to a pine tree, he perched on one of the two chairs in front of the trailer. With a forecast of rain, the sky above him was cloudy, but the air was still and he could hear the waves hitting the beach. He desperately wanted to call Poppie to see how her night went, but he decided against it. She didn't need to hear him slurring his words. He'd call her in the morning.

A knock at the door woke Jasper, and he groaned and hid his face in the pillow. When another knock came, he yelled, "I'm not here!" Then he was sorry he'd made such an effort as the aftereffects of his overindulgence appeared. He rubbed his head and tried to get comfortable on the pillow which suddenly felt hard as a rock.

"Jasper. It's me."

Poppie was the only person he'd open the door for, so he got up slowly and frowned at the clothes he still had on from last night. "I'm coming." He'd fallen into bed after taking off his boots and jacket. He opened the door and squinted at the gray light that filtered in. "Hey."

"Wow."

He leaned on the door frame. "I know."

The dogs rushed past him and greeted Poppie. The ground was still wet from the rain, but for the time being, it'd stopped. Jasper stepped outside and sat on the step in front of the door, then rubbed his face and ran a hand through his hair a couple of times.

"Do you want me to leave so you can go back to bed?"

"No. I'm glad you're here." He held up a hand, and she took it, then kissed him, lightly.

"What can I do?"

"I don't suppose you brought a gallon of coffee with you."

"No. But I can make you some. Unless I'm still banned from the trailer."

"I cleaned up a little. Sort of." He leaned to the side so she could go past him and open the door.

She stepped inside and said. "Oh my."

"No judgement."

"No. It's about what I expected."

"*Coffee.*"

"I'm on it."

When she came back out a few minutes later, Jasper stood to get out of her way, then headed for the porta potty. "I ah. I'll be back."

When he returned to the trailer, Poppie was sitting in a chair with a cup of coffee in her hand. She handed it to him as he sat in the other chair and took a drink.

"Thank you."

"You're welcome. So last night was a success?"

For a moment he thought the coffee was too much, too soon, but then his stomach stopped contracting and he took another sip. "I'd say, yes. It was great." He leaned back in the chair. "What time is it?"

Poppie checked her watch. "Eleven."

"Shit. I was supposed to be at work an hour ago."

"Whoops." She patted his arm. "So what did you guys do?"

"Um. Drank, mostly."

"Sounds fun."

"We watched a couple of movies."

"No way."

He shrugged. "It's a thing we do. Scary movies. Terrible ones."

"Oh, okay."

"You think we're lame."

"No. I just thought there would be strippers involved."

"That's what the chief said. Would you really rather I hired a stripper instead of binging horror movies?"

"No. Of course not. I was teasing."

He drank some more coffee and stretched his legs out. "What did you ladies do?"

"We had a sleepover."

"Oh. Not lame at all."

"Stop. It was fun. And I got to meet some more Gracie Island women."

"Like...?"

"Mandy, Tina, and Anna. So there were seven of us with Sarah and her sisters." She glanced at him. "We played Never Have I Ever."

He turned in his seat and smiled at her. "How'd that go?"

"Well, it seems that four out of the seven women have kissed Deputy Goodspeed."

"What? No way."

"Tina. Sophomore spring break bonfire?"

He thought for a moment. "Oh yeah. I'd just broken up with Sarah. It never went beyond that one kiss. In fact, she didn't speak to me all summer after that."

"Was it a non-consensual kiss?"

"No. Not at all. In fact, she kissed me. I was just…"

"An innocent bystander?"

"Something like that." He grinned. "I was sixteen, and a girl wanted to kiss me."

Poppie laughed. "Okay."

"Who was the other one?"

"Eighth grade dance."

Jasper grinned. "Mandy."

"Was she your first?"

He shook his head. "No." He finished his coffee and started to get up. "I need a refill."

She put a hand on his knee to stop him. "I'll get it. Just relax." She stood and took his cup. "Who was the first?"

Jasper squinted at her. She'd never let it go. "Mellie."

"Really. First kiss and first… Interesting."

"It was the summer before eighth grade. On the beach and spontaneous. Kind of surprised us both, actually."

"But nothing after that?"

"Not until junior year."

"You have so many secrets, Deputy."

"Well, at the rate you're dragging them out of me, there aren't many left."

She kissed him, then went into the trailer. When she came out with a fresh cup of coffee, Jasper was standing in the yard studying the cloudy sky.

She handed it to him. "Are we going to get more rain?"

"Yeah." He turned to her. "What are you up to today?"

"Sarah and I are taking the ferry to the mainland and picking up her dress."

"Don't stay too late. We're going to have a bit of a storm tonight. Don't want you to get stuck over there."

"What's too late?"

"Hmm. Don't miss the five o'clock ferry. Jake probably won't make the eight o'clock."

"Then I should go." She hugged him. "Sorry I woke you."

"It's fine. Like I said, I'm late for work. The chief's taking the noon ferry, too."

"Oh, great. I'll be sure to avoid him."

Jasper laughed. "Why? He's nice to you."

"Is he? It's hard to tell."

"Go on or you'll miss it."

"I'll see you later."

Jasper watched her drive away, then called the dogs and went into the trailer. He stopped inside the door. Somehow, in the small amount of time Poppie had spent inside making coffee, she'd managed to straighten things up.

He shook his head. "She just couldn't help herself."

Chapter Fifteen

"That's because you always had cookies."

The chief had already left when Jasper got to the station with his uniform on a hanger. He needed a shower and more coffee before he'd be ready to take on the day.

Maisy smiled at him. "Good morning, sweetheart. You look..."

"I know. Was he mad?"

"A little. But he was more upset about having to go to the mainland. You know how he hates meeting with the county supervisors."

"Better him than me."

She poured him a cup of coffee. "Someday it *will* be you."

"Hmm. Can't wait." He drank some coffee, then headed for the stairs. "I'll be ready to go once I shower."

"Nothing going on. Take your time."

The shower felt good, but it reminded him of Poppie, and he didn't say in as long as he thought he would. It just wasn't the same without her.

When he got dressed and went back upstairs, Maisy was on the phone. He gave her a nod as he refilled his coffee, then headed for his office. With the cloudy sky, he knew the internet wouldn't be working well, so he didn't bother turning on the computer.

James had left a couple of folders on his desk, so Jasper sat, took a sip of coffee, and opened one of them. It was a report, filed late yesterday, about a wild dog causing trouble at some of the residences on the edge of town. A few people had spotted him, but he was skittish and took off when they tried to approach him.

They tried to keep a handle on the feral animals on the island. But once in a while someone's pet would run off and never come home. They ran in the wilds, but occasionally came in to knock over garbage cans, and kill a chicken here and there. But they usually weren't too much trouble.

When Maisy appeared in his doorway, he closed the folder and smiled at her.

She came into the room and set a bottle of Tylenol on the desk. "Thought you might need these."

"Thanks." He washed two pills down with coffee.

"I got another call about the dog. Did you read the report?"

Jasper opened the folder again. "Yeah. Who called?"

"Warren Westly. Said he spotted him on Lighthouse Road this morning and it appeared the dog was hurt."

"Shot? Or hit by a car?"

"He couldn't tell. The dog ran off to the south."

"I'll take a drive out there and see if I can spot him." He stood and clipped his gun to his belt. "I'll try to stay in radio range."

"Okay. The chief won't be back until after five."

He gave her a wink. "Hold down the fort, Maisy."

Before heading out of town, Jasper bought three soft tacos from the deli. He was feeling a little closer to normal, and he figured putting some food in his stomach would help to get him the rest of the way there. He also bought a half-pound of ground beef. If the dog was hurt, he wouldn't get close to Jasper. But he might come in for a meal. Jasper brought a cage with him with a trigger under the food bowl that would close the door and safely trap the dog.

He headed to Harper's Fork, then took a right on Lighthouse Road. He'd lose radio contact in two miles, so he drove slowly looking for any sign of the dog. When he reached the two mile mark, he pulled over and took the trap out of the back of the Jeep. He carried it, and the ground beef out of sight of the road, picked a tree he'd remember, and put the trap at the base.

"Okay, you bastard. Come and get it." He set the trap, then backed away from it. "Of course, God knows what else I might trap in here." He glanced around. "You better come out before someone else eats this."

The wildlife on the island consisted mostly of a variety of birds, but there were small rodents, rats and mice that came over on boats and escape onto the land. However, they mainly stayed in town, where the food was readily available. In the wilds, it was mainly stray dogs and cats.

Jasper returned to the Jeep and drove two miles further down Lighthouse Road before turning back. When he got within radio range again, he called Maisy.

"I'm headed back. Did I miss anything?"

"Not a thing. Although, Wilda Meyers called and said her roof was leaking again and she was worried about the storm tonight."

"I'll stop by and see if I can do anything for her."

"Thank you, honey."

"So, Maisy. Someday, when I'm chief, are you still going to call me honey?"

"Jasper, I watched you grow up. I don't think I'll ever quite think of you as anything other than the skinny little boy who'd come hang out with me after school."

"That's because you always had cookies."

"Check in after you leave Wilda's."

"Yes, ma'am."

Jasper pulled up in front of the old house Wilda had lived in for forty years. She'd lost her husband, Ben, ten years ago, and her children had moved from the island years before that. She was alone and too old to keep up with the maintenance required to keep a house from deteriorating in the damp island weather.

She came out on the porch when Jasper got out of the Jeep.

"Deputy?"

"How you doing, Wilda? Heard you had a leak."

"Well, yes. But certainly you have better things to do than fix my roof."

"Do you have a ladder?"

"Around back."

"I'll take a look."

"You're an angel, thank you. I'll put some coffee on."

Jasper went around the house and found a ladder propped against the wall, looking like it'd been there since Ben died. He pulled away the weeds that had grown around it, then moved it to a low section of the roof. After giving the ladder a shake to test its stability, he climbed up and got onto the roof. It was all in bad shape, but there were missing shingles in one spot and he went to check it out.

When he heard, "Any luck?", he went to the front of the roof and smiled down at Wilda.

"I think I found the problem. Is it leaking into this corner room?"

"Yes. Ben's study. I don't want his books to get wet."

"I'll be right down." He went back to the ladder and climbed down, then went to the front of the house to find Wilda. "It's going to need a more permanent repair by someone who knows a lot more about roofs than I do. But I can keep the room dry temporarily."

She took his hand. "Thank you, dear."

"I'll go check in the shed for something to patch it."

Wilda checked the sky, which was getting darker with heavy clouds. "How soon is it going to rain?"

"We probably have an hour or so."

"If it starts lightning, you come down from there."

"Don't you worry about that."

Jasper went to the shed and found what he needed to apply a temporary fix to the leak. If the weather cleared tomorrow, he'd send Lance to fix it correctly. Lance knew his construction and would put the roof on Jasper's house soon.

It took him about forty-five minutes, and as Jasper finished, the first raindrops fell. He gathered his tools and went down the ladder, then went onto the front porch and knocked on the door.

Wilda opened the door and took his arm. "Oh my, it's raining. Come in and let me get you a towel."

"No. I'm fine. I just wanted to let you know I was done."

"Nonsense. Come inside."

Jasper stepped through the door and waited for Wilda to bring him a towel. After handing it to him, she motioned toward the kitchen. "Come sit and have some coffee."

She was obviously lonely, and he didn't have the heart to say no. He dabbed at his hair, then hung the towel around his neck. "Can I use your phone to check in with Maisy?"

"Of course, dear. Then come sit for a minute."

Jasper dialed the station and got the chief.

"Oh, hey. I didn't realize how late it was."

"Just got back. Where are you?"

"At Wilda's, she had a leak."

"Did you fix it?"

"Of course."

"Okay. Nothing going on. You might as well head home when you're through there."

"Did you, by any chance, see Poppie and Sarah on the ferry?"

"Yes. They're back."

"Thanks."

Since Wilda was busy in the kitchen, Jasper made another call to Poppie. "Hello?"

The sound of her voice made him smile. "Hey. Back safe and sound?"

"Deputy? Where are you? Your Jeep wasn't at the station."

"Are you checking up on me?"

"I wanted to make sure you weren't out getting into trouble."

He leaned against the desk. "I'm at Wilda's. She had a leaky roof."

"Did you bring her a bucket?"

Jasper laughed. "No. I fixed the leak."

"Wow. I didn't know that was in your job description."

"This is Gracie Island."

"Right. I hope you're done, because it's raining pretty hard."

"I am. Just need to visit for a few minutes."

"Is this Wilda someone I need to worry about?"

"She's closing in on eighty."

"Hmm. Okay. Then, aren't you the sweetest thing?"

He straightened. "I'll see you soon."

He hung up the phone and went to find Wilda in the kitchen. There were two cups of coffee and a plate of cookies in the middle of the table. She smiled and pointed at a chair.

"Have a seat. I just made the cookies this morning."

"Thank you." He took a sip of coffee and reached for a cookie. They weren't his mom's cookies, but they were good. "Mmm. My favorite."

"If I remember correctly, all cookies are your favorite."

Jasper laughed. "I do have a weakness for them."

Wilda had owned the bakery before she retired and sold it to Randy Steele. Every Saturday, he'd go to the movies, then get a cookie from the bakery. The theater closed when he was in high school and he missed it almost as much as getting cookies from Wilda's.

Wilda smiled. "I have a pot of stew on if you'd like to stay for dinner."

"Thank you. That's very kind. But I'm having dinner with a friend tonight."

She tilted her head. "That new girl? I heard you've been spending time with her."

"She's Lewis Jensen's sister. He's getting married on Thursday. Poppie's here for the wedding."

"Oh. How nice. I haven't seen her, but I hear she's very pretty."

Jasper nodded. "Yeah. She is."

"Well, good for you."

It was time to change the subject. "It seems you could use some help around here, Wilda."

"Oh. I do alright."

"I'll talk to the guys in the fire department. I'm sure they wouldn't mind coming and doing a few repairs."

"I don't want to be a bother."

"It's no bother. You know Lance, right?"

"Oh yes. He's even bigger than you. Though I remember when he wasn't. His family moved here when he was in elementary school."

"Yes, they did. He's very handy with repairs. He's helping me build my house. I'll send him by soon."

She patted his hand. "Thank you. You're too good to me."

"Just paying you back for all the free cookies you gave me."

She handed him a cookie. "Take another for the ride home."

Chapter Sixteen

"Thanks for listening."

With help from his friends, Jasper spent the morning putting up the exterior walls of the house. With the rehearsal dinner tonight and the wedding on Thursday, they wanted to at least get that done before Lewis was gone for two weeks on his honeymoon. Earl was scheduled to start wiring the house on Thursday. And on Monday, the plumbing would be installed. Jasper knew nothing about the electrical or plumbing, so he'd leave that to the experts. Once those things were done, though, the windows and flooring could be completed and then the drywall installed. It was all coming together, and after today, it'd look like a house.

He thought about his picnic with Poppie in the living room. No more watching the sunset through the walls. Although, with all the windows, they'd still have a good view from most any room. He smiled as he realized anytime he thought about the house, Poppie was in the picture. Living there alone didn't seem like an option anymore.

At noon, Poppie arrived and Jasper went to greet her. She seemed impressed with their progress. "Wow. You have walls."

He was happy to see her and he gave her a hug and a kiss, before taking a step back from her. "We'll have to watch the sunset from the front porch from now on."

She glanced at the small space in front of the door. "You'll need to actually build the porch first."

"Next week. I hope." He checked his watch. "I have to go into the station soon, but first I need to check on my trap. Would you like to take a ride?"

"Sure. What are you trying to trap?"

"A stray. He's hurt and possibly dangerous. Been raising a little hell the last week or so."

She seemed concerned. "What are you going to do with him if you trap him?"

"Take him to Doc Hannigan's. See what the damage is, and figure out if he's worth saving."

She frowned. "And if he isn't?"

"Let's not worry about that just yet. I need to find him first. Which hasn't been easy." He kissed her again. "Let me go talk to the guys. We're about done for the day."

Thirty minutes later, after Jasper sent the guys home and changed his clothes, he and Poppie left the house and turned on Lighthouse Road. When he spotted the tree where he left the trap, he pulled to the side of the road and stopped the Jeep.

"The trap is under that crooked pine." As he and Poppie got out of the Jeep, Jasper looked around. There was no sign of the dog and he'd gotten no reports about sightings or knocked over trash cans. If the dog was badly hurt, he could be dead by now. Jasper searched the sky. No sign of vultures, seagulls, or any other carrion-eating birds.

He took Poppie's hand, and they walked through the brush to the tree. The trap was empty, with the door still open, but the beef was gone.

"Dammit. Something not heavy enough to set off the trap got in and ate the bait."

"Like what?"

"Mice, rats, maybe a bird."

"Gross. Rats, not birds."

Jasper checked the sky again. "There *are* some gross birds. I didn't bring anymore meat, and it was a longshot, anyway." He picked up the trap, and they made their way to the Jeep. The bowl that held the bait smelled a bit like rotten meat, so he took it out of the trap and stashed it in a plastic bag. He then left the trap in the back and closed the rear door.

Poppie got into the passenger seat, then turned toward Jasper when he got in behind the wheel. "What now?"

He shrugged. "I guess we wait until someone spots him again."

"Do you think he's okay?"

Jasper shrugged as he pulled onto the road. He didn't want to share his fear that the dog may have died from his injuries. When he spotted the animal standing in the middle of the road about fifty feet away, he stopped the Jeep and turned off the engine.

He retrieved a rope with a slip knot on one end and a plastic bag with some old bacon in it, then opened his door. "Stay here." He stepped out of the Jeep and took his gun out of its holster. The dog growled when Jasper closed the door, then took an aggressive step toward him and snarled.

"Easy, boy. I'm not going to hurt you." Jasper took a step, and the dog snarled again. "I don't want to shoot you, but I will if I have to." He pointed the gun at the animal and took another step. The dog had blood coming from a wound on his side and when he moved toward Jasper, he favored his right leg. "I want to get you some help. Will you let me do that? I got a treat for you. Something I know you'll like." He shook the bag.

When he heard Poppie open her door, he glanced at her. "Stay in the Jeep."

"He's hurt. Don't shoot him."

Jasper kept his eyes on the dog, and said, "I'm not planning on it. Get back in the Jeep, dammit."

She circled the back end of the Jeep and came up behind Jasper. "I can help."

The dog seemed to feel outnumbered and he growled again, then suddenly charged. Jasper fired over the animal's head, and it stopped, then turned and ran off down the road.

"Dammit, Poppie. I said to stay in the Jeep."

"I just wanted to help."

"Well, you didn't. Now he's gone again. He'll probably die a slow death from his injuries or get taken out by another dog."

"Can we go search for him?"

Jasper studied her for a moment. "*I'll* go. You stay here."

"But..."

"But what?"

"I can..."

Jasper sighed. "Okay. Fine." He opened his door and sat. "Get in."

"Really?"

"Yeah. Get in the Jeep. Please."

Poppie went around the vehicle and got inside.

Jasper held out his hand, and she hesitated a moment before taking it. Before she realized what he was doing, Jasper put one end of his handcuffs around her wrist and the other around the steering wheel.

"Jasper!"

"I told you I was an asshole." He got out of the Jeep and peered at her through the window. "Stay here."

As he walked away, she yelled, "Like I have a choice."

With the bad shape the dog seemed to be in, Jasper felt the animal couldn't have gone far, so he followed the road, which took a curve around a stand of trees. He glanced over his shoulder at the Jeep before losing sight of it and almost went back. But when he heard a low growl in the brush ahead, he pulled his gun again, and moved toward the sound.

The dog was crouching in the brush, teeth bared, eyes crazy, and obviously in distress.

"Okay, dog. Let's get you to Doc Hannigan. He can at least give you a peaceful death."

The dog backed up and growled.

"Or we can do it the hard way." Jasper had never had to dispatch an animal, and he wasn't looking forward to doing it now. But if the dog wouldn't cooperate, he might need to. With the way the dog was bleeding, Jasper doubted he'd last another day.

He took a piece of bacon out of the bag and threw it near the dog. The animal seemed to have no interest in the food. Jasper took another step forward, and the dog moved toward him instead of retreating.

"Feeling brave, now, huh?" Jasper moved two more steps forward.

The dog charged again, and Jasper was out of choices. He fired and missed. The dog got to him and latched onto his arm before he could shoot again. His second shot hit the animal in the chest and he yiped then dropped to the ground. But the dog had gotten in a good bite to Jasper's arm before the second shot killed him.

"Shit." He scowled at the growing blood stain on the sleeve covering his right forearm. He turned and glared in the direction of the Jeep, even though it wasn't in his line of sight. He couldn't help but blame the whole situation on Poppie's stubbornness.

The dog was lying on his side in the dirt, bleeding from the chest. "You didn't have to die like this." He knelt and put a hand on the dog's head. "I'm sorry."

Jasper holstered his weapon, then turned away and headed for the Jeep. Without acknowledging Poppie, who was scowling at him through the window, he went to the rear of the vehicle and opened it.

Poppie turned in the seat. "I heard gunshots."

Jasper frowned. "The dog is dead. He didn't need to die like this. This is your fault. You did this."

Poppie started crying. "I'm sorry."

"You're sorry? Tell that to the poor dog."

She wiped her eyes, then pointed to Jasper's arm. "You're bleeding."

Jasper studied the blood on his sleeve, then unbuttoned the cuff, and pushed it up. The wound was big and deep. He didn't want to be mad at Poppie, but he couldn't help himself. He rolled the sleeve beyond the bite mark.

"You got bit."

"No, shit." He took out a first aid kit and opened it.

"Let me help you do that."

"You've done enough." He glanced at her. "Turn around and leave me alone. Or don't. Do whatever you want. You always do."

Without responding, Poppie turned in her seat.

The only thing he had to clean the wound was alcohol, which he knew would hurt. He held his breath and poured some on the bite. Growling the word he told Poppie he'd remove from his vocabulary, he sat on the bumper and waited for the pain to stop. He then wrapped it with gauze and tied it off.

He had an old blanket which he'd used for various things. Today, however, it'd be used to wrap a dead dog in. Without acknowledging Poppie, who he knew was watching him, he walked toward the dog. When he got to it, he put the blanket on the ground. He then lifted the animal onto the blanket, wrapped him up, and carried him to the Jeep.

He set the wrapped body in the Jeep and put a hand on it for a moment, before closing the door a little harder than he needed to.

When he got in behind the wheel, Poppie asked quietly, "Are you okay?"

"No. I'm not okay. The son of a bitch was probably rabid." He glanced at his bandaged arm. "I've probably got damn rabies."

"I'm sorry."

"Save it." He dug the handcuff key out of his pocket and removed the cuffs, then tossed them onto the dash.

They drove in silence and when they came to the fork, Jasper turned toward Lewis' house instead of town. He pulled in front of the house and Poppie looked at him.

"Jasper?"

He shook his head, and she got out of the car and closed the door. He pulled away before she got to the porch. As he got to the main road, he realized he was driving too fast, and he slowed down and took a deep breath as he looked at his bandaged arm.

"Shit." He glanced in the rearview mirror at Lewis' receding house. "Damn stubborn woman."

As he continued down the road, Jasper's hands started shaking violently and he stopped the Jeep. He got out and took a deep breath, then leaned against the vehicle.

"What the hell?"

He looked at the sky, then rubbed his face and stared at his boots, as he realized he wasn't mad at Poppie. He was scared for her. He was afraid of losing her. The whole situation could've been much worse. The dog could've gotten past him and kept coming the first time. It could've made it to Poppie.

"Why are you doing this to yourself again? Why are you offering up your heart, only to have it shattered *again*?" He shook his head. "She makes you so crazy you're talking to yourself."

He stood and started walking. He went fifty feet, then turned and went back to the Jeep. He needed to clear his head and think about the situation rationally.

He grunted. "*Rationally*? When it comes to love, there's no such thing." He leaned against the Jeep again and talked to a tall pine on the other side of the road. "Okay. Here's the deal. Would you give up the life you can have with her out of fear that someday you could lose her?" He looked at the blood seeping through the gauze on his arm. "Chances are, she'll get you killed long before something happens to her."

He got back in the Jeep and started it, then looked through the window at the tree. "Thanks for listening."

Jasper drove to the clinic and went inside. Amy was on the phone, and she gave him a smile and held up a finger.

He nodded and leaned on the counter while he waited for her to finish. When she hung up the phone, he straightened as she smiled at him. When she saw his bandaged arm, she lost her smile and came out from behind the counter.

"What happened?"

"A dog. Got me good."

"Blackjack?"

"No. A feral mutt out in the wilds. He was hurt, and I was trying to catch him."

She took his arm. "I'm going to take you right back to a room." She glanced at the only other patient in the waiting room. "Is that okay, Pete?"

Pete glanced at the blood and nodded. "Sure. Blood beats upset stomach."

Jasper followed Amy to an examination room and sat in one of the two chairs. Now that he'd gotten his emotions under control and the adrenaline rush was gone, the bite was starting to hurt. He leaned back and tried to relax.

Amy smiled at him. "The doctor is with another patient. But I'll send him in as soon as he's done. Can I get you anything?"

"No. I'm good."

Amy left him and he leaned back and closed his eyes. He was upset for getting so mad at Poppie, but he felt it was partially justified. All she had to do was listen to him.

While he waited for Dr. Hannigan, Jasper recalled all the times he'd asked Poppie to do something and she ignored him. It was a frustratingly long list. And he wasn't sure how it was all going to work if she didn't respect him enough to do what he asked in a situation where, clearly, he knew best. He didn't want to spend the rest of his life being fearful and throwing himself into dangerous situations to protect her. *You'll do it though, because you're an idiot.*

After twenty minutes, Dr. Hannigan came into the room with a sigh.

"What happened, now?"

"Dog bit me."

Davis unwrapped the gauze. "He certainly did. What dog?"

"A feral one. I caught up to him a couple miles past the fork."

Davis glanced at Jasper. "How was he acting?"

"Mean. Crazy. He was hurt, though. So maybe that's why. I don't think he would've lasted too much longer.

"Or he could've been rabid."

"I hope not. I brought him with me. You can test him, right?"

Davis took a step back and folded his arms across his chest. "Yes. But I'll need to send the samples to Augusta. So it'll take a few days." He went to the cabinet and took out some supplies. "I'm going to give you the first Rabies treatment dose. Don't want to take any chances."

"Okay. Do whatever you think is best."

"How'd you get him here?"

"In the back of my Jeep. I shot him when he charged me. That wasn't the plan. I was trying to bring him in to you, alive."

The doctor returned to the table. "Of course. You probably just put him out of his misery. Let's get this cleaned up."

As Davis cleaned the wound and took a few stitches to close the spots where the dog's teeth had sunk deep, he glanced at Jasper. "Seems your visits to me coincide with Ms. Jensen being in town."

Jasper shook his head. "It seems to be a pattern."

"Would it have anything to do with your overenthusiastic need to protect her?"

Jasper grumbled. "She wouldn't need protecting if she'd listen to me once in a while. The woman considers the words, 'please stay here,' as a challenge."

Hannigan laughed as he bandaged Jasper's arm. "Perhaps you should quit putting her in situations requiring you to tell her to stay put." He took a step back. "It'll be sore for a few days. I'm going to start you on antibiotics. And I've got two shots for you to get your preventative treatment started.

"Shots?"

"I know. Not your favorite thing."

"Are they going to make me sick? Lewis' wedding is Thursday."

"You should be fine. There might be a little soreness at the injections sites. But it's not going to hurt nearly as much as that bite must. Would you like some pain medication?"

Jasper thought about it for a moment. "I guess. I need to be pain free tonight and for the wedding."

"What's tonight?"

"Rehearsal dinner."

"Are you going to be drinking?"

"I was planning on it."

"Take a pill soon, then no more until you go to bed. Unless you drink a lot, then wait until morning."

"Got it."

Chapter Seventeen

"The tree told me the same thing."

Poppie's parents had arrived earlier in the day and gotten two rooms at the one motel in town. They wanted to give Poppie a place to get ready for the rehearsal dinner and the wedding other than Lewis' bachelorized bathroom.

She stepped out of the shower and wiped the steam from the mirror, still reeling from the confrontation with Jasper. But she'd gone from hurt and confused to mad and resentful. *How dare he cuff me to the steering wheel.*

During her long shower, she'd decided the best way to get back at him was to look absolutely irresistible at the rehearsal dinner. She'd bought two dresses for the dinner. The first one she loved, but then decided it was a bit too risqué. It was on the short side, with a lower neckline than she was used to wearing. So, she bought another she felt was more suitable for the occasion. But now, things had changed. She'd wear the slightly inappropriate dress and Jasper would love it. But he'd also hate the fact he wouldn't be getting near her tonight. Petty? Yes. Did she care? No.

She blew out her hair with a hot brush, leaving it straight with a slight curl on the ends. Then she applied a little more makeup than she normally wore. Last, she put on her lacy black underwear and bra. Knowing she was wearing it and he'd never see it somehow made her feel powerful. She slipped into the light blue dress, which was an almost perfect match to her eye color.

She backed away from the mirror. "Oh man. It's too much." She wished she could take a picture and send it to Sarah. But since this was 'no cell tower' Gracie Island, she didn't have that option. The next best thing was to call.

Poppie went to the room phone and dialed Sarah's number.

"Hello?"

"Hey Sarah. I'm sorry to bother you. I know you're getting ready."

"It's fine. What's up?"

"It's my dress. I'm thinking of wearing the light blue one."

"I love that dress."

"But it's so..."

"Perfect. Jasper will love it."

Poppie didn't want Sarah to worry about the thing with Jasper, so she said, "I know. But is it too, you know, with all the parents being there?"

"It's not that...whatever. It's classy, with a slightly sexy undertone. The only problem I see is that you're going to outshine me."

Poppie laughed. "That'll never happen." She took a breath. "Okay. I'm going to go for it."

"Good. See you soon."

Poppie put on a pair of strappy heels. Tonight, Jasper wouldn't be nine inches taller than her. She returned to the mirror.

"Okay. I hope this drives you crazy, Deputy."

The doctor had told Jasper to keep his bandage dry, so he wrapped his arm in plastic wrap before he took a shower. The pain pill was doing its job so far, so he was confident he'd be able to enjoy himself at dinner. Or at least pretend he was enjoying himself. He hadn't quite let go of his anger over the events with Poppie and the dog. He vacillated between being mad at her for her stubbornness, and being mad at himself for falling in love with her.

He scowled in the mirror. "All she had to do was listen. Is that so hard?" His reflection didn't have an answer for him, so he picked up his razor. Sarah had hinted that she'd like the men in the wedding to be clean shaven or at least not scraggly. Jasper ran a hand over his cheek. He didn't want to shave his beard completely, but he put his beard trimmer on the lowest setting and cleaned up his facial hair. His beard was still there, but it was neat and tidy enough to make Sarah happy.

The dinner wasn't formal, but Jasper put on one of his few dress shirts, with light grey slacks and a charcoal pullover sweater. He didn't often dress up. There was no reason to, but Thursday he'd be in a suit. He couldn't even remember the last time he wore a suit. He thought about it for a moment. "Grandpa's funeral. Five years ago."

He hadn't worn a suit to Ivy's funeral. Two days after she died, the island was hit with three weeks of rain. There was no reason to wear anything special under rain gear. Since her body was never recovered, they held a ceremony on the beach, in the pouring rain. Her gravestone was placed in the cemetery a month later, but there wasn't a casket under it. After the ceremony, her family had held a wake, but he didn't attend. He left the beach and went home, then didn't leave for a month.

He studied his reflection. "Yeah. You look stupid." He rolled his shoulders a couple times and ran his hands through his hair. "You can do this. Even though you want to strangle her when you see her. Don't. Be cool." He pointed at the mirror. "Be cool."

When Jasper arrived at the church, Lewis was outside waiting for him.

"You're late, man."

Jasper shook his hand. "Sorry. Had a bit of a mishap."

"Are you okay?"

"Yeah. Nothing to worry about."

They went inside to Sarah, Poppie, the minister, Sarah's two sisters, and her parents. Jasper nodded a hello to everyone, but avoided making eye contact with Poppie. She looked fantastic in a light blue dress that, for her, was edgy. He knew if he made eye contact, she'd be able to read his mind. And with what was going through it, he didn't want that to happen.

Pastor Mike gathered everyone. "Okay, I need the groom and the best man, or ah, woman, here on my left. Jasper, you and Amanda will come down the aisle first and then go to your respective sides, then maid of honor, Portia, followed by the bride and father of the bride."

Everyone nodded. They all knew basically what to do and Jasper felt this was all a waste of time, but he followed Amanda to the back of the church and then they walked together to the front again.

She nudged him halfway down the aisle. "You clean up rather well."

"Sarah insisted. Don't get used to it."

"I think Poppie approves, too."

Jasper glanced at Poppie, who was whispering to Lewis, but he didn't respond to Amanda.

He took his place next to Poppie, once more avoiding her eyes, and standing further away from her than he needed to. She smelled faintly of flowers, but he couldn't quite identify the scent. When he realized it was lilacs, he thought about last summer. He tried to clear his mind. No matter what it reminded him of, it didn't change the fact she was stubborn and willful. Even though she looked... *Stop.* And smelled so good... *How can the smell of shampoo be so intoxicating?*

To distract himself, he watched Sarah and her father walking toward them. She seemed happy, and it gave him something else to think about. Two of his friends were getting married, and no matter what was going on between him and Poppie, Lewis and Sarah's happiness was something to celebrate.

Pastor Mike glanced at Jasper. "Stand a little closer, son. I believe she's harmless."

If only you knew. Jasper sidestepped closer to Poppie, still avoiding her eyes.

Pastor Mike went through an abridged version of the ceremony, which Jasper only half listened to, and when Mike finished, he asked if they wanted to go over it again.

Jasper was relieved when both Lewis and Sarah said no.

"Okay, then. I'll see you all Thursday. I need everyone here by one." He glanced at Jasper. "Don't be late."

Jasper tried not to take offense to being singled out as he headed down the aisle. When Lewis caught up with him and put a hand on his shoulder, he stopped.

"Hold up." He took Jasper's arm and led him to a room off the main hall. It appeared to be the choir room, as there were a dozen robes hung on one wall, along with a piano, two music stands, and a microphone. "What's going on with you?"

"Me? Nothing."

Lewis folded his arms across his chest. "You're avoiding Poppie. You won't even look at her. Is this still about the other morning?"

"No. We're fine."

Lewis frowned. "I know you. And I know my sister. After the other day, you should be all over each other. Or at least want to be."

"Okay. We're not fine. But I don't want you to worry about it. It won't affect tonight or the wedding."

"What happened?"

"Nothing. It's...stupid. And we'll get past it." He sighed. "At some point. I think."

"Right. Nothing to worry about." Lewis leaned against the piano. "Not going anywhere until you tell me what happened."

"Fine. It was the dog. I'm facing down a crazy mean, and possibly rabid dog, and she wouldn't stay in the damn Jeep."

"You told her to stay?"

"Yes. Is that so bad? When the dog saw her, he charged. I could only stop him by firing my pistol over his head."

"So, the dog ran off?"

"Yeah. But he was hurt. So I had to go track him down. I didn't want him dying in the wilds from his injuries."

"Still, I don't see why that was such an issue."

"If she'd listened to me in the first place, the dog might be at Doc Hannigan's."

"So he's out there somewhere, possibly dying because Poppie didn't stay in the truck."

Jasper shook his head. "It's not that simple. You're making it sound...trivial."

"Well..."

"The dog is dead. I had to shoot it. But not before he bit me." He rubbed his arm. "Probably gave me rabies."

"Shit."

"Exactly."

Lewis scratched his head. "I can see why you might be upset with her. But why is she mad at you?"

"Well, it probably has to do with the fact that I handcuffed her to the steering wheel."

"You what?"

"I knew she'd try to follow me when I went to track the dog."

"So you handcuffed her?" Lewis started laughing. "That explains the dress."

"What about her dress?"

"It's not the one she was going to wear tonight. She wore it to tease you."

"She wouldn't do that."

"Ohh, yes she would. She's pissed. And..." He laughed again. "You're screwed."

"Whatever. I'm not that easily manipulated."

"Really? Okay." Lewis straightened and pushed away from the piano. "You know she doesn't like to be told what to do."

"Not even when it might save her life? Or at the very least, save her from bodily harm? Or me from bodily harm. This isn't an isolated incident. She never listens to me."

"Poppie's stubborn. As are you. You're going to have to figure out how to make that work, all the while keeping her from killing one or both of you."

"Her listening to me would be a much easier solution."

Lewis patted Jasper's shoulder. "That won't be easy." He studied Jasper for a moment. "But that's not all. It's not just about her listening to you."

Jasper sat on the piano bench. "After I dropped her at your house. I damn near had a panic attack."

"You panicking? That doesn't sound right."

"I know. Weird. Right? I couldn't stop thinking about what might've happened. If the dog got past me. If he—"

"Jasper. I can't even begin to imagine what you went through with losing Ivy. But I can tell you, we all have that fear. The fear of losing the ones you love. It's part of life. The only way to avoid it is to close yourself off from society. Do you really want to do that?"

Jasper shook his head. "The tree basically told me the same thing."

"The tree?"

Jasper got to his feet. "Never mind." He took a breath. "I'm fine. Poppie and I will be fine. Can we go eat, now?"

When they went outside to the front of the church to join the others, Lewis smiled at Poppie. "Maybe you could catch a ride with Jasper. That way we don't have to squeeze into the truck."

Poppie glanced at Jasper. "I'll walk."

Jasper sighed. "You don't need to walk."

"It's fine." She headed for the sidewalk in front of the church. "It's not that far."

Lewis looked at Jasper, who shrugged before getting into the Jeep. He pulled out and drove past Poppie without glancing in her direction.

"If you think that dress is going to make me regret what I did..." He looked at her through the rearview mirror. "Dammit."

Sarah took Lewis' arm. "What's going on? Do I need to panic about this?"

He patted her hand. "No. Of course not. It's fine. They're just having a spat."

She glared at him. "Lewis. Don't patronize me."

"I'm not. I swear. I talked to Jasper. It's all good." He kissed her. "I don't want you to worry about anything but getting to the church on time on Thursday."

She smiled. "We're getting married."

"Yes, we are." He took her hand and started walking toward the truck. "Come on. My parents are probably already at the restaurant."

He stopped at the truck and opened the driver's door for her. "I'm driving?"

"You take the truck. I'm going to catch Poppie."

Lewis watched Sarah drive off, then headed down the street. He had to jog to catch her, and when he reached her, out of breath, she frowned at him.

"Why does everyone think I'm incapable of taking care of myself?"

"That's not what I think." He took her arm. "Slow down."

Poppie slowed her pace and glanced at him. "Is it that obvious?"

"The fact that you don't want to drag Jasper into the coat closet and... Yeah. It's obvious."

"That's not—" She smiled. "Okay, maybe I often think about that when we're together."

"So, what's going on?"

She stopped and turned toward him. "I saw you take him into the choir room. I'm sure he told you."

"I want to hear it from you." They were in front of the grocery store and she went to the picnic table and sat down. Lewis sat across from her. "Apparently, there was an issue with a dog."

"It was so scary. And Jasper did his usual 'I'll save you, M'lady' and jumped in front of me."

"And why were you in danger in the first place?"

Poppie tapped her fingers on the table. "Because I didn't listen to him and stay in the Jeep."

Lewis pointed a finger at her. "Bingo."

"But then he... He handcuffed me to the steering wheel."

Lewis grinned.

"Shut up. It's not funny."

"It's kind of funny."

"Why is it so hard for me to do what he asks? I know he's not doing it to feel superior. He's doing it to keep me safe."

He laughed. "Only you can answer that question. But you better figure it out."

"Before he breaks up with me?"

"No. Before you get one of you seriously hurt."

She put her elbows on the table and rested her chin on her hands. "He's the one, Lewis."

"I know."

"I love him."

"I know."

She straightened. "He got so mad. And then I got mad. I didn't know what would happen when he arrived at the church. Then he was late and ignored me." She looked at Lewis. "Which I totally deserved. I need to fix this."

Lewis nodded. "You need to fix it."

"How?"

"Well, that dress is a start. Just be nice and not annoying. At least for tonight."

"I am annoying, aren't I?"

He grinned. "Just a little."

She shook her head. "More than a little."

"Yeah. But that's okay. It's what I love about you best. And I suspect it's what Jasper loves about you, too."

She got to her feet. "Poor guy."

"That's for damn sure."

Chapter Eighteen

"She thinks I'm a caveman."

When Jasper walked into The Sailor's Loft, Steve and Priscilla Jensen were in the foyer talking with Peg, who smiled when she saw him.

"Here's Jasper, now." She took his hand. "This is Steve and Priscilla, Lewis' parents."

Jasper shook with them. "Nice to meet you. I'm Jasper."

Priscilla patted his hand. "We've heard so much about you. Lewis goes on and on about you when he comes to see us."

"I'm glad you could make the trip to the island. Welcome."

Peg took Priscilla's arm. "Let me take you to the room." She led the way, and Steve and Jasper followed them. The dinner was in one of two rooms used for small gatherings. Jasper called it the Camelot room because of the large round table in the middle. Tonight it was set for ten with purple linens and a fresh centerpiece with lilacs and white daffodils. There was a piano in the corner, brought in for Sarah if she wanted to play something.

Priscilla took it all in. "This is wonderful."

Peg excused herself and Jasper tried to think of something to say to the two people he'd heard about, but never met. One thing was obvious, though: they had no idea he and Poppie were...whatever they were. He made small-talk, told them some things about the island, and talked about what a great guy their son was. As he was running out of things to talk about, and was getting uncomfortable, Poppie came into the room.

She went to her parents and greeted them, then nodded at Jasper, but he was sure it was for their benefit, not his. When Priscilla and Steve went to sit at the table, Jasper leaned in toward Poppie.

"They have no idea you and I are..."

She glanced at him. "When was I supposed to tell them? Should I have sent them a text? 'By the way, I'm doing it with Lewis' best friend.'"

"I'd go with something a little more subtle." He walked away from her as Lewis and Sarah arrived, followed by Sarah's sisters and her parents. Jasper melted into the background as introductions were being made. Then everyone but Jasper took a seat.

He stood behind his chair and rested his hands on the back of it. "We're short a bartender tonight. And I guess there's going to be champagne at some point, but if anyone wants something from the bar, I can get it for you."

After a few moments of deliberation and discussion, Jasper left with requests for four glasses of wine and three beers. He went to the bar and was pouring the beers when Poppie came up to the far side and sat on a stool.

Jasper set two drafts on a tray. "Did you want to add to the order?"

"No. I thought you might need help to remember it."

"Four wines, three beers. I think I got it." He poured a rum and coke and set it in front of her.

She pushed it toward him. "I didn't ask for that."

He pushed it back. "I think you need it. It'll take the edge off."

"I'm not on edge."

Jasper shook his head. "Poppie, you're always on edge. You're the most precarious person I've ever been around. Plus, you just reduced our relationship to 'doing it', so if you're not on edge, then I'd say we're screwed."

She studied the glass for a moment, then picked it up and took a sip. "I didn't mean it like that. It's not what I think."

He set another beer on the tray, then put four wine glasses down. He poured two Burgundies and two Chablis. "You have a bad habit of speaking before you think."

She took another drink, then stood. "Heaven forbid I should have a mind of my own."

"Jesus. That's not what I said." He took a bottle of bourbon from the shelf and poured a shot. He drank it, then picked up the tray and headed around the bar. "If I haven't made it clear how much I... How much I think of you, then you haven't been paying attention."

He headed for the door and Poppie picked up her drink to follow him.

"You handcuffed me."

He stopped walking and turned to her. "In retrospect, it might've been... No. I won't apologize for it. If I hadn't, you would've followed me and God knows what would've happened."

Jasper continued to the room and nodded at Lewis and Sarah, who both looked anxious about what might be happening in the bar. He passed out the drinks before sitting with one of the beers.

Sarah had put him next to Poppie, which is what they would've wanted prior to this afternoon. Poppie sat next to Jasper and leaned in toward his ear. "Can we just get through tonight, amicably?"

He turned to her. "I can. Not sure about you."

Jasper had taken a pain pill before leaving the house. He figured with the meal, he'd be fine drinking a beer or two. But he hadn't considered the effects of a shot of bourbon. So by the time the champagne came out with the dessert, he was feeling a little lightheaded.

He ignored it while he tried to stay engaged in conversation, but by the time he was finishing his piece of chocolate cake, he'd tuned out and was contemplating the floral design on the dessert plate. When he heard Lewis call him, he looked up.

"Yeah?"

"My dad asked you about crime on the island." Lewis' expression seemed to be trying to send a silent message, but Jasper couldn't pick up on it.

Jasper glanced at Steve. "Crime? Not much crime. Our little adventure last summer was the most excitement we've had around here in years." He glanced at Poppie, who nudged him on the thigh and shook her head. Lewis, across the table and two seats down from his father, was giving him the 'cut' signal.

Steve looked at his two children, who both stopped what they were doing. "What happened last summer?"

"Um." Jasper glanced at Poppie again and got a glare as she squeezed his thigh. He removed his napkin from his lap to buy some time while he wiped his mouth. "Small incident. A mainlander. Nothing, really. Like I said. Nothing happens around here. Fender-benders, cats in trees. Stuff like that." When Poppie let go of his leg, he took a breath, followed by a sip of champagne.

Sarah got to her feet. "How about some music?" She looked at Lewis. "You guys up for a couple of songs?"

"Sure, hon." He looked at Jasper and nodded toward the piano. "What'd you say?"

"I don't have my guitar."

"That's okay. Sarah can play the piano and I've got my harmonica." He took it out of his pocket, then raised an eyebrow at Jasper. "It'll be fun."

Jasper studied the distance between the table and the piano. It seemed like an impossible task without giving away his unintentional overindulgence.

Poppie seemed to figure out what was going on, and she got to her feet. "Come on, Deputy. Don't be shy. You sing in front of people all the time." She took his arm and pulled him to his feet. They headed for the piano as she whispered into his ear. "Are you on pain pills again?"

"Yeah. I got bit by a rabid dog today. Hurt like hell. Oh wait. You were there."

She walked with him to the piano and whispered, "I said I was sorry."

He nodded. "Oh. Right. That makes it all better."

She glared at him. "Even though I was handcuffed at the time." She leaned in close to his ear. "I've actually thought about being handcuffed by you. But it was under very different circumstances."

Jasper opened his mouth, but nothing came out.

She stepped back, looked at him for a moment, then returned to her seat.

Lewis came up to him. "Are you wasted?"

Jasper finally found his voice. "What?" He shook his head. "No. Well, slightly. I swear, I only took one pill."

Lewis shook his head. "You're such a lightweight." He turned to the table. "Mom and Dad, this will give you a taste of what Gracie Island is all about."

About halfway through the second song, Jasper started feeling a little more normal, and they sang two more before Sarah got to her feet.

"Okay, everybody. I know we're all having a good time, but a big day tomorrow preparing for the even bigger day, and I need my beauty sleep."

Lewis hugged her. "Nonsense."

She gave him a kiss. "The party will continue Thursday night."

As everyone prepared to leave and said their goodbyes, Lewis went to Jasper. "Will you have one last drink with me as a single man?"

Jasper grinned. "Sure."

Lewis kissed Sarah goodnight and promised to go home after one drink, then he and Jasper went to the bar.

Jasper poured them each a shot of bourbon, then raised his glass. "I wish you and Sarah all the best life has to offer."

They clicked glasses and drank their shots.

Lewis nodded toward the bottle. "How about one more?"

"Didn't you promise Sarah you'd only have one?"

Lewis thought for a moment. "One more."

Jasper filled their glasses again. "One more could go on all night."

As they drank their shots, Poppie came up behind Lewis and sat next to him.

He frowned at her. "Did Sarah send you?"

"No. But as your best man, I feel it's my duty to make sure you make it home sober and safe."

Lewis smiled. "Too late." He stood. "Just kidding. I'm fine. And I'm headed home." He hugged Poppie and shook hands with Jasper, then pointed at him. "This guy, however, is not fine. Make sure he gets to his mother's house."

Lewis left and Jasper looked at Poppie. "One for the road?"

"I think you've had enough."

Jasper put the bourbon away, then went around the end of the bar. "I don't need you to make sure I get home. It's two blocks. I think I can manage."

"I'm going to the hotel. It's on my way."

Jasper thought for a moment. "No it's not. The hotel is in the other direction. The town is six square blocks. How can you not know what direction the hotel is?"

"I'm not from here." She took his arm. "Come on."

As they went out the front door and headed down the street, Jasper glanced at Poppie. "Why are you staying at the hotel?"

"It's easier getting ready there instead of Lewis' house. I'm staying there through the wedding."

The fresh night air was clearing his head a little. "So what does a female best man wear?"

"You'll find out Thursday."

They got to Kat's porch and Jasper stopped at the bottom of the steps.

"Did you wear that dress for me tonight?"

"Of course not. I wore it for me."

Jasper scowled. "Bullshit." He contemplated kissing her. He was still mad, but he wanted to kiss her more than he didn't want to. He also wanted her to admit she'd dressed for him tonight to send a message.

She seemed to assess what he was thinking, and she took a step back. "No."

He stepped back as well.

She put a hand on his chest. "I want you to kiss me because you want to kiss me, not because you're under the influence of alcohol, pain pills...and this dress."

"I'm not *that* under the influence. And the dress is—"

"I'll see you tomorrow, Deputy."

"Now I feel like I should walk *you* home."

"I don't need you to protect me."

"I know, Poppie. God. I know. That's not what it is." He shook his head and went up the steps. "You just don't get it."

"Explain it to me."

He looked at her. "I shouldn't have to." He opened the door and went inside. He stopped inside the door, then turned and went back out. Poppie was still at the bottom of the steps.

He took a step away from the door. "I'll see you tomorrow."

"Get some sleep."

"I'm not drunk."

"I know."

He waved. "Good night."

When he went inside, the light was on in the kitchen, and he found Kat making a cup of tea. She turned and smiled at him. "Hi, honey. How was dinner?"

"It was great. You and Aunt Peg did a wonderful job, as always."

She nodded toward the table. "Sit. Do you want some coffee?"

He sat. "No."

Kat put some ice in a glass and filled it with water, then set it in front of Jasper. She then poured hot water into her cup and sat across from him. She dipped her tea bag several times.

"How much did you have to drink, honey?"

"I'm not drunk." He took the pain pills out of his pocket. "I can't seem to juggle these and alcohol."

She picked up the bottle and read the label. "Why are you taking pain pills again?"

"No big deal. Dog bite. Doc fixed me right up."

"Hmm. And why are you upset with Poppie?"

He frowned. "Who says I'm upset with Poppie?"

She tilted her head. "It's nine-thirty and you're sitting here with me instead of being out with her." She patted his hand. "When was the last time you went to a wedding?"

"You know the answer to that question, Mom. It's not a problem for me. I'm fine."

"It's only natural to think of your own wedding when you attend one for your friend."

He leaned back in his chair. "Whatever I may or may not feel about attending a wedding, it has nothing to do with Poppie." He took a couple of swallows of water.

"They're very different. Ivy and Poppie. Like night and day."

He sat up and leaned his forearms on the table, cradling the glass of water in his hands. "Mom."

Kat took a sip of her tea. "Ivy and you were like a classical composition. In perfect harmony. Predictable. No surprises."

"You make it sound boring. We weren't boring."

"I know that, dear." She drank some more tea. "On the other hand, Poppie is—"

"Heavy metal?"

Kat laughed. "No. More like jazz."

"Why jazz?"

"The music follows its own path. You never know what direction it's going to take. Each musician gets a chance to create something new and exciting, and it's never the same."

"Nah. Heavy metal is more accurate. Or something that makes you want to pull your hair out on a regular basis."

She ignored him. "Both are excellent choices. And one isn't more right than the other. Poppie challenges you. She's independent and—"

"Stubborn? Infuriating?"

"Intriguing."

Jasper shrugged.

Kat took another sip of tea. "She's passionate."

"Hmm."

"And you're in love with her."

He leaned back in his chair again. "I don't know what I am with her."

"You'll figure it out. You just need to let go a little."

"Let go?"

"Yes. You have the biggest heart of any man I've ever known. And I'm not saying that because you're my son. It's true. Plus, you're a warrior and a protector."

"She thinks I'm a caveman."

Kat laughed. "You need to figure out how to keep her safe without making her feel like she's not capable of doing it herself."

Jasper scowled. "I know she's capable. She's... Okay. I know what you mean."

"Good boy."

He got to his feet. "Can I go to bed now?"

"Yes. Come give your mother a kiss."

He kissed her, then headed for the living room. "I love you, Mom."

"I love you more, Son."

As he went down the hall, he mumbled to himself. "I'm surrounded by women who need to get the last word in."

Chapter Nineteen

"Tell her you're sorry."

After a restless night, Jasper got up early and went to the café for breakfast before going to the office. He'd ordered biscuits and gravy and was halfway through the meal when Poppie came in and went to the counter. He was out of her line of sight, but as he was debating on whether he should acknowledge her, she turned his way and spotted him.

Poppie gave him a nod, then turned back to the counter as the cashier approached. It appeared as though Poppie was picking up an order, and she waited a moment as the cashier retrieved it for her. After paying for it, she turned toward Jasper again.

After a noticeable sigh, she walked toward Jasper's table.

"Jasper."

"Poppie."

"Are you working today?"

Jasper glanced at his uniform and then frowned at the obvious question. "Yeah."

"Are you hungover?"

"I only had two beers."

"Right. And some champagne. And...a shot or two." She held up the bag she was holding. "I should get this to Lewis. He's finishing a project before he leaves on his honeymoon."

"Okay."

She took a few steps back. "I'll see you tomorrow, I guess."

"See you tomorrow." He watched her walk away. *Wow, that was really mature.*

They'd parted on decent terms last night, but now it was awkward again. He'd give them both the day to get over it. Then, hopefully, at the wedding, they'd figure out how to get back to where they had been.

When Jasper went outside, Sarah was leaning against his Jeep. "Don't you have anything better to do than waylay me in the parking lot? You're getting married tomorrow."

"I wanted to see how you were."

"I'm fine. You want to move out of the way so I can go to work?"

"Jasper Goodspeed, don't you be grumpy with me just because you're mad at Poppie."

Jasper folder his arms across his chest. "I'm not being grumpy."

She tilted her head. "I've known you since kindergarten. I know grumpy Jasper when I see him."

"Fine. I'm slightly grumpy. I just ran into Poppie."

"And?"

"It was...weird and stupid."

Sarah smiled. "You're both so stubborn."

Jasper shook his head. "I'm not stubborn."

She pushed away from the Jeep and straightened. "Sure you're not."
She pointed a finger at him. "You have one day. The wedding's tomorrow.
Make up with her. Tell her you're sorry."

"I didn't do anything."

She put her hands on her hips. "Handcuffs?"

Jasper sighed and cleared his throat. "Does Lewis tell you everything?"

"Of course."

He opened the door and got into the Jeep.

Sarah put her hands on the top of the door. "Apologize."

"Go do whatever brides do the day before their wedding."

"Jasper, I swear—"

"I'll talk to her." She let go of the door and he closed it. With a wave, he
drove away.

When Jasper went into the station, Maisy greeted him with a smile,
which quickly faded when she seemed to pick up on his mood.

"Are you okay, sweetheart?"

"I'm fine." Jasper nodded toward the chief's closed door. "Is he in?"

"No. He's at the marina. Apparently, the Murphy brothers got into a tiff
this morning."

"Hmm. It's not even a holiday. Have they been drinking?"

"I don't know. Duke called it in."

"Should I go down there?"

"I'm sure the chief can handle it."

Jasper touched his eye, which was only slightly discolored now. "Better
him than me." He headed for his office, but stopped when Maisy spoke
again.

"Hon, how's Poppie."

He turned to her. "Not you, too."

"Not me too, what?"

"Nothing. I just thought..."

"What happened? What did you do?"

"Why does everyone assume I did something? Maybe *she* did something."

"Are you two fighting?"

"No. We're disagreeing."

Maisy poured him a cup of coffee and handed it to him, along with a stack of forms. "Well, work it out. She's good for you."

Jasper looked at the forms. "What are these for?"

"The dog incident yesterday."

"Oh, right."

"The chief wants them done by lunch."

"I have a deadline now?"

Maisy smiled. "You tend to procrastinate when it comes to paperwork."

He started to argue, but knew she was right. "I'll do it now."

"Good. And call Poppie. Tell her you're sorry."

Without responding, Jasper turned and headed for his office. *Every time someone says that to me, I'm a little less sorry.*

He dropped the paperwork on the desk and sat down. As he took a sip of coffee, he glared at the phone. "No. I'm going to let it simmer. Simmering is good. Simmering lets everyone calm down."

Jasper spent the next hour grumbling his way through the paperwork. Maisy was right. He put it off whenever he could. It was his least favorite part of the job. This would be a problem, of course, once he became chief. Maisy did a lot, but there was a lot more the chief had to deal with.

"You're not going to need to worry about that for a while." He signed the bottom of the last page and leaned back in his chair. A normal report was pretty easy, but his one involved an injury and discharging his weapon. Much more complicated, which translated to much more paperwork.

He fingered the bandaged dog bite, which was still sore. "Dammit, Poppie."

When Maisy knocked on his door, and then opened it, Jasper got to his feet.

"What's up?" He brought the paperwork to her.

"Oh. Good job. The chief wants you to go to the marina."

"He's still there?"

"Yes, and he needs help."

"What happened?"

"I don't know. He said send Jasper right away."

When Jasper pulled into the marina parking lot, there was a crowd of people on the middle dock. He made his way through them until he found the chief. James was standing next to Lewis, who was sitting on a storage box and looked like he'd taken a swim. Sitting on the ground nearby, but ten feet away from each other, were Doyle and Reece.

The chief seemed relieved to see Jasper. "Did you bring cuffs? I secured Doyle, but you need to take care of Reece."

"It's that bad?"

James nodded. "Just do it."

Jasper went to Reece and cuffed him. "What did you guys do?"

"It was an accident."

"It always is."

Jasper returned to the chief and looked at Lewis. "Are you okay?"

Lewis shook his head. "Got knocked into the water when I tried to help the chief."

James glanced at Lewis. "He did more than take a swim. I think he might've cracked a rib."

Jasper knelt in front of Lewis. "Shit."

"No. No. I'm fine. I have to be fine. I'm getting married tomorrow."

The chief spoke up. "He says he doesn't want to go to the doctor. Maybe you can convince him. I'm going to clear this crowd, then take the Murphys to the station."

"You're arresting them?"

"Yes. I'm tired of their shit. And you keep letting them off with a warning. No more. I'm taking them in this time." James walked away and started telling the crowd to disperse. Jasper watched him for a moment, then turned back to Lewis.

"Do you need to see the doc?"

Lewis shook his head. "No. I can't. Sarah will kill me."

Jasper smiled. "There are quite a few folks here. Pretty sure she's going to find out."

"Yeah. But I can convince her I'm not hurt. If I go to see Dr. Hannigan, she'll definitely find out."

"Okay. What can I do?"

"She's busy with her mom and sisters today. And we aren't planning on seeing each other tonight. Can you drive me home, then track down Poppie?"

"Sure."

"And back up my story. I fell into the water. That's all."

"No problem." Jasper took Lewis' arm and helped him to his feet. When Lewis groaned and favored his left side, Jasper hesitated. "You're really hurt."

Lewis straightened. "No. I'm good."

The crowd had dispersed, and the chief had loaded the Murphy brothers into his Bronco. So Jasper and Lewis had a straight shot to the Jeep. They took it slowly, and Jasper helped Lewis into the seat before going around the front end and getting in behind the wheel.

He glanced at Lewis. "I'm not sure you're going to be able to pull this off."

"Trust me. I got it." He laid his head back against the seat.

Jasper opened the glove box and took out the bottle of pain pills he'd gotten yesterday, then handed them to Lewis. "These might help."

"You sure you don't need them?"

"You need them more. Just careful with the alcohol consumption."

"Got it."

Jasper drove Lewis to his house, then helped him inside and set him on the couch. After fetching him a glass of water, he left to find Poppie. He drove through town and spotted her in front of the grocery store. She was at a picnic table with Amanda, halfway through a meal of chicken nuggets and potato wedges, deep in conversation. She didn't notice him until he was a foot away.

Poppie seemed surprised to see him. "Oh. Hey."

"Can I talk to you for a moment?"

She glanced at Amanda. "Sure."

Jasper gave Amanda a small smile. "Alone."

Poppie got to her feet. "Okay."

Jasper started walking, and she followed him. "We're not going to be able to fix things on the street in front of the grocery store."

He stopped walking and turned back to her. "That's not why I'm here." He took a breath, as he was hit with the urge to kiss her again. "It's Lewis. He needs you."

"Why? What's wrong?"

"Go tell Amanda you need to help Lewis with something, then I'll explain on the way."

Poppie went back to Amanda, then returned with her purse and a bag with the rest of her lunch. He didn't even bother trying to open the door for her. She'd only take it as an attempt to undermine her in some way.

She got in, then turned in her seat as he started the engine. "What's going on?"

"Lewis got hurt."

"What?"

"And he doesn't want Sarah to know."

"Hurt how? What happened?" She glared at him. "Was he with you?"

"No. And I resent the inference. I wasn't anywhere near him. And people only seem to get hurt when *you're* around." He pulled onto the street. "The Murphy brothers got into it at the dock. The chief went to break it up, and somehow Lewis got in the middle of it. I wasn't there. You'll have to ask him the details. By the time I got there, it was all over. I drove him home and came to find you, per his request."

She faced the windshield. "Sarah's going to be so upset."

"That's why he doesn't want her to know."

Poppie glanced at Jasper. "Sounds like a great way to celebrate a wedding."

Jasper shrugged. "There's no way he's going to be able to keep it from her. But humor him for now and see him for yourself."

They drove the rest of the way in silence and when they got to the house, they both got out of the Jeep.

Poppie looked at Jasper. "What are you doing? I can take it from here."

"I want to see if there's anything he needs."

"Fine."

They went up the steps to the porch and Poppie went through the door before Jasper could open it for her. He caught the door as it was closing and went in behind her.

She went to the couch and sat next to Lewis. "What did you do?"

He looked at Jasper. "Thanks."

"No problem. Do you need anything else? Can I bring you anything?"

Poppie glanced over her shoulder. "We're good. Thank you, Deputy."

Lewis put a hand on her arm. "Chill, Sis." He looked at Jasper again. "No. I think we're good. But I'll call if I need you."

Jasper nodded. "Okay. I better go check in with the chief to make sure he got the Murphys locked up without incident." He took a few steps back. "Take it easy."

Chapter Twenty

"I don't have a hero complex."

J asper left Lewis and Poppie, but instead of going to the station, he went to the clinic. Amy greeted him with a shake of her head.

"What now?"

"It's not me this time. Is the doc around? I need to talk to him for a moment."

"He should be done soon." She glanced at the empty waiting room. "And there's no one waiting."

Jasper took a seat and waited ten minutes for Dr. Hannigan to come talk to him. He got to his feet as the doctor approached.

Hannigan offered his hand. "What's up, Jasper? Everything okay?"

"Lewis got between the Murphy brothers at the dock and got a pretty good bump to the ribcage. Is there anything he can or should do to relieve the pain?"

"Isn't he getting married tomorrow?"

"Yes. That's why he's not here. He doesn't want Sarah to know."

"I see. Is he at home?"

"Yeah. Sarah's spending the night with her sister."

Hannigan thought for a moment. "I'll stop by and see if I can do anything for him."

"Thank you. That's not why I came."

"I know. Don't worry. By law, I can't tell anyone. Not even his bride-to-be."

"Thanks, Doc."

When Jasper returned to the station, he went to the chief's door and knocked. After receiving a gruff, "Come in," he opened it and went inside.

The chief was at his desk and took a moment before looking up from his paperwork. "How's Lewis?"

"He's in pain. I stopped by the clinic and Doc Hannigan is going to go check on him."

"Good." He returned his eyes to his desk.

"So, you got the Murphys downstairs without too much trouble?"

"Of course." He looked at Jasper again. "Did you think I wouldn't?"

"No. Just asking." The words came out a little sharper than he meant them to.

"I know you grew up with those boys and have a soft spot for them, but their fighting is getting out of control. And it's not just happening during holiday celebrations, anymore. And when other people get hurt..." He nodded toward Jasper. "It can't be overlooked anymore."

"I understand. I'm not questioning your call to arrest them this time."

"You can't let friendship and loyalty get in the way of you doing your job."

"I realize that. I came in here to see if you were okay, not to get a lecture on procedure."

The chief studied him for a moment. "Why are you in a mood?"

Jasper scowled. "I'm not in a mood." He backed up toward the door. "Checking in. That's all" He turned away and headed out of the office.

"Jasper."

Jasper stopped walking and turned back. "What?"

"Take the rest of the day off."

"Why?"

"Because I don't want the mood, you say you're not in, to interfere with you doing your job."

Jasper wanted to argue with him. He wanted to argue with someone. Anyone. But instead he took a breath, nodded his head, and left the room. He went to his office, refrained from slamming the door, and sat at his desk.

"He's the one in the mood. Not me. He's eternally in a mood." When he heard a knock, he glared at the door. "What?"

The door opened and Sarah walked in and approached the desk. "What happened to Lewis?"

Shit. "What do you mean?"

She sat in the chair. "Three people have come up to me and asked me how Lewis is. What happened?"

"Did you try calling him?"

"No. We have a pact. No contact until we see each other tomorrow at the wedding."

Jasper glanced around the room. "Lewis is fine."

"Jasper. Look me in the eye and tell me that."

Jasper looked at her. "What do you mean?"

"You're incapable of lying. At least right to my face. So look at me and tell me everything's fine."

Jasper sighed and looked at Sarah. "Lewis... Shit."

"I knew it." She leaned forward. "What happened to my husband?"

"Okay. He's fine. Just a little banged up."

"Oh my God."

"Not in a bad way. Not visibly. He's as pretty as he was the last time you saw him."

"What happened?"

"The Murphy brothers were getting into it at the marina. The chief showed up and Lewis tried to help."

She got to her feet. "This was your fault?"

"How's it my fault? I wasn't even there."

"Your hero complex is wearing off on him."

Jasper leaned back in his chair. "I don't have a hero complex."

"You want to save everyone. People, animals, you can't help yourself." She started to tear up. "And now, my Lewis is hurt the day before our wedding." Her tears turned into full blown sobbing.

"No, no, no, no." Jasper got to his feet and came around the desk. "No crying. He's going to be fine."

Sarah stood, too, and put her arms around Jasper. "Do you promise?"

Jasper hugged her. "I promise. He's a little sore, that's all."

She took a step back. "Where?"

Jasper handed her a napkin from his desk. "His ribs on the left side. I think. Anyway. Dr. Hannigan is going over to check him out."

Sarah wiped her eyes and blew her nose, then tossed the napkin in the trash can next to the desk. "Thank you."

"For ratting out my friend?"

"No for helping *this* friend." She returned to the chair. "I won't tell him you caved."

Jasper sat as well. "Thanks." He swiveled back and forth a couple of times. "I don't have a hero complex."

"So, you going out on a motor boat in a hurricane to save Poppie last year wasn't being a hero?"

"No. I was trying to save her. But it wasn't heroic. It was... Well, actually, it was stupid."

"Taking care of Burt. Helping Wilda. I could go on and on."

"That doesn't make me a hero."

"To them, you're a hero. Just as though you were wearing tights and a cape."

"I do look pretty good in tights."

"I'm sure you do. But I don't want to know how you know that."

Jasper grinned. "Seriously, Lewis didn't want to worry you. He's not going to let it slow him down for the wedding."

"How about for the wedding night?"

"Umm. I'm sure he'll manage to...man up and do what he needs to do."

"You make it sound like a chore."

"Can we talk about something else, please?"

"Yes." She crossed her legs. "Poppie. Have you talked to her?"

"Something besides that."

"Jasper."

"I've talked to her, yes. Had a conversation with her, no."

"What are you waiting for?"

"Well, I've been a little busy saving your fiancé."

Sarah stood. "For a hero, you sure are a coward."

He went around the desk and gave her a hug. "Go do your night before the wedding stuff. I'll make sure Lewis is taken care of and gets to the church tomorrow in tip top shape."

"Thank you."

"You're welcome."

"Talk to Poppie."

"Yeah, yeah, yeah."

Jasper left the office with no further conversation with the chief and drove to Lewis' house. On the way, he spotted Dr. Hannigan leaving. Jasper stopped and rolled down his window, as the doctor pulled up next to him.

Jasper gave him a smile. "What's the prognosis?"

"If he takes it easy today, he should just be a little sore tomorrow."

"Good news. Thank you for checking on him."

"That's what I do. Take care, Jasper."

"See you later. Or hopefully not."

Dr. Hannigan waved, then drove away, while Jasper continued to Lewis' house. When he arrived, he went onto the porch and took a moment to decide whether or not to walk in. Normally, he'd go inside, but with Poppie there, and the current situation with their relationship, he chose to knock.

Poppie opened the door a few inches. "You're back."

"I wanted to check on Lewis. I saw the doc on the road."

"He said it appeared nothing was broken. Just bruised."

"Good. Can I come in?"

She sighed, then took a step back and opened the door for him. He came through and nodded at Lewis, who was reclining on the couch with a hot water bottle on his ribcage.

Jasper went to the couch. "I wanted to check on you again."

"Doc says I'll be good as new tomorrow."

"Great. Can I bring you anything? Dinner from the Loft? Something from the deli?"

Poppie stepped up next to him. "I'm making dinner. We're fine."

Lewis raised an eyebrow at her. "He's just trying to help. Don't be rude."

Poppie glanced at Jasper. "Sorry. I didn't mean—"

"Don't worry about it." Jasper took a few steps back toward the door. "I'll see you tomorrow, then."

Lewis frowned at Poppie. "Thanks, Jasper. See you tomorrow."

When Jasper closed the door behind him, Lewis studied Poppie for a moment. "Geez, get over it already."

"I know." She sat on the arm of the couch. "I'm being a B, aren't I?"

"Yeah, you kind of are."

"He probably hasn't left yet. Go talk to him."

Poppie got up and went to the door, then glanced back at Lewis before she opened it. Jasper was getting into his Jeep, but stopped when she came out the door.

She went to the edge of the porch. "Can we talk for a minute?"

Jasper closed the door and went to the bottom of the steps. "Okay. So what do you have to say?"

"Me? Um...I thought you might have something to say to me."

He shook his head. "You want me to apologize, don't you?"

"Well, it would be appropriate."

Jasper rested a foot on the first step. "How so? This was all you. Or seventy-five percent you."

Poppie folded her arms across her chest. "How do you figure?"

"Stay in the Jeep, Poppie. That's all I asked you to do."

She sat on the top step. "You think handcuffing me to the steering wheel was only worth twenty-five percent?"

Jasper started laughing. "Okay, how about sixty-forty?"

"I suppose I'm the sixty?"

He shrugged. "Take it or leave it."

She got to her feet. "I'll have to think about it."

"Okay. Think away." He started for the Jeep, then turned back to her. "By the way, I saw Sarah, and she knows about Lewis' mishap."

"You told her?"

"No. I mean, not at first." He took a breath. "She got it out of me."

Poppie shook her head.

Jasper went on. "She's not going to tell him she knows. So, keep it on the down low."

She folded her arms again. "So, you can't lie to Sarah, but you want me to lie to my brother."

"Do whatever you want." He turned toward the Jeep again. "I'll see you at the wedding."

Poppie watched him get into the Jeep and start the motor. She knew she should go to him. She also knew she was being stubborn and the sixty-forty split in responsibility was probably correct. But she couldn't bring herself to stop him.

Just look back before you drive away. The Jeep started to move. *Please look back.*

He didn't look back. "Of course he didn't look back. Why would he? You're being a B."

Chapter Twenty-One

"We should put money on that."

J asper left Kat's house at twelve-thirty dressed in a charcoal suit with a lavender shirt and a dark purple tie. He assumed Sarah's two sisters would wear lavender, but he had no idea what Poppie would be wearing, and was eager to find out. He wasn't mad anymore, at least not as mad as he was yesterday. He was ready to let it go, if she had.

Since his Jeep was still parked by the restaurant, he walked to the church, which was a block to the east and a street to the north. He arrived by twelve-fifty and went inside. Pastor Mike had offered his private office for the men to gather in until the ceremony, so Jasper went to the office and opened the door.

Lewis was inside, along with his father and Poppie. Jasper stopped inside the door and smiled at Poppie.

Mad or not, he was glad to see her. "You look...amazing."

"You don't look bad yourself, Deputy."

She was wearing a tailored grey suit, with wide-legged, high-waisted pants. Under the fitted jacket, she wore a lavender silk shirt with pearl buttons. The skinny tie, hanging loose around her neck, was dark purple. There were lilacs and baby's breath tucked into the French braid crown in her hair. Like at the rehearsal dinner, she was wearing more makeup than she usually did. But it was subtle, and she was beautiful.

Lewis came up beside her and put his arm around her shoulders. "Only my sister could pull off the perfect best man attire."

Poppie kissed him on the cheek. "It was a team effort with your lovely bride."

Jasper put a hand on Lewis' shoulder. "And how's the groom?"

Lewis patted his left side. "About eighty percent. Nothing I can't handle."

Steve took out his phone. "Okay, I know there will be pictures, but if I don't get a couple of the three of you, Priscilla will kill me."

Poppie held up her hand. "Wait. My tie." She looked at it and frowned.

Jasper went to her. "Let me."

He saw a touch of stubbornness reflected in her eyes. "I can do it."

"Just..." He stepped up to her, and she sighed, but let go of the tie and dropped her hands to her side. He studied her for a moment, then started to tie it. He shook his head. "I have to do it from behind." He went behind her and put his arms around her. As he secured the tie, he took in the scent of the flowers in her hair, and he felt her relax. *Alright, Penelope, I can play jazz with the best of them. Bring it on.*

He moved to her side and Poppie glanced at him, then briefly brushed his hand with hers.

Steve looked at them. "Okay, Lewis, get on her other side. Let's see some love."

Jasper put an arm around her waist, while Lewis stood on the other side and Poppie put her arm through his. Steve took several pictures of them, then returned the phone to his pocket.

"It's strange that I can't send these to her."

Lewis went to him and put a hand on his shoulder. "Dad, you're more teched out than I am. I don't even own a cell phone anymore."

Steve looked at Jasper. "How do you stay in touch with your office?"

"Radio. Telephone. There are only so many places I can be."

Steve smiled at Poppie. "What do you think of all this, honey?"

"It works for them, Dad. They've gotten along fine for a hundred years or so."

"Interesting." He went to a bottle of bourbon sitting on the desk next to four shot glasses. As he filled the glasses, Lewis took Jasper aside.

"I need you to get a message to Sarah for me."

"I'm not sure how easy that'll be."

"It's important."

"Okay. Sure. What's the message?"

Lewis took a moment, then smiled. "Grilled cheese."

Jasper cocked his head. "Come again?"

"Grilled cheese. She'll know what I mean. And don't pass it on to someone else. I want you to tell her."

"Okay."

Steve handed them each a shot glass, then hesitated before giving Poppie one. "I know you're not fond of whiskey."

She took the glass. "It's fine, Dad. I'm not sitting out on the toast to my big brother."

Steve smiled and held up his glass. "To my son. Twenty-eight years ago, your mother told me this day would come sooner than I thought possible.

At the time, I didn't believe her. But here we are, on your wedding day, quick as a wink. Where did the time go?"

They all drank their shots and Jasper nodded at Lewis. "Just remember this day, man. Keep it with you, always."

Poppie coughed, then set her glass down. "Okay. Enough." She took a tissue and dabbed at her eyes. "I promised myself I wouldn't cry today."

Lewis grinned at Jasper. "We should put money on that."

"I know it's a losing bet, but I'll put ten bucks on her not crying during the ceremony."

Lewis went to him and shook his hand. "Great. I can use ten bucks."

Poppie put her hands on her hips. "Hey. That's not cool." She looked at Steve. "Dad?"

Steve laughed. "All in good fun, honey. All in good fun."

Poppie sighed. "Whatever."

Jasper checked his watch. "Okay. I should go connect with the women."

Lewis smiled. "See you on the other side."

Jasper shook his hand, then pulled him in for a hug. "You've got this."

Jasper left the office and went to the room reserved for the bride, then tapped on the door. After a moment, Portia opened it a few inches.

"No men allowed."

"I have a message for Sarah from Lewis."

"What is it?"

"I need to give it to her directly. No middlemen. Or women."

She closed the door. A few moments later, she opened it again, and glanced behind Jasper, then opened it wide enough for him to come inside.

He smiled and shook his head when he saw Sarah in her non-traditional gown. It was a cocktail length, strapless dress, with a full skirt and a corseted bodice. The color was a light champagne with tiny purple flowers embroidered on the corset. "Wow."

"Thank you."

"Lewis is going to...flip." He went to her and took her hands.

She allowed him to kiss her on the cheek, then took a step back from him. "What is Lewis' message?"

Jasper leaned toward her. "Grilled Cheese?"

Sarah started giggling. "Perfect." She hugged Jasper. "Thank you."

"Are you going to tell me what it means?"

She shook her head. "Go on now."

Jasper left the room and sat on a chair in the entrance hall. The wedding was due to start in ten minutes and he took the time to get himself into the right mindset. Even though he'd told his mother he was fine attending a wedding, he couldn't quite shake the memories of his own. He closed his eyes and allowed himself to take a moment to remember.

He and Ivy hadn't gotten married in the church. They'd said their vows on the beach. It was a bit of a gamble, but they'd brought umbrellas in case it rained. Ivy loved the rain as much as Jasper did, and it wouldn't have ruined the day. But the rain held off, the sun was shining, and it was a perfect day. And like he'd told Lewis, Jasper had kept the memory in his heart. His day-to-day life with Ivy was fading, but that day would stay with him always.

The pastor's wife, Evelyn, interrupted Jasper's thoughts when she came up to him along with Sarah's father.

"Okay, the men are ready. Let's get the girls." Jasper stood and straightened his tie, then tugged on his jacket while Evelyn knocked on the door. "Ladies, it's time."

Amanda came out and took Jasper's arm, and Portia stood behind them. Evelyn led them to the closed double doors leading to the sanctuary.

Evelyn said quietly, "When the music starts, I'll open the doors. Then you're on."

Jasper nodded, and Amanda dabbed at her eyes with a tissue.

Jasper whispered to her. "Are you okay?"

"Yes. Dammit. I thought I'd at least make it until the ceremony starts."

He smiled and patted her hand. "Take a deep breath."

She did as he said, then looked closely at him. "How're you doing with all this, Jasper?"

"All what? The wedding?"

"Yeah."

"I'm good."

"Hmm. Stoic as always."

The music started and Evelyn opened the doors. Jasper and Amanda both took a breath, then started walking down the aisle. When they got to the front of the church, they split and Jasper went to stand next to Poppie. He gave her a small smile, but she turned away from him and glanced at Lewis.

Jasper took his place and watched as Sarah and her father came down the aisle. He couldn't see Lewis' face, but he heard him gasp as Sarah got closer.

As the ceremony began, Poppie sniffled and dabbed at her eyes. Jasper took a handkerchief from his pocket and put it into her hand. She glanced back at him, and he gave her a wink. This seemed to make her cry more, and she wiped her eyes with his handkerchief. He leaned into her ear. "You just cost me ten bucks."

By the time Pastor Mike introduced the couple as Mr. and Mrs. Jensen, all the women in the wedding party were crying. The guests all cheered as

Lewis and Sarah headed down the aisle, followed by the wedding party. When Jasper got to the entry hall, he went to Poppie.

"Are you okay?" She nodded and tried to give him his handkerchief back. "Um. You can keep it."

She gave him a little smile, then seemed to remember they were supposed to be mad at each other, and turned away from him. He stayed by her side, though, while the guests filed by. She didn't know many of them. He knew them all.

They spent the next thirty minutes shaking hands and greeting people. At some point, Poppie wandered off while Jasper was stuck in a conversation with Peg and Beryl. By the time Jasper broke away from the crowd of well-wishers and stepped outside, Poppie was gone, apparently whisked away to the reception by her parents.

Lewis and Sarah came through the doors and he gave them a smile.

"Hey you two. You did it."

Lewis put his arm around Sarah. "We certainly did."

Jasper shook Lewis' hand and kissed Sarah. "Now for the fun part."

Lewis laughed. "Party time."

Sarah took his hand. "Not too much partying. I want you conscious for what comes after everyone goes home."

"Oh honey, you don't need to worry about that."

Jasper grinned. "Okay, you two. Go on. I'll see you there."

Lewis shook with him again. "You're coming right behind?"

"Yeah. Right behind."

Jasper watched them get into Sarah's car and drive away. He waved, then went to his Jeep. But instead of going right to the reception, he headed to the marina and parked in the lot. As he walked to the end of one of the piers, there was a cool breeze blowing and he could see rain clouds over the water. If his rain prediction radar was working, he figured it'd be raining within the hour.

He stuck his hands in his pockets and watched the seagulls for a few moments. There were two boats on the horizon, most likely fishing vessels returning for the day. He sighed. As frustrating as Poppie could be, he knew he didn't want to be without her. He was in love with her. And if what Lewis said was correct, she was in love with him, and had been since last summer.

"Penelope Jensen, you drive me crazy. But we'll figure this out."

As he headed back along the pier and got near the Jeep, he saw someone he didn't recognize standing next to it.

He approached the man. "Hi. Can I help you with something?"

"Are you Deputy Goodspeed?"

"Yes. And you are?"

The man held out his hand. "Evan Jeffers."

Jasper shook with him. "Sam's son. We've been trying to track you down."

"The alumni association got a hold of me. Not sure how you knew to contact them."

"Facebook." He shrugged. "I had help from a mainlander."

Evan took in Jasper's suit. "I guess this is a bad time."

"Um, yeah. My friends just got married. The reception is starting."

"Oh. Of course. I'm staying in town a few days. Can we talk tomorrow?"

"Sure. Is tomorrow afternoon okay?"

Evan smiled. "Yeah. The afternoon is fine."

"I'll be at the station." He took Evan's hand again. "I'm sorry about your father."

Evan shrugged. "I haven't seen him in several years. I'm just here to tie up any loose ends he might've left."

"Okay. I'll help however I can." Jasper opened the door of the Jeep.

Evan put his hand on the top of the door. "One more thing. Where's he buried?"

"Um. I'll take you to his grave tomorrow."

"You can just tell me."

"No. It's better if I show you." He got into the Jeep. "Tomorrow afternoon."

Chapter Twenty-Two

"No handcuffs involved."

Poppie was talking with Portia and Amanda when she spotted Jasper arriving at the reception thirty minutes after everyone else. She watched as he greeted several people, then headed for the bar. Lewis and Sarah had opted for an open bar, and with The Sailor's Loft losing their bartender, Mellie offered to fill in for the event.

Amanda glanced over her shoulder at Jasper. "So, you two...?"

Poppie smiled at her. "What about us?"

"Well obviously there's a massive connection. It's like being in the middle of an electrical storm when you two are in the same room together."

Poppie shrugged. "That's a little exaggerated, isn't it?"

Portia patted her hand. "No. Amanda's right. Go get him."

Poppie took a sip of her champagne. "Hmm. Not sure he wants my company. We had a bit of a...misunderstanding." She felt a tinge of jealousy as she watched Mellie laugh at something Jasper said.

Amanda smiled. "Misunderstandings are great. Because then you get to make up."

"I think I'll give him a little more time." What she really wanted was for him to come to her. She reprimanded herself. *Really? The whole thing was your fault.* She smiled at the women. "I'm going to go see if Kat needs any help."

Mellie set a beer in front of Jasper. "So, why are you sitting here by yourself?"

"Just wanted to say hi to my favorite bartender."

"I see." She glanced toward Poppie. "You two were pretty cozy at the plunge. What's going on?"

"A little...setback. No big deal."

Two customers came to the bar and Mellie leaned toward Jasper. "Don't go anywhere. I'll be right back."

Jasper took a sip of his beer. Mellie had always been there for him. Of all the people he had to lean on after Ivy died, she was the one he'd found comfort with. She was a good friend, and it was her who got him through the first rough year.

When she returned, she smiled. "What happened?"

"Just a stupid fight. Not even a fight really." He took another sip of beer. "She never listens to me."

"How do you mean?"

"Like... 'stay in the Jeep so the rabid dog doesn't attack you.'"

"*Rabid* dog?"

"Potentially rabid dog." He rubbed his arm where the dog had bitten him. "I got bit and had to shoot the dog, because she wouldn't stay in the damn Jeep."

"You got bit by a rabid dog?"

"Yeah."

"And it's because she got out of the Jeep?"

"Yeah."

"So, the dog wouldn't have attacked you if she'd stayed in the Jeep?"

Jasper shook his head, then smiled. "Honestly. I don't know. He might've." He shrugged. "He probably would've."

"Therefore...?"

"Shut up." He studied the label on his beer bottle. "So, why'd you and I break up?"

"Because I wanted to see the world and this island *was* your world."

"Oh, right." He reached for her hand. "I hope you're happy, Mellie."

She smiled. "I am."

"You deserve to be with someone who appreciates your...individuality."

Mellie laughed. "Hmm. Well, if you must know. I'm working on someone."

He raised an eyebrow. "Really? Who?"

"Not saying, just yet."

"Not even to me? He's local right? You're not going to run off with some online guy, are you?"

"He's a local."

"Good." He took another drink. "How about a hint?"

She shook her head. "You'll be the first to know when and if it gets to that point."

"It's not Duke, is it?"

She pulled her hand away. "Eww. No."

Jasper laughed. "There's a woman out there somewhere for him."

"I doubt it." She glanced toward the restaurant. "They're getting ready to start the dancing."

Jasper swiveled in his seat for a moment, then turned back to Mellie. "I should..."

"Yes. You should."

He took a last sip of his beer, then slid the bottle toward Mellie. "Wish me luck."

"With that suit, you don't need luck. You just need to stand there and smile."

"You're the best, Mellie."

"As are you, Jasper."

Jasper gave her a wink, then headed for Poppie. He came up beside her while Lewis and Sarah started dancing in the middle of the dance floor.

He nudged Poppie with his shoulder. "Beautiful couple."

She glanced at him. "Don't. I'll start crying again."

When the song ended, Pastor Mike, who'd taken on the MC duties for the night, asked the father of the bride and the mother of the groom, to come dance with their respective children.

As they started dancing, Jasper leaned close to Poppie. "Your dad's getting a little misty."

Poppie glanced at her father. "You're right, he is."

"Go ask him to dance."

She nodded then circled the dance floor and went to her father. Jasper watched them dance. He couldn't get over how perfect Poppie looked in her best man attire. Only she could pull that off. The dress at the dinner was provocative, but this... He smiled. This was fascinating.

When the song ended, Lewis went to Poppie for the next dance. The parents were joined by their spouses, and Jasper went to Sarah.

"I think it's my turn."

She smiled. "I think you're right." They started dancing. "So, are you done being stupid?"

"You think I'm being stupid? Maybe she's being stupid."

Sarah glanced at Poppie and Lewis. "I think you're both being stupid."

Jasper sighed. "What do I do about that?"

"Quit being stupid. After this dance, go dance with her."

"Hmm. I guess I could do that." After a few moments, he said, "Thanks for filling her in on my dating profile, by the way."

Sarah laughed. "She asked. And I didn't see the harm in letting her know how popular you were in high school."

"I wasn't popular. I was skinny, shy, and five-foot-eight, until half-way through Sophomore year."

"And by the time we started Junior year, you were an even skinnier and slightly awkward six-foot-something."

"Well, you grow seven inches in six months and see how awkward you feel."

"The good news is, you filled out." She patted his chest. "Very nicely, I might add."

"Sarah, you're a married woman."

"Which means I can safely flirt."

After a few moments of silence, Jasper said, "So, I need to know. Grilled cheese?"

Sarah laughed. "It's a running joke. A list of safe words."

Jasper leaned back and looked at her. "You need safe words?"

"No. In awkward or stressful situations, one of us will come up with a ridiculous word or phrase that theoretically could be used as a safe word. If we needed one. Which we don't."

"Hmm. Seems thou protesteth too much."

She shook her head. "We're probably the least kinky couple around."

"I'm sorry."

Sarah pinched his arm. "Shut up."

The music ended and she stepped away from him. "Now, go make up with Poppie."

Jasper approached Lewis and Poppie. "I think your bride wants to dance with you again."

Lewis grinned. "She can't get enough of me." He kissed Poppie on the cheek then left to dance with Sarah.

The music started again and Jasper smiled at Poppie. "I can't just leave you here on the dance floor all alone."

"Are you going to escort me off?"

He held out his arms. "No. I thought we could dance." She looked at him for a moment, and he added. "No handcuffs involved."

She stepped close as he put his arm around her waist. She was quiet for a few moments before saying, "I accept that I'm sixty percent responsible."

"Hmm. Well, on further consideration, I'd say fifty-fifty is more accurate."

"So, you're sorry for the handcuffs?"

"Yes." He pulled her in a little closer. "Did you mean what you said about...?"

She leaned back. "No. I was just trying to—"

"Right. I know." He sighed. "I do usually have them on me though. If you ever change your mind."

"Don't hold your breath, Deputy."

He glanced at her parents who were dancing, as well. "Have you told your parents we're...doing it?"

"Stop. You know I didn't mean that." She looked at him. "I'm going to tell them in the morning."

"Are you also going to tell them you're staying?"

Poppie laid her head on his shoulder. "Do you still want me too?"

He leaned back and looked at her. "Of course. It was a stupid argument. It doesn't change anything." He pulled her back in and she laid her head on his chest, again.

"We need a safe word."

He glanced at Sarah and Lewis. Never in his life had he had a conversation about safe words. Now, twice in five minutes? "So. You *do* want to use the handcuffs?"

Poppie giggled. "No. Not that kind of safe word. You are...slightly...overprotective."

"Only slightly?"

"And we need a word that you use only when real danger is present."

"Okay. That might work." He thought for a moment. "How about Penelope?"

"Perfect."

"We should try it out." He took a breath. "Penelope, kiss me." She turned her face to him and he kissed her. "Mmm that worked really well. Let's give it another try."

"No. We don't want to pull attention away from the bride and groom."

"What's next on the agenda?"

"The buffet comes out in about thirty minutes."

"Okay. I can work with that." He stopped dancing and took her hand. "Come on."

"Where are we going?"

"I want to show you something." He headed for the kitchen and went through the swinging doors.

"You want to show me the kitchen?"

Jasper took a key from a board on the wall with several sets of keys. He then opened a door on the far side of the kitchen.

Poppie peered through the door at the dark set of stairs. "Okay. That's not creepy at all."

Jasper started up the steps. "Trust me."

Once the door closed behind them, the stairwell became even darker and Poppie held onto Jasper's hand with both of hers as he led her up the stairs. They came to a landing, which was a little lighter due to a door with a window at the end letting in the late afternoon sun. They were in a hallway with two more doors and Jasper unlocked one of them and pulled her inside. He kicked the door closed and took her in his arms.

After a kiss that seemed to make her forget she was ever mad at him, she tried to peer around the room. With the curtains closed and blinds drawn, she could only see the outline of furniture. "You wanted to show me a storeroom?"

"It's not a storeroom. It's Diedre's apartment."

She looked at the dark shapes in the room. "Is it available?"

He slipped off his jacket and dropped it onto the floor. "You really want to talk real estate right now?" He loosened his tie and pulled it off over his head.

"Deputy Goodspeed. Just what do you think is going to happen here?"

He helped her out of her jacket and untied her tie. "I missed you."

"We've seen each other every day since I got here."

"Yeah. But for the last forty-eight hours, you've been mad at me." He started unbuttoning her blouse.

"We're going to get caught, again."

"The door's locked, and I have the key. Besides, why would anyone want to come to an empty apartment?"

She cocked her head and said, "For a quickie in the ex-bartender's bed?" Then she unbuttoned his shirt and he let it drop to the floor. "We're going to have to put all this stuff right back on."

"Yeah. But not yet." He kissed her. "Penelope, stop talking."

"Yes, Deputy Goodspeed. Whatever you say."

Jasper and Poppie managed to get mostly dressed in the dark room, then went into the hall to fix their ties, tuck in their shirts, and straighten their hair.

Poppie patted her braid. "Oh my gosh. Is my hair a mess?"

Jasper fixed a couple of the flowers and tucked in a stray hair or two. "It's fine." He fixed her tie and buttoned a button she missed. "No one will ever know."

"Hmm. Not so sure about that." She put her arms around his neck. "You are a very bad boy."

"It seems to me, I wasn't the only one in that room. So if I'm bad, so are you."

She stepped away from him and took his hand. "Come on. I'm starving."

They went down the dark stairs and opened the door to the kitchen, finding Peg on the other side of it.

Jasper stopped short. "Oh. Hey."

Peg put her hands on her hips and cocked her head while she studied him for a moment. Then she held out her hand.

Jasper dug the key out of his pocket and put it in her hand.

She looked at it for a moment, then nodded toward the doors to the dining room. "Get on out there while there's still food left."

Jasper kissed her on the cheek, then led Poppie through the swinging doors, while Poppie mumbled.

"*We won't get caught. I have the key.*"

He smiled at her. "Aunt Peg is cool."

Poppie sighed as they got in the buffet line. "We should make an announcement. Pastor Mike can do it for us. 'Poppie and Jasper are doing it.'"

"I'll go talk to him."

Poppie took his arm. "Don't you dare."

Chapter Twenty-Three

"How about a mimosa?"

P oppie kissed Jasper, then got out of bed, taking the blanket with her, and wrapping it around her shoulders

He groaned. "Where are you going? Checkout isn't until noon."

"I need to meet my parents for breakfast."

He rolled onto his side and patted the bed. "Can't you tell them you overslept?"

"They're leaving town in two hours, and they think I'm going with them."

Jasper raised onto an elbow. "Oh. Right. They don't know about me."

"They will in about thirty minutes." She headed for the shower. "I'm going to pay for another night so, don't go anywhere."

"I should show up for work at some point. And I need to meet with Evan Jeffers."

She stopped and turned back to him. "He's coming to town?"

"He's here. I saw him yesterday before I got to the reception."

She went back to the bed and sat on the edge. "And...?"

"He's here to tie up loose ends, or so he said. And he wants to see his father's grave."

"Uh-oh."

Jasper shrugged. "It'll be fine. He knows how his father was." He tugged on the blanket. "You sure you can't be a little late?"

She stood. "Yes. Just wait for me. I'll make it worth your while."

"Yes, ma'am. I'll be right here." He laid back down. "Actually, I need to go walk the dogs. But I'll be back."

When Poppie got to The Sailor's Loft, Steve and Priscilla were at a table waiting for her. Priscilla was half-way through a mimosa.

"Hi, honey."

"Good morning, Mom." Poppie kissed her on the cheek, then hugged her dad. "Morning, Dad."

"Hi, sweetheart. You all packed and ready to go?"

Poppie sat and took a sip of the water in front of her napkin.

Priscilla patted her hand. "Would you like a mimosa, honey? Dad's driving so we can enjoy breakfast."

"No thanks. Um, I need to talk to you guys about leaving today."

"Oh, we have to, dear. Steve has to be back to work on Monday. And he needs a couple of days to unwind."

"I know. I meant about me leaving. I'm going to stay awhile."

Steve leaned forward in his chair. "Stay? Your brother's going to be gone for two weeks on his honeymoon."

"I know." Poppie straightened her silverware and took another sip of water. "I'm not staying for him." She glanced at her mother.

Priscilla tilted her head. "It's the cute deputy, isn't it? I saw you two dancing last night."

"Um. Yeah. Jasper."

Steve shook his head. "Wait. What about the deputy? I thought he was Lewis' friend."

"He is, but—"

"He's Poppie's friend, too." Priscilla smiled at Poppie. "Isn't he, honey?"

"A good enough friend to stay here? Just like that?"

Priscilla frowned at her husband. "Your daughter's in love. Can't you see that, dear?"

Poppie tried to protest. "No. Well, maybe."

Steve studied his daughter. "What do you know about this young man? Aside from him being your brother's friend and in law enforcement."

"That isn't really an issue here. And what difference does it make? He's Lewis' best friend. Lewis trusts him. Lewis approves of us." She frowned. It wasn't exactly what she meant to say.

Priscilla patted Poppie's hand. "Didn't Jasper lose his wife recently?"

Steve shook his head. "What? He was married? He's a widower? Does he have kids?"

Poppie got to her feet. "Dad. Please."

Priscilla looked at her. "Sit down, honey. Your father's done talking for a while."

Steve didn't seem to agree, but he leaned back in his chair and drank some coffee.

Poppie sat. "Yes. He was married. He tragically lost his wife a little over two years ago. Last summer, when we met, he wasn't ready. But he is now. He's ready to move on and he wants to move on with me."

Priscilla smiled. "He seems like a very nice man."

Steve wasn't ready to concede. "You've only known him a week."

"No, Dad. I met him last summer. And we've kept in touch. I need to stay and see this through. I think he's the one. But I can't find out if he's here and I'm in Boston."

Priscilla patted her hand again. "Of course. You stay as long as you need to."

Steve looked at his wife. "Prissy!"

"Steve, she's a grown woman. She doesn't need our permission. She needs our support."

Steve sighed, then turned to Poppie and took her hand. "You'll always be my sweet, little Poppie. I can't help trying to protect you."

"Dad. You don't need to protect me from Jasper. He's a much better person than I am."

"I don't believe that."

"Well, it's true. So, be happy for me and hope it all turns out the way I want it to."

"And how's that?"

"That you'll need to come to Gracie Island to visit both of your kids."

"Did he grow up here? Does he have family?"

Poppie glanced around the restaurant. "His mother and aunt own this place. It's been in the family since 1975. He plays music on Friday nights in the bar with Lewis and Sarah. His father is the chief deputy sheriff and there has been a Chief Goodspeed in town for three generations. Jasper will be the fourth when his father retires. He doesn't have children, but he has a chihuahua he loves. And he recently took in two more dogs. What else do you want to know?"

Steve smiled at her. "That he makes you happy, which he clearly does." He leaned toward her and kissed her on the forehead. "Just don't be too hard on the poor boy."

Poppie smiled. "Oh, don't worry. He can hold his own."

Priscilla smiled. "How about a mimosa?"

Jasper sat on the old wooden bench he'd dragged to the high tide line the first summer in the house. He'd spent many hours sitting on it, with and without Ivy. Today, he felt she was sitting beside him while he watched the dogs run on the beach and chase the waves as they rolled in.

"Two years ago, I never could've imagined having this conversation with you. But you were always the one I went to when I needed advice. You always knew the right thing to say. I didn't think it'd be possible to fall in love again. But I have." He looked at the sky. "God help me, I love her." He watched the dogs for a moment. "The funny thing is, I think you'd love her, too. And I'm pretty damn sure you're up there laughing your ass off at how much she frustrates me." A breeze blew up from the water and he closed his eyes for a moment as he felt it on his face.

"Mom was right. You and I were in perfect harmony and we would've had a wonderful, stress-free life together. I'm sorry I couldn't protect you. I'm sorry...I couldn't save you." He swiped at a tear. "I'll always love you, and you'll always be with me."

Penny came up to his feet and put her paws on his boot. He picked her up, and she wiggled, then barked. "I know. Thank you." Penny barked again. "Alright. That's enough."

When Penny barked a third time, Jasper looked over his shoulder to find James approaching.

"Chief?"

When Jasper started to stand, James held up a hand. "Stay put." He walked around the bench and stopped several feet in front of it.

"Is everything okay? Did you need me for something?"

"No. I was driving by and I saw your Jeep." He glanced at the wooden frame of the house. "It's coming along."

"Yeah. Should be done in a month or so."

"It's going to be a great house."

"Thank you." Jasper watched his father shift from one foot to the other. Something was definitely up. He couldn't remember the last time the chief had dropped by to say, "hi." And his house wasn't on the main road. You had to turn onto his street to get there. There was no 'driving by.'

"So your friend's wedding was yesterday?"

"Yeah." Jasper put Penny down. "Seriously, what's up? Why are you here?"

"Just wanted to check in." James put his hands in the pockets of his jacket. "I'll see you at the office later. Sam's son is in town."

"Right, I saw him last night. I'll be in this afternoon and I'll take him to the house."

James nodded. "Okay." He started walking. "I'll see you then." He passed the bench and headed for his Bronco.

Jasper sat for a moment, then sighed and got to his feet. "Dad?"

James stopped.

"Are you okay?"

"I'm fine, Son. I'll see you at the station."

Jasper watched James until he got into his Bronco and drove off.

When he sat back down, he watched the waves for a moment. "What the hell was that?"

Jasper was dressed and in a chair with a magazine when Poppie came through the door. She smiled at him and then went and sat on his lap as he tossed the magazine aside.

"Why are you dressed, Deputy?" She started unbuttoning his shirt.

He smiled at her. "What did you drink for breakfast?"

"I couldn't let Mom drink mimosas by herself."

"How many did you have?"

"One. Or... possibly three."

"Three? Wow." She'd made it halfway through his buttons, and he pulled the shirt off over his head, along with his t-shirt. "And how many did your mother have?"

"I don't know, but she probably won't remember much of the drive home."

"So what do they think about..." He lifted her arms and took her shirt off. "Us?"

"Mom thinks you're cute and Dad told me to be nice to you."

Jasper laughed. "I like your parents." He stood, taking her with him, then dropped her gently onto the bed.

She looked at him. "Can we stop talking about my parents now?"

He laid next to her. "Yes."

She touched his bandaged arm. "Jasper?"

"Yes?"

"Can we never fight again? Sparring is fine. But fighting is stupid and I don't like it."

"I wish I could say yes. But realistically, probably not going to happen."

"Can't you just humor me?"

"Okay. Sure. We'll never fight again."

"Thank you."

Jasper woke from the light sleep they'd both fallen into and rolled away from Poppie. She

reached for him. "Where are you going?"

"I'm not going anywhere. I just need to call my mom."

Poppie sighed. "You and I are much too attached to our parents."

Jasper laughed. "It would seem so. I want to show you the apartment."

"Oh. In the daylight?"

"Yes. You need a place to stay, right?"

"Once Lewis is back, yeah." She sat and wrapped the blanket around her shoulders. "And we've already broken it in."

Jasper dialed The Sailor's Loft. "Hey, it's Jasper. Is Mom available?"

Peg hesitated on the other end of the line. "No. She's out."

Jasper checked the time on the bedside table. "It's noon."

"She had an appointment, honey. She'll be back soon. What do you need?"

"Um... I wanted to show Poppie the apartment."

"In the daylight?"

"Yeah."

"Bring her by, honey. I'll go to the fuse box and turn the power on."

"Okay. See you soon." He hung up the phone and dropped onto the pillows. "Hmm."

"What's wrong?"

"Mom wasn't there."

Poppie shrugged. "Does she have to show it to us?"

"No. That's not the problem." He rearranged the pillows and sat up more. "I can't remember the last time Mom took off in the middle of the day."

"Sounds like she's due, then."

"I told you something was going on with her."

"You're hungry, right?"

"Starving."

"So, let's get dressed and go get some breakfast. When she comes back, I'm sure she'll have a perfectly good explanation."

Jasper sat on the edge of the bed. "Okay. I also need to check in with the chief." He dialed the station.

Maisy answered in her usual chipper mood. "Sheriff's office."

"Good morning, Maisy."

"Good afternoon, honey."

"Right. Is the chief in?"

"No, he's out."

"Can you get him on the radio?"

"He asked not to be disturbed unless it was an emergency. And even then, to call you first."

"He doesn't want to be disturbed? Since when?"

"Do you want to leave a message?"

"No. I'll be in around two. And Evan Jeffers will be in. If he gets there before I do, will you call me at the Loft?"

"So he must have gotten one of our messages. I'll call you if he comes by and keep him occupied until you get here."

"Thank you, Maisy." Jasper hung up the phone, then turned to Poppie. "Seems the chief is indisposed as well."

Poppie smiled. "They're together."

"No way." He stood and started walking around the room. "That's not possible." He looked at her. "What?"

"It's hard to hold a conversation with you when you're walking around in all your glory."

He glanced at his naked body. "Do you want me to get dressed?"

"No. Carry on."

He sat on the end of the bed. "Mom would never go back to that situation again."

Poppie crawled to the end of the bed and put a hand on Jasper's back. "Maybe the situation has changed."

He glanced back at her. "Let's go eat."

She smiled. "You *will* need to get dressed for that."

Chapter Twenty-Four

"Baby's breath."

Jasper got the key to the apartment from Peg and took Poppie upstairs to show it to her. His mother wasn't back yet, and Peg still wasn't being forthcoming with any information. When he unlocked the door and opened it for Poppie, she stepped in and gasped, as he flipped on an overhead light.

"Oh, my gosh. It's wonderful."

The apartment was, in effect, a studio, but it covered the whole second story, making it a large, open living space. It was furnished with a four-poster bed in one corner, which they'd tested last night, a couch and two chairs next to a woodstove, and a small, fully equipped kitchen. There was a breakfast bar separating the kitchen from the rest of the room, with two barstools. The large bathroom was between two walk-in closets. And there was a sliding glass door opening to a small balcony.

Jasper smiled at Poppie's enthusiasm. "Pretty great, right? I haven't been up here for a while, before last night. I actually lived here for about six months after I came back from Augusta. Of course, it was empty, and I slept on a mattress on the floor."

Poppie went to him and gave him a hug. "I love it."

When the door opened, they both looked to see Kat come through it.

She smiled at them. "I hope this means you're planning on staying with us for a while."

Poppie glanced at Jasper. "As long as he's willing to put up with me."

"Well, the apartment is yours for as long as you need it."

"Thank you so much."

Kat looked at Jasper. "Are you okay, honey?"

This wasn't an ideal time to have the conversation he wanted to have with her. But his mother could always read him, and she'd bug him until he came clean. "Can I talk to you for a moment on the balcony?"

"Sure, dear." She smiled at Poppie. "Excuse us, honey. Look around. Make yourself at home."

Kat followed Jasper to the balcony, and he closed the door.

There was no sense dragging it out, so he came right to the point. "What's going on, Mom?"

She held his gaze for a moment, then looked away. "What do you mean?"

"The last time you took off in the middle of the day was when I sprained my ankle in eighth grade."

She sat in one of two matching wooden chairs. "Jasper, there's nothing going on." She patted the chair next to her. "Come sit down."

Jasper sighed, then sat.

She was quiet for a moment, then seemed to give in. "I didn't intend to keep this from you, but I've been spending time with your father."

Jasper got to his feet. "What the hell, Mom?"

"Please sit and calm down. This is why I didn't tell you sooner. Let me explain."

He sat again. "Why would you put yourself in that situation again? The drinking? The solitude? Being the only one who cares?"

Kat patted Jasper's knee. "Your father's been going to AA for six months. He hasn't had a drink in seven."

"What?" Jasper tried to remember the last time he needed to go check on the chief after missing work. It'd been at least that long. "Why didn't he tell me? Why didn't *you* tell me?"

"He's having trouble figuring out how to talk to you, Jasper."

"I see him every day." He leaned back in the chair. "That's why he was being so weird this morning."

"What happened this morning?"

"He showed up at the house. He never comes to my house unless it's on fire."

"Honey!"

"Well, it's true."

"As the chief deputy, he knows how to talk to you. As your father, he has no idea how to approach you. He knows he's failed you. He'd really like to make amends. I'm sure that's what he was trying to do this morning."

Jasper stood again and looked at the alley below. Despite the apartment facing an alley, the view was beautiful. There was only one building between The Sailor's Loft and the shoreline, and it was the mercantile which had a rooftop garden. But Jasper wasn't there to admire the view. "Why change after twenty-plus years of drinking?"

"Almost losing you last summer had a big impact on him."

He turned back to her. "Bullshit."

"Honey."

"Sorry." He sat again. "I want you to be happy, Mom. Are you sure the chief does that for you?"

"Yes. You know, I never really stopped loving him."

"No. I didn't know that. You've barely talked to each other in fifteen years. You're hardly ever in the same room together." He glanced at her. "I guess that's changed." He rubbed his face. "Oh, God. Don't answer that question." He took a deep breath. "Okay. I sort of see where you're coming from. There aren't a lot of eligible bachelors on the island. And you deserve to be happy if that's what you want. But just so you know. If he screws this up..."

"I know, dear." She took his hand. "Now, enough about that. Talk to me about Poppie. She's staying?"

"Yeah. We need to see where this is all going."

"And where do you think it's going?"

Jasper shrugged. "I don't know. One minute I want to strangle her and the next minute... Well, I don't. Thanks for letting her rent the apartment."

"Does she need a job?"

"I told her I could train her to work the bar. Or maybe she could wait tables. She wants to work, and she's still got her apartment in Boston to pay for."

"Well, she doesn't need to pay rent here."

"I'm pretty sure she'll insist on it."

"I'll talk to her and we'll figure something out."

"Thanks, Mom." He squeezed her hand. "It's going to take me a while to wrap my head around this 'you and dad thing.'"

"I know."

They went back inside and found Poppie in the kitchen area.

Kat went to her. "What do you think?"

"It's great. I love it. You must have a waitlist a mile long for it."

Kat smiled. "This is Gracie Island, dear, not a lot of turnover. It's yours if you want it."

"Of course I want it!"

"The furniture all stays. But if you have your own things, we can put this stuff in storage." Kat glanced around the room, then frowned at the bed and went to it. She straightened the quilt and fluffed the pillows.

Jasper winked at Poppie. When Kat picked up something from the bed, he asked, "What do you have there?"

"Baby's breath."

"Hmm." He took it from her. "That's weird."

Kat cocked her head. "Jasper?"

"What?" He tucked the sprig into his pocket.

She glanced at Poppie. "You can move in anytime."

"Thank you, Kat."

"And there's always work to be done, so let me know what you want to do."

"You're the best. Thank you so much."

"I'll leave you two to get settled in." She patted Jasper's cheek. "Come down and eat when you're ready."

"See you in a few minutes, Mom."

Poppie waited for Kat to leave, then went to Jasper. "So much for our secret rendezvous. Does anyone in Gracie not know we were in here last night?"

Jasper grinned. "I think she was the last one." He took the baby's breath out of his pocket and stuck it in her hair. "Let's put this back where it belongs."

She put her arms around his neck. "Can I tell you something that will probably freak you out?"

"Sure. Why not?"

"I didn't realize it until this morning. Or maybe I didn't want to admit it to myself." She kissed him. "I'm pretty sure I'm falling in love with you, Deputy Goodspeed."

"Hmm. It doesn't freak me out."

She smiled. "Really?"

"Yes. I have a small confession to make to you, which might freak *you* out."

"What is it?"

"When I need advice, I usually go to my mom. But sometimes, when it's really important and something I don't necessarily want to share with my mother, I talk to Ivy."

Poppie put a hand on his cheek. "That doesn't freak me out. I think it's sweet."

"You don't think it's weird I talk to my dead wife?"

"Not at all. What did you talk to her about?"

"I told her I was in love with you." He smiled. "Actually, I said, 'God help me, I'm in love with her.'"

Poppie cocked her head. "God help you if you don't kiss me right now."

Jasper kissed her, then stepped away.

She pulled him back. "Where are you going?"

"I'm starving. Let's go eat."

Poppie sighed. "Wow. We declare our love and all of a sudden, you want to go eat. Are we going to turn into one of those couples now?"

Jasper grinned. "What couples would that be?"

"Sex once a week, couples?"

He stepped close and put his arms around her waist. "I'll tell you what. If you let me eat and regain my strength. We can go back to the hotel and have all the sex you want."

She smiled. "Bed sex?"

"Yes."

"Shower sex?"

"Sure."

She leaned in and whispered in his ear.

He took a step back. "Maybe I'm not as hungry as I thought."

Poppie laughed. "Come on, Deputy, let's get you fueled up."

As they sat at the table waiting for their food to arrive, Jasper took Poppie's hand. "So, I found out where my Mom was today. And why the chief showed up at the house this morning."

"The chief came to see you this morning?"

"Yeah. Weird, I know."

"So, what's going on?" She looked at him, then smiled. "I was right. They're seeing each other."

Jasper took a breath. "Yes. You were right."

"Oh, my gosh. That's so cute."

"Is it?"

"Yes. And you need to be happy for them. And supportive."

"I can try to be supportive. But happy? I'm not so sure."

Peg arrived with burgers and fries and set them on the table. "Here you go. Can I get you anything else?"

Jasper smiled at her. "No. All good. Thanks."

Peg left and Poppie took his hand. "Are you worried about his drinking?"

Jasper picked up his burger and took a bite. When he finished chewing, he said, "Apparently, he's been sober for seven months. And going to AA for six."

"That's wonderful!"

"Hmm."

"You don't think it'll take?"

He looked at his burger. "Time will tell." He took a bite, then washed it down with some water. "If he fails, I just don't want him to take Mom down with him."

"She survived the last time, and she still had a son to raise. Your mom is tough. She'll be fine."

"I suppose." Jasper finished his burger while trying to picture his parents together. It didn't feel right. They weren't together even when they were married. What had changed? Surely it wasn't because he'd nearly died in a hurricane, as his mother had suggested.

When he realized he'd been lost in thought, he smiled at Poppie. "Sorry. Just a lot to take in."

"I understand."

He ate his last fry, then wiped his mouth with his napkin. "So, what do you think about bartending?"

"Might be fun."

"It is, mostly. It can get crazy once in a while. But nothing you can't handle."

"Will you teach me?"

"Sure. Mom has had a lot of temporary help since Deidre left. And I haven't been available for the last two nights. But I told her I'd cover the next few days. If you want to join me tonight. You can be my assistant and see what you think."

"Sounds fun."

"You're going to make a hell of a lot of money, too."

"Really?" She smiled at him. "More than you?"

"Hell, yeah. I'm a county employee."

Chapter Twenty-Five

"Things were so much easier when I was twelve."

J asper finally made it to the station by two-thirty and when he walked in the door, Evan was there talking to Maisy.

Jasper went to him and shook his hand. "Sorry. Have you been waiting long?"

"No. Just got here."

"Come into my office."

Evan nodded and followed Jasper, then sat in the chair in front of the desk while Jasper went to the coffee machine.

"Coffee?"

Evan shook his head. "No, thanks."

Jasper poured himself a cup, then sat at his desk. He took a sip, then set the cup down. "So, I checked the county records, and your father didn't write a will. Or at least he didn't file one. But he owned the house and the three acres it sits on, free and clear. He had no bank accounts, credit cards, or debt of any kind. He wasn't reliant on any county resources, he was completely self-sufficient." Jasper shrugged. "He paid his property taxes every year, and that's about it. Not sure where the money came from, but he kept a tab going at the grocery store and the mercantile. Gave me cash once a month to settle his accounts. And a list every Saturday of what he needed me to bring."

"So, he never came into town?"

"Not in the last eight years. The chief says it's been ten or twelve."

"Wow." Evan leaned back in his chair. "I had no idea he'd completely withdrawn from society." He looked at Jasper. "If it wasn't for you—"

"Someone else would've stepped up. Gracie Island takes care of their own." Jasper took a sip of coffee. "I can take you to the house if you want."

Evan took a moment. "Um. Sure. I'd like to see his grave first, though."

Jasper cleared his throat. "About that." He picked up his coffee cup, then set it down without taking a drink. "I was the one who found Sam. I got to his house late morning, and he'd died sometime during the night. I made a decision maybe I didn't have a right to, but I couldn't see bringing him into the cemetery to be buried among people who he'd spent a decade or more staying away from."

"So what did you do?"

"I buried him on the property, not long after I found him. I dug the grave, wrapped him in a blanket, and buried him under the trees."

Evan got to his feet and went to the window. Jasper watched him and tried to figure out what might be going through the man's head. But he wanted to give Evan time to process what he'd been told, so Jasper drank his coffee and straightened his already tidy desk.

Evan stood at the window for several minutes, before turning around to Jasper. "Will you take me to the house now?"

Jasper stood. "Of course." He still didn't know how Evan felt about his father's unorthodox burial, but Evan didn't seem mad or particularly upset by the information.

The drive to Sam's house was a quiet one. Evan seemed lost in thought, and Jasper thought it best to leave him to it. When they pulled onto the property and stopped in front of the house, Evan took a moment before getting out of the Jeep.

Jasper got out, closed his door, then went to the empty goat pen and secured the gate. When Evan got out of the Jeep, he came up beside Jasper.

"He had animals?"

"Yeah. Four goats and a dozen chickens. The neighbor Bo has them. But technically, they're yours if you want them."

Evan shook his head.

"He also had a dog. A Lab. I figure he's a couple of years old. He's at my place, if you—"

"Can't have a dog in my apartment."

"Right. I'm happy to keep him."

Evan turned toward the house. "Is there anything in there worth saving?"

"Not really. Do you want to go inside?"

Evan shook his head. "No." He glanced toward the trees. "He's over there?"

"Yeah."

Evan started walking and Jasper followed him. When they got to the grave, Evan stopped a few feet away and knelt on one knee.

"So, he died in his sleep?"

"Near as I can tell, he went peaceful."

"I guess that's all we can hope for." He got to his feet, then turned to Jasper. "Thank you."

"For what?"

"For taking care of him." He glanced at the grave. "Not only for this, but for coming to see him every week. I don't imagine he was very welcoming."

Jasper gave him a little smile. "I figured out pretty early on, if I brought a bottle and a carton of cigarettes, he'd at least come onto the porch and talk for a minute."

"Whiskey?"

Jasper nodded. "Yeah."

"That always was his drink."

"You can take some time to think about it, but you'll need to make a decision on the property."

Evan studied the house for a moment. "Is it worth anything?"

"The house isn't, but the property is, to the right person, I guess." He glanced toward the trees. "Bo's property backs up to it halfway through that stand of trees. He might be interested in buying it. Most people around here are settled on land their parents and grandparents lived on. Anyone new, which is rare, prefers to be by the water."

"You've done so much, I hate to ask, but could you check around? See if there's any interest?"

"Of course. No problem."

"What happens if no one wants it?"

Jasper looked across the grassy property. "Then it'll sit here."

Evan sighed. "Okay. Well, I won't expect much. I didn't come here thinking I'd come into some big inheritance or anything."

"Of course."

"But, if the neighbor wants it. Maybe you could get a fair price for it."

"I'll take care of it."

Evan held out his hand. "Thank you."

Jasper shook with him. "I'm sorry there wasn't more for you here."

"I didn't really expect any more than this."

The ride back to town was just as quiet, and Jasper dropped Evan off at the marina in time to catch the five o'clock ferry.

Evan got out of the Jeep and looked in at Jasper. "Thanks again. I gave my contact information to your...ah...the woman at the station."

Jasper smiled. "She's our Gal Friday. Pretty much runs the place."

"I figured."

"Have a safe trip back. I'll keep in touch."

With a wave, Evan closed the door and headed down the dock toward the ferry. Jasper watched him until he boarded, then pulled away and drove to the station.

The chief was at Maisy's desk when Jasper came through the door.

James nodded at him. "How'd it go?"

Jasper shrugged. "As good as it could, I guess. He seemed okay with Sam's final resting place."

"Good. It could've been a problem if he wasn't."

"He seems like a decent guy. Hard to believe he's Sam's son." He headed for his office. "I've got some paperwork to work on, then I need to go man the bar at the Loft."

Jasper spent the next hour filling out his monthly report that was twenty-seven days overdue. As small-town as they were, they still had to follow protocol. At least most of the time.

As he was finishing, James knocked on the open door. "Are you about done?"

"Yeah. Just finished."

James stepped into the room with a coffee cup in his hand. "Can we talk for a moment?"

"Sure."

James went to the coffee machine and filled his cup, then brought the pot to Jasper's desk. "Can I top off your cup?"

Jasper nodded and watched James pour coffee into his mug. If they were going to be drinking coffee, then this would be more than a brief conversation. He suspected he knew what the chief wanted to talk about. He took a sip of fresh coffee while James settled into the chair in front of the desk and took a sip from his own cup.

When he set it on the edge of the desk, he glanced at Jasper. "I, ah, talked to your mother this afternoon. She said she told you about...well, about us...seeing each other."

It was hard enough talking to his mother about it. But having this conversation with his father was uncomfortable and just plain wrong.

"She told me."

James sighed. "She said you had some reservations."

I have a hell of a lot more than some. "Um. Yeah. A few."

James picked up his cup again and stared into it before taking a sip. "Such as?'

Jasper was trying to stay patient. "She said you've been sober for seven months."

James set his cup down. "That's right."

"Well, that's great, of course, but it's kind of soon to—" He rubbed his face. "Shit. I'm worried. I'm worried about Mom. Honestly, I guess I don't understand why she's willing to trust you again."

"I see." He leaned back in his chair. "So, I'm assuming *you* don't trust me."

Jasper drank some coffee. "As chief, I trust you implicitly. As a husband, not so much."

"How about as a father?" Jasper tilted his head and James raised a hand. "Never mind. Forget I asked." He got to his feet. "Leave that paperwork with Maisy, then go help your mother. She needs you with Deidre gone." He started for the door.

"Dad."

James stopped and looked back. "It's okay."

"No. It's not."

James turned for the door again. "I'll see you tomorrow."

Jasper glared at the doorway after James went through it. "Nice talk, Dad."

James had left his cup on the desk, so Jasper picked it up along with his and took them to the coffee station behind Maisy's desk. It had a small sink, and he poured the coffee from both cups down the drain. Like Jasper's favorite mug, the chief always seemed to drink from that one. Jasper had never paid much attention to it, but now, under closer observation, he saw it was ceramic and crudely made. When he saw the letters J G scrawled on the bottom, he nearly dropped it into the sink.

He turned to Maisy. "Where did the chief get this mug? It looks hand-made."

Maisy gave him a queer look, then took the mug from him. "You made it for him, honey, in fourth grade. He's used it ever since."

Jasper leaned against the sink. "I don't remember that."

"It was a long time ago." She sat on her stool behind the reception desk. "I know the chief can be difficult. And he's a man of few words, especially if they're personal. But he—"

"Did you know about him and Mom?"

She gave him a small smile. "I suspected."

"I never saw it coming."

"Kids never do. No matter how old they may be. It's hard to picture our parents having lives and interests outside of being our parent. Your mother deserves to be happy."

"I know. That's why I have a problem with it."

"The chief has always loved her."

Jasper shook his head. "He sure has a funny way of showing it."

"Just give it some time."

Jasper pushed away from the sink and stood. "Time enough for him to screw her over again?"

"No. Time enough for them to figure out what they want. Whether or not you like it, there's not much you can do about it." She stood and went to him, then put her arms around him and gave him a hug. "It's going to be fine."

"Do you have any cookies to go along with this heart to heart?"

She stepped back and smiled at him. "No. I think this is probably beyond cookies."

Jasper sighed. "Things were so much easier when I was twelve."

Chapter Twenty-Six

"That's not exactly what I said."

The traffic at the bar was a little heavier than it had been once word got out Jasper was pouring drinks. He was sure Poppie felt a little like they had thrown her into the deep end without swimming lessons, but she did alright. And contrary to her nature, she listened to everything he said, followed his directions, and did remarkably well, considering she'd never been on the business side of a bar.

Jasper was glad it was busy, though. Every time it slowed down a little, he'd start thinking about his conversation with the chief. The man could face down an armed suspect without hesitation. But when talking to his son, he always had one foot out the door.

When they got a small break, Jasper took Poppie into the storeroom and put his arms around her.

"You're doing a fantastic job."

She shook her head. "I don't feel like I am."

He kissed her. "Trust me, you are."

"There's so much to learn. I had no idea."

"You'll get it. No one's in a hurry around here."

She stepped back and studied him for a moment. "You seem distracted tonight."

"Nah."

"You met with Sam's son today."

He leaned against a stack of beer cases. "It went fine. I'll tell you about it later."

"You sure?"

"Yeah. We better get back out there."

During the week, the restaurant closed at nine, and the bar was open until ten. But when they still had a full-house at nine-forty-five, Jasper decided to stay open until eleven. The regulars missed Deidre, and even though the bar had been open since she left, Lance and a few of the other guys filled in, but they weren't Deidre. Jasper, however, knew what he was doing, and the customers were glad he was there.

The response to Poppie becoming the new full-time bartender was mostly enthusiastic, with a few grumblers mentioning nepotism. But Jasper was sure it wouldn't be long before she won them all over. When he caught her pouring the wrong draft into a glass, he stepped up behind her.

"Is that for Derek?"

"Yeah."

He took the glass and poured out the beer, then set it under the right tap.

She frowned. "I swear he said—"

"He probably did. He gets confused sometimes, but this is what he wants. No matter what he asks for."

"How am I going to remember all of this?"

"You will. You're doing fine."

"You're going to work with me tomorrow, right?"

"Of course. I'll work with you as long as you need me to."

"Even though you're working all day, sheriffing?"

Jasper laughed. "Even so."

By ten-fifteen, no new customers were coming in, so Jasper turned off the open sign and announced last call. They took a few last orders, but most of the customers knew it was time to leave.

By ten-thirty, everyone had gone.

Poppie sighed as the last two men left, then looked at Jasper. "Phew."

"Just need to clean up, and close out the register."

She gave him a hug. "I'll leave the money counting to you." She picked up a tray and went to gather the empty glasses and wipe down the tables, while Jasper went to the cash register. When she finished, she began sweeping the floor.

When Jasper came and took the broom from her, she smiled. "You want to sweep?"

"I'd rather sweep and mop, then wash glasses." He handed her sixty dollars.

"I already have a pocket full of money."

"This is from credit and debit sales."

"Geez."

"I told you."

"Isn't some of this yours?"

"I'll keep the cash I got. You take this. You earned it."

"I'm not so sure about that. Everyone was here because you were, not me."

"Take it. Consider it my contribution to your rent, seeing as I'll probably be spending a lot of time in your new apartment until my house is done."

She smiled at him. "You think so?"

"I think we need to bring the dogs over so they don't get lonely."

She kissed him. "I best get those glasses washed then, if this night is just beginning."

They were done cleaning by eleven, and Jasper locked the door behind them as they headed for the Jeep. They drove to his house and parked in front of the trailer. When they got out of the vehicle, they could hear the dogs inside, excited by their arrival.

Poppie stuck out her bottom lip. "Poor babies, all cooped up."

Jasper opened the door, and the dogs piled out. After greeting their humans, they ran off to do their business. Penny was the first one back, and she put her paws on Jasper's leg. He picked her up and let her lick his cheek.

"Okay, that's enough." He handed the dog to Poppie, then whistled for Blackjack and Sam. They'd wandered beyond the headlights which Jasper had left on. When the dogs returned, he put them in the back of the Jeep, then went inside the trailer and retrieved their food and bowls.

"Okay, I think we're set." He hesitated for a moment. "Oh, wait. I need a clean shirt for tomorrow." He went into the trailer and packed a small bag with fresh clothes. He glanced around. "I'm not going to miss you."

After a shower, Jasper climbed into bed next to Poppie and she snuggled into his side.

"You must be tired."

"It's been a long day." He kissed the top of her head and patted the hand she had resting on his chest.

"Do you want to tell me about it?"

"Everything went fine with Evan. I took him to the house, and showed him Sam's grave, which he seemed to feel was the best thing to do for his father."

"What's he going to do with the property?"

"He has no interest in it. He asked me to see if I can find a buyer."

Poppie nodded, then looked at him in the dim light of the apartment. "So, it doesn't seem like that's what's distracting you tonight."

Jasper took a breath and blew it out slowly. "No. It was the damn chief. He came into my office right before I left and attempted to have a conversation with me."

"It didn't go well?"

Jasper shook his head. "I don't understand why he has such a problem talking to me. I've never confronted him about our relationship, or lack thereof. I've never pressured him for more than he was willing to give. But I don't think it's asking too much for him to talk to me about something outside of sheriff's office business. He just can't do it."

"I'm sorry."

"Yeah. Me too." He sighed. "Anyway, that's not what I want to talk to you about tonight."

"Okay. What do you want to talk about?"

He stroked her hair, then kissed it, again. "I've been working on my house for six months now. The first several were planning and making sure it was everything I wanted it to be. Mom helped me, of course, with the kitchen and the extra bedroom. Though I'm pretty sure I would've added the second room without her telling me to." He took a moment to adjust his pillow. "But through the whole process, the planning and the building,

I always felt there was something missing. But I couldn't put my finger on it."

"I can't imagine what it could be. It's perfect."

"Well, it came to me last week when you showed up." He rolled to his side and raised onto his elbow. "The thing I was missing was you."

She smiled. "Really?"

"I don't want to live in the house by myself."

"You don't?"

He ran his hand through her hair and touched her cheek. "There's two ways to look at our relationship. One is that we've actually only spent two to three weeks physically together. The other is we've known each other for almost eleven months. That's damn near a year."

"Those are two very different views."

"So, how do you see our relationship?"

"Well, to quote a smart and sexy deputy sheriff I know, I'd say we've known each other almost a year."

"That's not exactly what I said. If you're going to quote someone, it should be word for word. *Damn* near a year."

Poppie smiled. "Are you asking me to move into your house with you?"

Jasper peered around the room at the shadows of the furniture. "Well, you just moved into this great apartment, but yes. When you're ready, I'd love for you to be the thing that completes it."

She pushed him onto his back and kissed him. "When is the house going to be ready?"

"With this dry weather we've been having, it's coming along faster than we thought it would. I'd say in three weeks it'll be time to finish the inside. Paint, flooring, furniture."

She laid her head on his chest. "So, if I'm going to live there, do I have any say in any of the finishing stuff? The paint, for instance?"

"You mean something other than off-white?"

"Boring."

"You may paint the walls any color you want. Within reason."

Poppie grinned. "Awesome."

"I'm going to regret this, aren't I?"

"I won't go crazy. Just a little subtle color here and there."

"Okay. Emphasis on subtle."

"I'm very excited."

"You want to show me how excited you are?"

"I thought you had a long day."

"I didn't actually go to the station until mid-afternoon. Someone kept distracting me."

She kissed him. "Like this?"

"Yeah. Something like that. It was a little more involved, though."

She kissed him again. "Well, let me see if I can figure it out."

Chapter Twenty-Seven

"Classic James Goodspeed."

J asper and Poppie were sitting on the tailgate of Lewis' truck, eating blueberry muffins from the bakery. The dry weather had continued and once the roof was done, they'd get to work on the interior. At that point, it wouldn't matter if it rained or not.

Poppie spent the last week perfecting her bartending skills by night, and looking at decorating magazines by day. After working six days straight, Kat insisted she and Jasper take the night off, and tomorrow, Poppie would tend bar by herself. She was nervous, but Jasper was confident she'd be fine.

Lance, who was on the roof of Jasper's house, called down to them.

"When you asked me to help you today, I figure you were actually going to be up here with me."

Jasper grinned at him and held up his partially eaten muffin. "Sorry, I'll be right up."

"By all means. Finish your muffin first."

"Do you want me to bring you one?"

Lance waved at him and went back to work.

Jasper looked at Poppie. "Was that a yes or a no?"

"I think it was a 'just get up here.'"

Jasper put the last bite in his mouth and slid off the tailgate. He wiped his hands on his jeans, then drank the last of his coffee, before giving her a smile and a kiss.

"Are you sticking around for a while?"

"Yeah. I enjoy watching big, strong men doing manual labor."

He flexed his bicep. "You like that?"

She laughed. "Go before Lance gets mad and leaves."

When he turned to go, the radio cackled, and he went to the Jeep and picked up the receiver.

"What's up, Maisy?"

"Kat's been trying to reach you."

He leaned against the open door. "Is everything okay?"

"I'm not sure, but it probably has something to do with the chief not showing up this morning."

"Christ."

"Call her and let me know what she says."

"Okay. I'll be in as soon as I can."

"Thank you, honey."

He tossed the receiver on the passenger seat and closed the door as Poppie came to him.

"Is everything okay?"

"No. I need to call Mom." He headed for the trailer. "I'll be right back."

Jasper went into the trailer and dialed Kat's house. She answered on the first ring.

"James?"

"No, Jasper. What's going on, Mom?"

He heard her sigh. "When I woke up this morning, he was gone. I found a note in the kitchen."

Jasper tried not to let the overshare from his mother bother him. "What'd it say?"

"He said he needed to clear his head, and he took the boat to Puffin to fish."

Jasper sat at the table. "The fishing is horrible around Puffin."

"Honey."

"Oh, right. Dad doesn't fish. And he doesn't decide last minute not to show up for work. Unless..."

"Jasper. I truly don't believe—"

"Mom. Are you sure?"

"I'm sure that as of last night, James hasn't had a drink in over seven months."

Jasper tapped the table. "Okay. What do you want me to do?"

She sighed again. "I guess nothing. I just panicked and needed to talk to you about it. Let's give it some time. He'll probably be back this afternoon."

"And if he's not?"

"Then we'll figure out what to do next."

Jasper stood. "I'll be available all day, either on the radio of at the station. If you need anything, call me."

"I will, honey."

"Love you, Mom."

"I love you more."

As he hung up the phone, Poppie opened the door. "Is everything okay?"

"I'm not sure."

"Can I come in?"

"Of course." He went back to the table, and she sat across from him. "The chief didn't show up for work this morning."

"Oh, no."

"Yeah. He left a note for Mom this morning—don't even get me started on that whole situation—said he was going fishing. Needed to clear his head. Whatever that means." He looked at her. "He doesn't fish. And if he did suddenly get the urge to take it up, he'd go somewhere else. Not Puffin Island."

She took his hand. "Are you afraid he's fallen off the wagon?"

Jasper shook his head. "I don't know. Mom seems to think that's not what it is."

"So, what do you need to do?"

"Go to work and wait to hear from her. Hopefully, he'll be back soon." He kissed her hand, then got to his feet. "I need to get dressed."

Poppie folded her arms across her chest and smiled at him.

"Are you going to help?"

"No. I'm going to watch."

He took off his plaid flannel and put on his uniform shirt, then glanced at her as he stepped out of his jeans. "Are you enjoying yourself?"

"Immensely."

He put on his olive cargo pants and tucked in his shirt, then buckled his belt. "Show's over."

She got up and put her hands on his chest. "You wear this uniform very well."

"You said that about my suit at the wedding.

"I liked that, too. But my favorite outfit is your birthday suit."

"That old thing? I've had it for thirty years."

"It still looks great."

When they went outside and started walking toward the house, Lance moved to the edge of the roof and knelt.

"Wow. You'll do anything to get out of helping me today."

"Sorry. Apparently, the chief decided to take the morning off. Duty calls."

Lance shook his head. "Whatever. You were just going to get in my way."

"Hey."

"Just kidding. Go do what you gotta do. I'll get this done for you."

"Thanks, Lance."

Jasper spent the morning trying to stay busy, but there really wasn't much to do. When a fender bender was called in, he jumped at the chance to get out of the office. He drove two blocks and found Bindi Anderson and Skeeter McDonald standing next to their vehicles. Jasper parked across the street and crossed over to them.

"Everyone okay?"

Bindi glanced at Skeeter. "Yes. No thanks to Mr. McDonald."

Skeeter put his hands on his hips. "Hey. I didn't see you. You stopped in the middle of the road."

"I was parallel parking."

Jasper raised his hands. "Okay." He surveyed the damage on both vehicles. "Nothing major here. Let's get them off the road."

Skeeter got into his truck and backed into a space next to the bakery, while Bindi finished her parallel parking, then got out of the car.

Jasper went to the Jeep and retrieved a clipboard with statement forms. "Okay. One at a time. Bindi, what happened?"

Bindi gave her accounting, followed by Skeeter, and both statements were similar enough for Jasper to conclude it was nobody's fault. He handed them each an accident report.

"Give that to Rick at Haven Insurance. He'll take care of that end of it."

Bindi put a hand on Jasper's arm. "Thank you, Jasper."

Skeeter shook Jasper's hand. "Appreciate it." He nodded at Bindi. "Sorry, Mrs. Anderson. I guess I wasn't paying attention."

She gave him a smile. "No harm done."

As they drove off, Randy came out of the bakery. "A little excitement for the day?"

"Very little. How you doing, Randy?"

"Hanging in there. How's the house coming?"

"Getting there. Lance is shingling the roof today."

"Do you want a cup of coffee?"

"No. Thanks. I need to get back to the station."

"What's this I hear about the chief and your mom?"

Jasper shook his head. "Well, it's not a rumor. And I'm having a little trouble being the supportive son."

Randy laughed. "I hear ya. Parents. What are you gonna do?"

"See ya, Randy."

Jasper crossed the street and got into the Jeep, then checked in with Maisy. Someone had called in to report some boys roughhousing at the gazebo, so Jasper headed to the park. When the boys in question saw him pull up, they ran off.

"Yeah, you little punks. I know where you live." He wrote down the boys' names, but didn't plan on calling their parents. He'd give them this one.

When he was twelve, he'd climbed to the roof of the gazebo and was taking a bow when the chief arrived. His friends all ran off and he'd nearly broken his neck trying to get down, but he wasn't quick enough and the chief was waiting for him on the grass below. Jasper thought he was going to get reprimanded, but all the chief said was, "You know, your mother's rather fond of you and I don't want to be the one to tell her you cracked your skull open falling off the gazebo."

Jasper started the Jeep. "Classic James Goodspeed."

It was mid-afternoon, and he hadn't eaten yet, so Jasper told Maisy he'd be at the Loft for the next hour to eat lunch. Peg greeted him when he went inside and she took him to a table. After he ordered a burger and fries, Peg left him with water and a cup of coffee. A few minutes later, Kat came and sat at his table.

Jasper smiled at her. "Any word?"

"No."

He picked up his cup. "I can fly over there. It'll take twenty minutes at most."

"What if he didn't go to Puffin Island?"

"Well, then it might take longer, but I'll find him." He drank some coffee and set his cup down. "He's not going to go too far in his boat. Certainly not out into the blue water. He'll stay between the islands and the coastline."

Kat rested her elbows on the table. "What if he's really just fishing?"

"We've already established that's a long shot."

"But if he is. He'll be mad I sent you out looking for him."

"If he gets mad because you were worried about him, then screw him."

"Honey."

Jasper raised a hand. "I know. Sorry."

"Okay. Do it. I guess. But eat first and come back before the sun goes down, whether or not you find him. I don't want to be worrying about both of you."

"If I don't get back before sunset, I'll be spending the night on the plane. I can't land her in the dark."

"Just make sure you're back."

After Jasper finished eating, he used the restaurant phone to call Poppie.

"I wanted to let you know I'm taking the plane up to see if I can track down the chief."

"Wow. Okay. Will you be back tonight?"

"Ideally, yeah. The landing strip isn't set up for landing in the dark. It's a tricky approach and a short runway. If I absolutely had to, I could land her in the marina. But that's not ideal."

"So, be back before dark."

"That's the plan." He took a moment. "I don't suppose you'd like to come with me?"

"No flying for me."

"It's pretty fantastic scenery and we'll be flying low. Hardly flying at all. More like skimming the water."

"Sounds super safe. I also imagine you wouldn't mind having a buffer between you and your father."

"Never crossed my mind."

"Right."

"Will you at least meet me at the landing strip and see me off?"

"Sure. When?"

"I'll be there in thirty minutes. Just need to check in with Maisy and change out of my uniform."

"See you there."

Chapter Twenty-Eight

"I don't remember you mentioning this part."

Jasper was finishing his pre-flight check when Poppie arrived in Lewis' truck. She parked next to the Jeep, then walked over to him. The plane was small and oddly shaped, with enough room in the cabin to seat four people.

He gave her a hug, then took a step back. "What?"

She sighed. "I'm sort of, possibly, maybe thinking about—"

"Coming with me?"

"I just know I'm going to regret it. How safe is it?"

"Super safe. Like I said, we'll be staying low. If the engine stalls, we won't have far to fall."

She stepped away from him. "That's not what I want to hear."

"I'm kidding. We're flying over water. The plane's amphibious I can put her down on water or land. Pretty damn safe." She sighed deeply, and he added, "We'll be home in less than four hours."

She covered her face and groaned, then took a big breath. "Okay. I'll go."

Jasper grinned. "Yes!"

Poppie put a hand on his chest. "But I swear, if we—"

He put a hand over her mouth. "Don't even say it. It's bad luck." He went to the Jeep for supplies. "I promise you, you're going to love it."

As soon as Poppie buckled into the seat next to Jasper, she began to regret her decision. She thought about bailing, but when she saw how excited he was that she was coming, she couldn't do it.

He patted her knee. "Are you ready?"

She nodded as she glanced around the tiny cockpit. It looked bigger from outside the plane.

"Okay. Here we go."

The takeoff was smoother than she thought it would be and it wasn't until they were in the air and Jasper banked the plane and flew over the water that her stomach flip flopped and she started to panic. She closed her eyes and held her breath.

Jasper took her hand for a moment. "Hey, you're fine. Open your eyes. You can see all of Gracie Island."

Poppie opened her eyes and looked out the window. The island was below and she could see it all, including the lighthouse. The town and residential areas seemed small compared to the wilds. And she was surprised the island was egg-shaped, with the smaller end being where the lighthouse was. There were more trees than she thought, and on the west side, there was a bay surrounded by rock outcroppings.

"Oh, my gosh." She pointed to the bay. "Is that where the Dragonfly was?"

Jasper glanced out her window. "No, that's the west side. The little indent on the east, about a quarter of the way down from the lighthouse, is Bay Harbor where Roger found the Dragonfly. If you look closely, you can see the original Gracie house. Or at least the fireplace."

He made some adjustments and turned the plane south. "We're going to head toward Puffin Island. It's about ten miles to the south. But I'm going to hug the coastline, because honestly, I'm not convinced he went all the way there. There are four islands between Gracie and Puffin. He could've stop at anyone of them. Or just be moving around."

She patted his thigh. "We'll find him." She was still scared, but the beauty of the water and the coastline of Maine in the distance was a great distraction.

They came to the first island, which was small, mostly wooded, and uninhabited. There was no sign of James' boat, so they kept going. The second and third, both small, flat, and grassy, were also clear. As they approached the fourth, Jasper spotted a small boat on the west side of the island pulled onto the sandy beach. He dropped in altitude and determined it was the chief's runabout. The island was bigger than the first three, and seemed to be a mix of grasslands and trees, with a sandy beach most of the way around it. Jasper circled the island and came in toward the small bay behind the boat and landed the plane a hundred yards out. He then powered the plane to within twenty feet of the shore and turned it off.

Poppie looked at the water surrounding them. "Um. Do we swim from here?"

Jasper laughed. "Unfortunately, I can't pull her onto the beach. But it's not deep. You'll get a little wet, though."

"Hmm. I don't remember you mentioning this part."

"Sit tight...please. I'll go tie off the plane, then come back for you."

"Oh, how sweet."

"I know." He opened his door and stepped onto the pontoon, then jumped into the water and it hit him just below his waist. He sucked in his breath and said, "Oh shit, it's cold." He glanced at her. "I'll be back."

She watched as he secured a line to a metal strut on the pontoon, then waded to the beach and tied the other end to a tree. He then came back to the plane and opened her door.

He held out his arms. "Good thing you're a tiny little thing or you'd be wading your ass to land."

She stepped onto the pontoon and put her arm around his neck as he picked her up. "Hmm. This reminds me of last summer."

"Only you weren't quite so obliging."

"I didn't know you yet."

He carried her to the beach and set her down. "Next time, *you* carry me."

"Sure. No problem."

He walked to the boat. There wasn't much in it to tell him the where or why behind the chief suddenly taking the day off.

Poppie came up beside him. "No alcohol."

"And no fishing gear."

He turned away from the boat and looked inland, then called, "Chief!" He shook his head and called again, "Chief, it's Jasper." He looked at Poppie. "Bastard."

He went to the backpack he'd taken from the plane and slipped it on. "You up for a hike?"

"Sure."

They headed for a sandy trail meandering through the low brush and left the beach. "There's nothing out here but birds and insects, but stay close." He glanced at her. "Penelope."

"Right behind you, Deputy."

Every few minutes, Jasper stopped and called to James, but he never got a response. They kept going until they reached the beach on the far side of the island. Jasper took off the backpack and took out two bottles of water, then handed one to Poppie.

"I'm starting to believe I wasn't so off base about him falling off the wagon."

Poppie took his hand. "We'll find him."

Jasper put the pack back on. "Okay. Right or left?"

"Um." Poppie glanced both ways down the beach. "Right."

He started walking along the shore. "I swear, if he's passed out somewhere, I'm gonna be pissed."

It took an hour for them to circle back to where the boat and plane were. When they rounded the last area of high brush, Jasper stopped walking.

"Son of a bitch."

Poppie stopped too. "Is that—"

"Yes."

James was sitting on the bow of the boat and turned toward them when he heard them coming.

Jasper called out as they got closer. "What the hell are you doing here?"

James got to his feet. "I could ask you the same thing."

Jasper and Poppie approached James. "Mom was worried and couldn't decipher your cryptic message."

"I told her I was going fishing."

"Right. Something you haven't done in years, and apparently without any gear."

James sat. "I've been on my own for fifteen years. I'm not used to reporting my every move to someone else."

Jasper slipped off the backpack and let it drop to the ground. "She's not someone. She's Mom, your ex-wife, and apparently your...partner again. She deserves a little respect and communication from you. And on top of that, you ditched work and left me to cover for you on my day off."

"Jasper, you've had plenty of time off lately with the wedding..." He glanced at Poppie. "And such."

"That's not the point, Chief."

James stood again and looked at the sky behind Jasper. "I hope you brought camping gear with you."

Jasper checked the sky. "We'll be fine if we leave right now." A bolt of lightning crackled from the dark clouds, and he looked at James.

James shook his head. "It's not safe."

Jasper glanced at the sky again. "Surely you heard me calling you."

"Better get set up before the rain starts." He started walking toward the brush.

Poppie stepped in front of Jasper. "I don't understand you, Chief." Jasper took her arm, but she pulled it away. "We came here to make sure you were okay. Kat's worried about you. Maisy's worried about you. Jasper flew here because he cares what happens to you, and you have nothing to say?" She took a breath. "Do you have any idea what an amazing man your son is? Or how much he does for the town way beyond what's expected of a deputy. He's respected and loved by everyone. You may be Chief Deputy Whatever, but Jasper is the glue holding Gracie Island together." She swiped at a tear. "And you can barely be civil to him, let alone be thankful he cares enough to fly out here and look for you."

James stared at the sky for a moment, then turned and went up the trail.

Poppie turned to Jasper and growled. He put his arms around her. "Thank you. But he couldn't care less." He kissed the top of her head. "So you think I'm amazing?"

She laid her head on his chest. "I guess I shouldn't have said anything."

"No. It's fine. I'm impressed."

"Is he right about the storm?"

Jasper studied the clouds. "I'm afraid so." He stepped away from her and gave her a small smile. "We need to spend the night."

She frowned. "A campout. Yay."

"With the chief." He looked at the plane. "I need to get some supplies."

"Do you have to wade again?"

"No. I'll use the boat."

Jasper pushed the boat off the sand and jumped into it, then started the trolling motor. He moved slowly toward the plane, then pulled up beside the pontoon and shut down the motor. After tying the boat off, he stepped onto the pontoon and opened a cargo compartment. He took a tarp and a tent and dropped them into the boat. He then retrieved two sleeping bags and a canvas tote.

After depositing those items into the boat, he moved to the door of the cabin and went inside. A few moments later, he came back out with their coats and Poppie's purse. He got into the boat and headed for shore.

As he reached the beach, James came up beside Poppie and pulled the bow onto the sand. Jasper handed him the items he'd gotten from the plane and James set them in the dry sand above the waterline.

Jasper stepped out of the boat. "I've only got one tent. And I'm not sharing it with you."

"I'll make do."

Jasper handed him the tarp and one of the sleeping bags. James hesitated. "You sure you can spare them?"

"Just take them."

James took the tarp and sleeping bag with a nod, then returned to the trail. "You've got fifteen minutes before the rain starts."

Poppie looked at Jasper and he shrugged. "It's hereditary."

She picked up the canvas tote. "Well, that's the only thing you got from him."

They headed up the path and found James in a small clearing, rigging the tarp to protect him from the rain.

Jasper stopped. "I have a little food. Nothing much. I wasn't expecting to spend the night."

"I have my own. Thank you."

"Okay." Jasper started walking again. "We'll be about fifty feet further in the clearing on the left."

They arrived at the clearing and Jasper dropped the tent and sleeping bags, then took Poppie's hand. "You're awfully calm about all this."

"When I'm with you, it doesn't matter where we're at or what we're doing."

"Freezing our asses off during the plunge? Freezing our asses and risking our lives on the Dragonfly during a hurricane?"

"Having our first kiss on St. Patrick's Day. Picnicking in your house. Sneaking up to the apartment during the reception."

Jasper smiled. "Yeah. Okay. Let's go with your memories."

When he pulled the tent out of its case, Poppie asked, "Do you need help?"

"It's pretty self-erecting. Or... Is that a word?'

Poppie laughed. "I don't know, but I get what you mean."

The tent popped open and Jasper used a rock to pound the stakes into the dirt. Just as the rain started to fall, they tossed everything else into the tent and got inside.

Poppie looked around. "This is cozy."

"Just the way I like it."

She nodded toward the canvas tote. "So, what's in the bag?"

"Survival food. Nothing too exciting." He handed it to her.

She searched through the contents. "Not bad. We'll make it through the night."

"I don't suppose you've replaced that tiny bottle of rum in your purse."

"No. Sorry."

"Probably for the best."

The rain started coming down hard and Poppie put on her coat. "So, do you want to play Never Have I Ever?"

"We don't have any alcohol."

She handed him a bag of chips. "We'll substitute."

"Not nearly as fun." He opened the bag. "Can I go first?" She nodded, and he thought for a moment, then said, "Never have I ever ridden a bike."

"You're kidding." She took a chip and ate it. "How is that possible?"

"The weather and the condition of the roads aren't really conducive to bike riding."

"I suppose." She took a second to think. "Never have I ever...gotten intimate in a tent."

He smiled, then took a chip and ate it, then set the bag aside. "Seems like that's something we have the time and the opportunity to correct."

Chapter Twenty-Nine

"It's not too late."

The rain fell most of the night, but the wind wasn't too bad and the tent protected them and kept them dry. They talked for hours, mostly about Gracie Island and Jasper's experiences growing up on it.

Poppie was amazed and a bit jealous of the idyllic childhood the island seemed to offer to the children lucky enough to grow up on it. Jasper's story seemed to be from another time far away from the modern world she was raised in. It solidified her secret desire to live with Jasper on the island and raise their children there.

They were lying down, sharing the sleeping bag, and had just eaten granola bars and fruit leather. She put her head on his chest and snuggled into his side.

"You had a wonderful childhood, despite the chief."

"I did. And someday, if I'm lucky enough to have a kid or two, I can't see raising them anywhere else."

Poppie thought about Jasper's comment last summer about not planning on having children. Now that she knew he'd lost a baby when he lost Ivy, the statement made sense. But now, it seemed he'd changed his mind.

"So, you'd like to have children?"

He was quiet for a moment. "Yes. I would."

Poppie let the subject rest. She didn't want to push him. She hoped he meant with her. But she still wasn't sure, and didn't want to assume they'd get to that point. Marriage. Children. Although, them moving into the house together would be a major step in that direction.

When she heard his breathing become deep and regular, she knew he'd fallen asleep. Despite the storm outside the little tent they occupied, she felt safe in his arms. She wondered for a moment how the chief was faring, but she wasn't about to let it keep her awake. She pulled the sleeping bag a little higher over them, and let herself drift off to sleep.

When Jasper woke up, the rain had stopped, and by the light coming through the blue nylon tent, he assumed the sun was shining above them. He kissed Poppie on the cheek, then slid out from under the arm she'd thrown over his chest.

She mumbled, and he kissed her again. "Go back to sleep."

She moaned, then turned onto her side, putting her back to him. He tucked the sleeping bag around her, put on his coat and shoes, and unzipped the door.

The sun was indeed shining, and the drops of rain on the surrounding brush glistened in the light. The ground was wet, but sandy enough not to be muddy, so he stepped out and stretched, before zipping the door closed.

It was brisk, as most mornings in the spring were, but he loved it and he took in a deep breath of ocean air.

He went about twenty feet into the brush to relieve himself, but stopped short when he saw James doing the same.

"Oh. Sorry."

James held up a hand, then zipped his pants and turned to Jasper. "Pick a spot, Son."

Jasper went another ten feet, then turned his back to James. When he was done, he turned to find the chief still standing where he'd found him.

Jasper walked back to him. "Are you okay?" He looked closely at his father, who seemed tired and was pale.

"Sure. I'm fine." He rubbed the back of his neck. "Just a little stiff. Haven't slept on the ground in a while."

Jasper nodded. "I'm going to get Poppie up, then I guess we'll take off. Are you staying or…"

"You can tell your mother—" He stopped short and coughed, then rubbed his shoulder. "Tell her…"

"Chief?" Jasper started moving toward James, but wasn't quick enough. The chief crumpled to the ground before Jasper could break his fall. "Dad?"

James fell face first and Jasper turned him over and wiped the sand off his face. "Dad?" The color had drained from James' face, and his skin was cold and clammy.

After what seemed like forever, but was probably only a few moments, James opened his eyes. He groaned and rubbed his chest, then mumbled, "What the hell is wrong with me? I feel like an anvil is sitting on my chest." He tried to get up.

"Stay put, Dad."

"I'm okay." He swiped at the sweat on his forehead.

"No. You're not. You're having a heart attack." Jasper had never witnessed someone having a heart attack, but he knew the signs. He re-certified his first aid training every year, and James had all the classic symptoms.

James looked at Jasper. "Shit. Are you sure?"

"Pretty damn sure. I'm going to get you to the hospital."

"No. I'm fine. I just need to rest for a minute." He grimaced and grabbed his chest. Dammit." James took a hold of the front of Jasper's coat as the look on his face changed from disbelief to panic. "I can't die. Not here. Not now. Not before I—"

"No one is dying here today." Jasper patted James' arm. "Stay put." He got to his feet. "I need to go get Poppie."

"But I need to talk to you. There are things—"

"There will be time later, at the hospital." He turned and headed for the trail.

"Jasper."

Jasper didn't stop. He couldn't stop. Having this conversation now, meant there might not be time to have it later. And that was something he wasn't prepared to deal with. He jogged back to the tent and zipped it open. "Poppie." He stepped inside and she rolled over.

"Is it time to go?"

"It's the chief. I think he's having a heart attack."

Poppie sat up. "Oh my god"

"Get your coat and your purse. We'll leave everything else and I'll come back for it later."

Poppie put on her coat and shoes, then got her purse. "I'm ready." She stepped out of the tent. "Where is he?"

Jasper took her hand and started walking. When they got to James, he was leaning against a smooth, mossy rock. He was even more pale, and he was having trouble catching his breath.

Jasper knelt beside him. "We'll get you to the mainland. We just need to get to the plane." He took James' arm and helped him to his feet. Poppie took his other arm, and they headed for the beach. "Did you leave anything you need to bring? Do you have a gun with you?"

James shook his head. "Nothing of value." He stumbled and Jasper put his arm around him. "Didn't bring my firearm."

"Okay. Almost there." The thirty feet to the beach seemed much farther, and they were nearly dragging James by the time they reached the shoreline.

The tide had gone out, leaving the boat almost completely on dry land and the plane only ten feet from shore. Jasper contemplated his choices. He didn't want to drag the chief through the water if he could avoid it. But putting him into the boat first was an extra step and could cause more stress to James' failing heart.

Jasper decided the extra step would be better than wading through the cold water and climbing onto the plane's pontoon.

He looked at Poppie. "Can you take him for a minute while I push the boat into the water?"

She nodded and then buckled under James' weight. But she quickly adjusted as Jasper let go and went to the boat. It wasn't a big boat, only a twelve-footer, but it was still heavy when on dry land. Jasper put all he had into it, and after a moment, it seemed as though it wasn't going to budge. But adrenaline, along with a dose of stubbornness, took over, and the boat slid toward the water. Once it was halfway afloat, it became easier, and Jasper stopped pushing when just the bow was on the sand.

Jasper took a moment to catch his breath, then he and Poppie got James into the boat without too much trouble. Poppie sat next to James on the front bench seat, while Jasper shoved the boat another foot, then jumped in and started the trolling motor.

Reaching the plane, Jasper once again, tied the boat off and opened the passenger door on the plane. "Dad. I'm going to need you to help a little."

"I'll do my best."

Jasper climbed onto the pontoon, then James stood with Poppie's help, and Jasper was able to pull him up. Jasper then backed into the rear door and pulled James into the passenger seat. He buckled him in, then went out and helped Poppie, and she sat in the seat next to James.

Jasper looked in through the door at her. "I need to secure the boat, I'll be right back." He dropped into the boat and motored to the shore. Once there, he pulled it up as high as he could, then secured a line to a medium sized tree. He waded to the plane, hoisted himself onto the pontoon, then got into the cockpit.

He glanced at James and Poppie. "Okay, here we go."

James nodded, then closed his eyes. Poppie gave Jasper a small smile. "We're good back here. You concentrate on getting us to the mainland."

Once he was in the air and close enough to Gracie Island, Jasper radioed the station.

Maisy answered with, "Praise God. You're okay! What happened?"

"I'm pretty sure the chief is having a heart attack. I'm flying him to Colter Point. Can you have an air ambulance meet us there? Portland is probably your best bet."

"Right away. What else can I do?"

"Call Mom and fill her in. Tell her I'll be back this afternoon and figure out how to get her to Dad."

"Okay, honey. God speed."

"Thank you, Maisy. I'll check in when we land."

Jasper glanced over his shoulder. Poppie was talking to James, but Jasper couldn't hear what she was saying. When James nodded and almost smiled, Jasper sighed. *Maybe he's going to be okay.*

Poppie thought the best thing she could do was keep James talking, so since Jasper's childhood was fresh in her mind, she asked James if he had any anecdotes to share.

James took a breath and winced. "I wasn't around much when Jasper was growing up. But there is one thing that sticks in my mind."

Poppie patted his arm. "Tell me."

James glanced at her. "You're trying to keep me distracted."

"Yes. I am. So tell me."

James rubbed his left arm and hugged it to his chest. "He was about nine, I guess. Took it into his head to climb the mast in front of the Loft."

"Oh my goodness."

"He made it all the way to the cross piece. That's about twenty feet off the ground." James glanced at her. "He always was a stubborn kid."

"What happened?"

"Climbing up, he was only looking skyward. But once he got there, he made the mistake of looking down."

"Uh-oh."

"He froze." James shook his head at the memory. "His friends ran into fetch Kat, but she couldn't talk him down. So she sent the kids to get me." He closed his eyes for a moment and tried to catch his breath, which seemed to be inadequate. "By the time I arrived, there was a crowd of people watching and Jasper was fighting back the tears."

"Poor little thing. Were you able to talk him down?"

"No. Had to call Earl." He glanced at Poppie again. "Our electric guy. He has a truck with a lift and a bucket to get to the power lines. I went up in the bucket, but Jasper still refuse to let go. Said he wanted his mom to come get him." He took another moment to cough and catch his breath. "I could've forced him. But that didn't seem right. So I went down and Kat, bless her soul, climbed into the bucket without a second thought. Earl sent her up and Jasper went right to her, of course."

"They're very close."

James nodded. "That they are. When he was a kid, I figured that was enough. The boy had his mother."

Poppie shook her head and took James' hand. "He needed his father, too."

James nodded. "I know that now."

"It's not too late."

James closed his eyes. "I'm afraid it might be."

"I promise you, it's not. We'll get you better, then you need to talk to your son."

"Do you think he'll listen?"

"I know he will."

Chapter Thirty

"I prefer my pilots fed and hydrated."

J asper landed the plane in the water, then drove it to the end of the pier. A medical transport helicopter was waiting on the oversized dock, designed for that purpose. Jasper had brought several people here over the years to be transported to Portland or Augusta, but never a family member or even a friend. For most of them he also provided a return trip home, but a few never left the hospital. He hoped this wasn't a one-way trip for his father.

He shut down the plane as two men approached and tied it off. As he stepped out of the cockpit, two paramedics came toward him with a gurney, and Jasper went to greet them.

He shook their hands. "Thank you for getting here so quickly." He glanced at his plane. "He's in the back, and seems to be okay, considering."

"Any health issues we should know about? Medications?"

"He was a smoker for thirty years. Quit about ten years ago. He's also an alcoholic, but has been sober for seven or eight months. Medications, I have no idea."

"Okay. Thanks, that helps."

"He's been healthy other than that, though. I think."

"We'll take care of him." They continued to the plane and Jasper opened the door for them. James seemed worse than he had on the island as the medics helped him out of the plane and laid him on the gurney.

James reached for Jasper. "Call your mother."

"I'll get her here."

"You're chief, now. The town is in your hands."

"I'll take care of it until you get back."

James put a hand on Jasper's chest. "Son—" He coughed and gasped for a breath.

"I know, Dad." He held James' hand for a moment, then tucked it into the blanket covering him. "I'll talk to you soon." He took a step back as Poppie came up to the gurney.

She patted James' hand. "We'll see you soon."

James nodded. "Take care of him."

Poppie glanced at Jasper. "I will."

Jasper and Poppie followed the paramedics to the chopper, then stood back while they loaded James. Before they took off, one of the men came to Jasper and shook his hand again.

"We'll be there in twenty minutes or so. Will you be coming to the hospital?"

"I need to get my mother first. She'll be there in a few hours."

"Okay. You can call the hospital for information once he's checked in."

"Thank you."

Poppie took Jasper's hand, and they watched the helicopter take off. Once it was out of sight, Jasper bent forward and rested his hands on his knees.

"I need to sit down."

Poppie took his arm. "I've got you." She led him to a faded wooden bench and sat him down, then sat next to him. "Just breathe."

Jasper tried to take in a breath, but his lungs didn't seem to work. He felt dizzy and weak, and his head was swimming. "Shit." He took a shallow breath. "I should've let him finish saying what he wanted to say."

Poppie laid her head on his shoulder. "You'll get the chance to hear it."

He glanced at her. "Will I?"

"Yes."

"I'm having a panic attack, aren't I?"

"I believe so, yes."

He sighed. "I thought it only happened when you were...panicking."

"It happens when you're feeling overwhelmed. You just sent your father off in a medical helicopter. I think that qualifies."

"Second time in a week. I'm not the panicking type."

"I know. But sometimes you need to let go and let the emotion do its thing."

"Okay, Dr. Jensen." He got to his feet and tried to shake it off as he successfully took a deep breath. "I'd prefer emotion didn't run me over."

He walked to the edge of the pier and looked at the water. There were several boats visible, something he didn't see on the island any more. Colter Point was a thriving fishing community with a population five times that of Gracie.

As Poppie came up beside him, Jasper nodded toward a large vessel with 'The Dancing Dolphin' painted on its stern. "That's Matt Wembly's boat.

He left Gracie about ten years ago. His parents still live down the road from Lewis."

"I didn't think anyone ever left Gracie Island."

"Our population used to be about seven-fifty. When the fishermen had to go out further and further to make a good haul, they left. A few of them ended up here. The Gracie fishermen are scattered up and down the coast."

"Well, that's kind of sad."

"Back when the chief was a deputy, there were two of them under my grandfather." He took another breath. He was almost back to normal. "Now, we barely need the two of us."

"The chief enjoys having you do all the running around."

Jasper smiled. "Yeah. So he can sit on his ass in his office."

When a man came up behind them, they turned and greeted him.

He gave them a smile as he shook Jasper's hand. "Sorry to bother you. I'm Terry Grove. Are you Chief Goodspeed's deputy?"

"Yeah. Jasper...Goodspeed."

"Right, you're his son. How's he doing? He's going to be alright, I hope."

Jasper shrugged. "I think so."

"Well, we'll all be praying for him. He saved our town a few years back."

This was news to Jasper. "How so?"

"The fire. Ten years ago. He arrived with a crew from the island just in time. If they hadn't showed up, we would've lost the whole town."

"I wasn't aware of that."

"I guess you were at the academy at the time. At least, that's what he said. He was damn proud you were carrying on the family legacy."

Again, news to Jasper. He wasn't sure how to respond, so he just nodded.

Terry patted him on the shoulder. "I'm sure you're headed home, but if you need to eat first, we have the freshest seafood on the coast." He pointed toward a restaurant. "Salty Sam's. You tell them Terry sent you. It's on me."

"That's very kind, but—"

"No buts. You go get some food, and we'll make sure your plane's ready to go. We'll gas her up and such."

"Thank you."

"Don't mention it."

Poppie shook Terry's hand. "Thanks. We haven't eaten much. We'd love a quick bite before we take off."

"You're welcome, Miss...?"

"Poppie."

"Alright, Poppie. Nice to meet you both."

They headed to the restaurant and a young waitress greeted them.

"Two today?"

Jasper glanced at Poppie, feeling awkward about mentioning Terry's offer. "Yes, thanks." But the waitress seemed to know who they were.

She picked up two menus and started walking. "You came in with Chief Goodspeed."

"Yeah."

"Well, we'll all keep him in our prayers." She stopped at a table. "You sit right here and order whatever you like. It's on the house."

Poppie gave her a smile. "Thank you."

Jasper took a menu from the waitress. "We're in a bit of a hurry. So, can you recommend something that won't take too long?"

"Of course. The blackened halibut is always good. Rich can get that started right away." She glanced around the nearly empty restaurant. "Not too busy this time of day."

"Thank you. I appreciate it. And I need some coffee."

"Iced tea for me," Poppie added.

"Right away. Baked potato okay?"

"Yes. Thanks."

Poppie waited until the waitress left, then looked at Jasper. "So, you didn't know about the chief helping with the fire?"

"I heard something about some of the guys coming to help. I was never told they saved the day."

"And your father was bragging about you?"

"I find that hard to believe."

She reached across the table and took his hand. "I think the chief is, and has been, more invested in you than you think."

"Hmm. It would've been nice for him to verbalize it from time to time." He let go of her hand and leaned back in his chair. "Sorry."

The waitress returned with their drinks and a basket of rolls. After she left, Jasper took a roll and pulled it into two pieces, then took a bite. "I'm starving."

"I think lunch yesterday was our last meal."

"I need a phone. I should call Mom."

Poppie took her phone out of her purse and handed it to him.

"You carry this on you?"

"Of course. A habit I'll get over after a while, I'm sure. It's charged, too."

He looked at the phone for a moment, then turned it on.

"Do you want me to dial the number for you?"

Jasper frowned at her. "I know how to use a cell phone."

"Okay. Just asking."

He found the correct screen, then dialed the number for the restaurant.

Peg answered. "The Sailor's Loft."

"Hey, Aunt Peg, it's Jasper."

"Oh, honey, how's James?"

"He's on his way to Portland."

"And how are you and Poppie?"

"Fine. Getting something to eat real quick, then headed back. Can I talk to Mom?"

"Of course. Hold on."

In a few moments, Kat came on the line, sounding worried. "How is he?"

"He's on his way to the hospital. He was awake and talking."

"When will you be here?"

"We're leaving here in about thirty minutes."

"Okay. Be safe."

"We will. Love you, Mom."

"Bye, honey."

Jasper ended the call and handed the phone to Poppie. "First time in my life she didn't respond with 'I love you more'."

"She's distracted."

"I guess." He glanced toward the kitchen, then drummed his fingers on the table. "We should've left. I could've lasted another hour without eating."

Poppie handed him another roll. "I prefer my pilots fed and hydrated."

"I guess you'll never want to fly with me again after this trip."

"It's been an adventure. But flying's not too bad. I'm pretty sure you'll be able to talk me into going with you again once everything settles down."

"I'm going to hold you to that."

The waitress returned with their meals and set them on the table. It looked good, and Jasper was glad they had taken the time to eat. He picked up his fork and cut into his halibut.

After tasting it, he smiled at Poppie. "Okay. This is really good."

They ate quickly, and after leaving the waitress a generous tip, they returned to the plane. Terry greeted them. "It's all ready to go."

Jasper shook his hand. "Thank you. What do I owe you?"

"Just take care of your father."

Jasper sighed. "I don't know what to say."

Poppie took Terry's hand. "Thank you."

"No problem. Let us know how he does."

She nodded and put her arm through Jasper's. "Will do."

Jasper did a quick pre-flight check, then they boarded the plane. With a wave to Terry, they took off and headed for Gracie Island.

Chapter Thirty-One

"It fits, you know."

W hen Jasper and Poppie returned to the Island, Kat was packed and ready to go. Beryl had volunteered to go with her, and they'd take the ferry, then drive three hours to Portland. Kat hadn't owned a car for years since the restaurant was so close to her home. But Beryl kept a car on the mainland for shopping trips and such.

Jasper was glad Kat wasn't going alone. If Beryl wasn't taking her, Jasper would've considered saying "screw it" to keeping an eye on the town, and drove her himself.

They'd been gone a day now, and Kat had called Jasper several times with updates. It seemed the chief was doing well and was out of danger. But Jasper still wasn't convinced the danger had passed. He'd feel better when they were all back together on the island where they belonged.

Jasper didn't want to bother Poppie on her first night alone behind the bar. He was confident she'd do well, but Lance was on standby if she ran into trouble. So when he left the office after his first day as interim chief, he took the fire escape stairs on the back of the building to the apartment.

The day had been slow, and he spent most of it trying to make sense of James' filing system. Maisy took care of the general paperwork, but James handled and kept track of chief business and filed it in an old three-drawer wooden cabinet, which, as far as Jasper could tell, had no rhyme of reason to its order.

When a call came in late in the day, Jasper was thankful for the chance to leave the office. The call from Mrs. Waters was to report a suspicious sound coming from her mud room. It's the type of call the chief would've sent his deputy on. Since Jasper didn't have a deputy to send on the frivolous calls, he went himself.

The suspicious sound turned out to be a rat couple procreating behind the washing machine. Jasper chased them outside and then had to spend thirty minutes drinking a cup of coffee with the lonely Mrs. Waters, whose husband was in Augusta for the week visiting his mother. Apparently, Mrs. Waters wasn't too fond of her mother-in-law, and chose to stay home. It was all more information than Jasper wanted or needed to hear, but the coffee was good, and by the time he got into town, it was time to call it a day.

So, at seven o'clock, he climbed the dangerously steep steps hanging off the back of the Loft, then went down the hall to the apartment. The dogs heard him coming and met him at the door. He squeezed by them and closed the door before they could escape.

"Okay, guys. I know. I just need to change my clothes, then I'll take you out."

Appearing as though they understood him, the three dogs sat by the door and watched him change out of his uniform and into a pair of jeans and a flannel shirt.

Since they were in town, and not at his property, he carried Poppie and put Blackjack and Sam on leashes. It was a bit precarious going down the fire escape, with Sam wanting to go full speed and Blackjack unable to do so. But they made it safely to the alley, then headed to the beach two blocks away. Once there, Jasper let the two big dogs off their leashes and put Penny down. Sam, the free spirit, took off running toward the surf and started chasing the waves as they rolled onto the sand. Blackjack watched and seemed jealous, but then settled for smelling a large piece of driftwood. Penny quickly took care of business, then wanted to be picked up again.

The breeze coming off the ocean was too chilly for her, so Jasper put her inside his jacket, then started walking down the beach. Blackjack followed him and after a few minutes, Sam joined them. They went a quarter-mile before turning back. Blackjack was just shy of two weeks into his recovery and Jasper didn't want to tire him. When they arrived at their starting point, Jasper leashed the two dogs and they headed for the apartment. On the way back, they ran into Dr. and Mrs. Hannigan on an evening stroll.

The doctor took a quick look at Blackjack. "He's doing well."

"Yeah. We took a short walk on the beach. He did fine."

"Good to hear." He patted Sam's head. "And who's this?"

"Sam Jeffers' dog."

"Ah. I see. Seems you're quite the dog magnet these days."

"Not sure how that happened. But, yeah. Went from one tiny mutt to three dogs in two weeks."

Hannigan laughed. "Why are you here in town? I thought your house was about done."

"I've been staying at the apartment above the loft...with Poppie."

Mrs. Hannigan smiled. "That's great news, Jasper. She's a lovely girl."

"Yeah. It's ah... Yes, she is."

The doctor patted Jasper's shoulder. "We'll see you around. Hopefully not in the office."

"Hey, it's been almost a week."

By the time Jasper got the dogs settled in, it was after eight. Having missed dinner, he went down to the kitchen to find something to eat. Peg was pulling double duty what with Kat being in Portland, and she gave Jasper a tired smile when he came through the stairwell door.

"Hi, honey. How was your first day as chief?"

Jasper perched on a stool next to the prep table. "Slow."

"Well, good. Are you hungry?"

"Yes. I'll take anything."

Peg glanced at Ben, one of the cooks. He usually worked on the days Peg didn't, and with her on busy nights. While Kat was away, he'd be working more, while Peg took over Kat's baking duties.

"Can you throw one of those steaks on the grill for Jasper, hon?"

"Sure thing." Ben looked at Jasper. "Medium?"

"Perfect."

Peg filled a bowl with clam chowder and set it in front of Jasper. "I talked to Kat not long ago. James is doing well, but they want to keep him a couple of days."

Jasper nodded. "I talked to her this afternoon. She said they'd be home Thursday if he continues to improve." He blew on a spoonful of chowder. "I'll be glad to have them back. Doesn't seem right for them not to be here."

"I know what you mean. This is the longest Beryl and I have been apart in years."

"It was great of him to go with Mom. I didn't want her going alone. But I really wasn't in a position to take her."

Peg picked up three plates of food. "I'll be right back. These are going to the bar. I'll check on Poppie."

"Thanks."

By the time she returned, Jasper had finished his chowder and was eating a slice of bread. She set a beer in front of him. "This is from Poppie. She said to tell you, she's doing fine."

"Thank you. I didn't want to bug her, but I was curious how she'd do on her own."

"She's had a good teacher."

Ben brought the steak with a side of fries and handed it to Jasper. "Enjoy, Chief."

"Thanks, Ben."

Peg leaned on the counter. "It fits, you know."

"Chief?"

"Yes. I know you didn't expect it this soon, but you'll be fine."

Jasper cut into his steak. "It's just temporary."

"I'm not so sure. They'll want him to take some time off. I'm not sure he'll want to come back."

Jasper thought about the prospect of being chief for real, then shook his head. "He'll be chomping at the bit to come back. What's he going to do if he retires? He'll go stir crazy."

Peg smiled. "Don't count on it. He's got something else to occupy his mind now."

Jasper grumbled. "Don't remind me."

"Sweetheart, it's a good thing. They really want it to work this time."

He jabbed his fork into a bite of steak. "I don't know."

"Give it a chance. I know you don't trust James. But trust Kat. She's no fool."

"I know that."

"Then trust that she knows what she's doing."

Jasper frowned. "I'm trying."

Peg squeezed his shoulder. "Try harder."

He put on a smile. "Better?"

"Yes. Much."

The day Kat, James, and Beryl returned to Gracie, Jasper went to see them after work. The chief looked better, but he still wasn't back to normal. Even though he was sixty and had smoked and drank most of his life, Jasper always thought James looked pretty good for his age and had never thought of him as old. But now, he seemed to have aged ten years. He was still pale, and he appeared to be tired.

Jasper smiled and hoped his father couldn't read his thoughts. "Welcome home." He kissed Kat and shook James' hand, which still felt a little clammy.

As Jasper took a seat in one of the chairs, James leaned back on the couch. "How's everything been? Any problems?"

"Absolutely nothing going on. The most exciting thing I did was round up Mace's horse when it got loose and was running down the highway."

"Well, good. I didn't want your first week of interim chief to be too crazy."

"No too much danger of that."

James smiled. "I guess you're right. Not every day we get to work a murder case."

"That's a good thing."

James sat forward and was quiet for a moment. "I'm a bit tired from the trip. But I'd like you to come see me tomorrow, if you get a chance."

"Um, sure. Tomorrow afternoon?"

"That'll be fine." Kat was in the kitchen and he glanced in that direction. "Go spend a minute with your mother, and I'll see you tomorrow."

Jasper stood. "Okay. Get some rest." James nodded, and Jasper escaped to the kitchen, where he found Kat making coffee. "Is he supposed to be drinking that?"

Kat glanced over her shoulder. "It's decaf."

"Eww. He's going to hate that."

She turned and leaned against the counter. She too, seemed tired.

Jasper went to her and took her hand. "Are you okay?"

"Just glad to be home. For a day or two, I wasn't sure he'd be coming back with me."

"He did. And he's going to be fine. It's going to take some time."

She leaned into him and laid her head on his shoulder. "When Maisy called me. I thought the worst. I thought...we'd lost him."

"I know. Me too." He leaned back. "But we didn't. You two have a lot of years ahead of you...together."

"You're still not sure about that, are you?"

Jasper shook his head. "I'm working on it."

She stepped away and poured a cup of coffee. "Do you want a cup?"

"No. I'm going to go home and make some real coffee. Ten bucks says the chief will be drinking real coffee before the weekend's over."

"You think I'm that easy?"

"No. I think he's that stubborn." He took a moment, then asked. "Do you know what he wants to talk to me about tomorrow?"

Kat shook her head. "No. But I know you should come find out."

"I will." He kissed her on the cheek. "See you tomorrow, Mom. Love you."

"I love you more."

Chapter Thirty-Two

"I'll have what he's having."

Jasper tried not to bother Poppie too much while she was working, even though she repeatedly told him to come see her. Thursdays were generally slow, so after he left Kat's house he spent another hour at the station, then went to the Loft.

There were a few couples at the tables and four men at the bar. Poppie spotted Jasper when he came in and gave him a smile. He went to a stool at the end of the bar, away from the customers, and sat down. Poppie delivered a beer, then went to him.

"Chief Goodspeed. You finally made it."

"I figured you wouldn't be too busy tonight."

She took his hand. "I'm never too busy for you." She put a napkin in front of him. "Is it a beer night or a shot night?"

"Beer's fine." She started to leave, but he held onto her hand. "It's also a kiss the customer, night."

Poppie looked at the other patrons. "Okay. If you insist."

Jasper grinned. "Just this customer."

"Oh." She leaned across the bar and he raised in his seat to meet her halfway across. They kissed, then he sat again.

Duke, one of the four men at the bar, called out. "Hey. I'll have what he's having."

Poppie shook her head. "Sorry. That was a special order for law enforcement only."

"Bummer. I guess I'll just take another beer, then."

Poppie left Jasper to serve Duke, then returned with a beer for Jasper. "Have you seen your mom and dad?"

"Yeah. They're both glad to be home."

"How's he look?"

"Like he had a heart attack a week ago."

"He's going to be fine, though, right?"

"I think so." Jasper took a sip of his beer. "He wants to talk to me tomorrow."

"That sounds promising."

"How so? If it's anything personal, he'll chicken out."

"I don't think so. Things have changed."

"Hmm. We'll see."

Poppie gave him a sly grin. "I have some news that might distract you from a conversation with your dad."

"Lay it on me. I could use something else to think about."

"I know who Mellie's mystery man is."

Jasper smiled. "Who? And how the hell did you find out?"

She leaned on the bar and whispered. "I overheard Lance and Mark talking." She smiled. "Seems Lance is pretty happy with his...tough and unpredictable lady."

"No way."

Poppie nodded. "He didn't know I heard him. But I know what I heard."

"Mellie and Lance?" He thought about it for a moment, then nodded. "Okay. I can see that."

"They're a bit of an odd couple."

Jasper tilted his head. "Some might say that about us."

"Yeah. But they're like Jasper and Poppie 2.0."

Jasper spent an hour at the bar, but when it started getting busier, he left so Poppie wouldn't be distracted. After a second beer and another kiss, he went upstairs to walk the dogs and read a book until she was off at ten.

When Poppie came into the apartment, she found Jasper asleep on the couch with an open book on his chest. She watched him for a few minutes.

"Sound asleep at ten-thirty."

He stirred, and she kissed him on the forehead, then took the book from under his hand. Jasper opened his eyes and gave her a smile.

"Hey."

"Hey, back." Poppie set the book on the table, then crawled between his outstretched legs and laid her head on his chest.

Jasper yawned. "I tried to stay awake."

"Tell me about your day."

"Not much to tell. I took Lance to Wilda's, and he made a list of all the repairs she needed for her house. Then, of course, we had to stay for coffee and cookies."

"Of course."

"Also, I got a report of another stray causing trouble."

She tilted her head up to him. "I'll let you handle that one on your own."

"Thank you."

"Bo got back to me about Sam's house. He's decided not to buy it. So, I called Evan and told him I'd keep trying to find a buyer."

"So, let me get this straight. Today you were a home repairman, dog catcher, and realtor. Chief Goodspeed, you wear many hats."

"I also did the monthly expenditure reports. Actually, I watched Maisy do the monthly expenditure reports."

"You've learned how to allocate. That's good."

"I'm learning." When the phone rang, Jasper groaned.

"Do you need to get it?"

"I'm dispatcher tonight."

"Another hat." She got up so he could sit and he reached for the phone.

"Chief Goodspeed." He listened for a moment. "Okay, Mellie. I'll be right there. Don't do anything stupid." He laughed. "See you in a few."

As he hung up the phone, Poppie watched him. "Trouble at the Pelican?"

"Tom Evers."

"Oh, boy." She watched Jasper attach his gun to his belt and drop his badge into his shirt pocket. "Will you be long?"

"I hope not." He kissed her. "In case you're asleep when I get home."

When Jasper came into the bar, Tom had Bryant Witmer in a headlock and Mellie was moving toward them with her bat. Jasper came up behind Mellie and put a hand on her shoulder.

"I don't want to have to arrest you, too."

She relaxed a fraction and stepped back while Jasper approached the men.

"Let him go, Tom."

Tom glanced over his shoulder. "This is a private conversation. It doesn't concern you."

"I'm pretty sure Bryant would disagree. What do you say, Bryant?"

"Get him the hell off of me."

Jasper took another step closer. "Give it up, Tom."

Tom hesitated a moment, cursed, then shoved Bryant into a table with three empty glasses on it. The table fell over and the glasses all broke when they hit the floor, along with Bryant.

Jasper moved toward Tom, took his arm, and bent it behind the man's back. When Tom struggled, Jasper said, "Don't fight me. It's only going to get worse from here."

Tom relaxed and let Jasper cuff him, then Jasper set Tom in a chair, and glanced at Bryant, who was still on the floor but sitting up. "Are you okay, Bryant?"

Bryant nodded and stood. "I'll live."

Jasper pulled Tom to his feet. "Let's go. I think this time you'll be spending some time in the county lockup in Portland. I hear it's not nearly as nice as our jail."

"Don't care."

Jasper nodded at Mellie. "I'll come back to help you clean up."

"Don't worry about it. I got it."

"I'll be back in thirty."

Jasper put Tom into the Jeep, then drove to the station. Since all of Tom's information was recent from his last visit on St. Patrick's Day, the booking process was quick and Jasper put him in a cell, then left a note for Maisy, letting her know they had a guest. She'd make sure Tom got breakfast in the morning, and when Jasper came in, he'd contact Portland and arrange for a transfer. This was Tom's third strike in two months, so he'd be spending some time as a guest of Cumberland County.

Jasper got back to the Pelican, just short of thirty minutes later, and finding the door locked, he tapped on the window. Mellie came to open the door for him, and he took the broom from her hands as he went inside.

He went to the pile of broken glass and swept it into the dustpan Mellie held for him. As she disposed of the glass, Jasper picked up the table and two chairs. After making sure they weren't broken, he joined Mellie at the bar.

"Was Bryant okay when he left?"

"Yes. He was fine. Just pissed off."

Jasper sat on a stool and Mellie set a shot glass in front of him. "I should probably go."

"One drink. I owe you."

He nodded toward the glass. "One drink." He watched her pour, then took a sip. "I'm pretty sure I know who your secret guy is."

She took a sip of her whiskey and then tilted her head. "Really? Did someone open his mouth?"

Jasper didn't want to get Lance in trouble with Mellie, so he shook his head. "No. I used my awesome powers of deduction. They're part of the whole law enforcement package."

"You're so full of shit. Okay. Who do you think it is?"

"Will you come clean if I'm right?"

"Maybe."

Jasper laughed. "Well, then maybe I won't tell you."

"Fine. If you're right. I'll let you know. But if you're wrong, I'm not going to tell you who it is."

"Fair enough." He finished his shot. "Lance."

"Dammit. How'd you figure it out?"

Jasper shrugged. "Like I told you. I'm good at my job."

"And like I said. You're full of it." She filled their shot glasses again. "What do you think?"

He picked up his glass. "Put that bottle away." He took a sip of the second shot. "Not many local guys could handle you. And of those that could, only Lance is worthy of you."

"Well, we'll see about that."

Jasper downed the rest of his whiskey, then set the glass on the bar. "I need to go home."

"Which is Poppie's apartment?"

"Yes. Until the house is finished."

"And then?"

"Then she'll be moving out of her apartment and into my house."

Mellie smiled. "That makes me very happy."

Jasper stood. "Me too." He tapped the bar. "I'll see you, Mellie."

"Bye Jasper. Don't go spreading the news about Lance around."

"I won't tell a soul."

Poppie was in bed when Jasper got back to the apartment. He quietly undressed, then slipped into bed next to her. She rolled toward him and put her arm across his chest.

"How'd it go?"

"Tom's spending the night in jail."

"Did he go peacefully?"

"Mostly. After he threw Bryant across the room."

"He's the town black sheep."

"Only when he's drinking. Which is more often than not, lately."

Poppie kissed Jasper. "Were you drinking with him? You smell like whiskey."

"Sorry. I guess I should've brushed my teeth again." He kissed her on the forehead. "I had a quick drink with Mellie."

"Hmm."

"Hmm? What's that mean?"

"Nothing."

"Poppie. You don't need to be jealous of Mellie."

She laid her head on his shoulder. "I'm not." She sighed. "Okay. I'm a little jealous of her."

"Mellie and I are friends. She's been a really good friend to me, actually."

"I know. She's so...cool and interesting."

"You're the only woman I find interesting."

"Thank you. You're sweet. But that's probably not true."

"Trust me. It's true."

"What makes her a really good friend?"

Jasper took a moment. "Two people got me through the last two years. Mellie was one of them."

"Will you tell me about it?"

He stuffed another pillow under his head and pulled Poppie in closer to his side. "On the day of Ivy's funeral, I went home and didn't leave for a month. I wouldn't even let Mom or Aunt Peg come into the house. They checked on me every day and left me food and necessities on the porch, but I didn't want to see them or talk to them. On January fifth, Mellie showed up with a couple dozen tiny tacos from the deli and a bottle of whiskey."

"You let her in?"

"Not at first. But she wouldn't leave. She sat on the porch and waited. About forty-five minutes in, it started raining. Thirty minutes later, I opened the door. She stayed for hours and listened. I talked, I ranted, I...cried. No argument or judgement from her. She just listened."

"She is a good friend."

"For the next year, she was there for me. Whenever I wanted to talk, I went to her. She got me through."

Poppie was quiet for several moments. "Who was the other person?"

"Lewis. He was the other side of the coin. When I needed a distraction, I went to him. I'd help him on a boat, or show up at his door. We'd eat chili or junk food, drink beer, and not talk. We'd play cards, or take a hike. It didn't matter what we did. It only mattered that we did it together."

"I love my brother."

"So do I."

Poppie sat. "I'm glad you had them."

"Me too. I'm not sure where I'd be right now if it wasn't for them. Certainly not here with you."

Chapter Thirty-Three

"That's Chief Deputy Sweetheart."

J asper went onto the porch of his mother's house with trepidation and opened the kitchen door. James was sitting at the counter with a cup of coffee, and Kat was cutting a slice of poppyseed bread, fresh from the oven. They both smiled at Jasper when he entered the room.

"Hope it's not too early. I wanted to come by before I went to the station."

Kat set the bread in front of James, then went to Jasper and hugged him. "Of course not, honey. Take a seat. I'll cut you a slice of bread."

Jasper sat at the counter, leaving an empty stool between himself and James.

Kat set the bread in front of him. "Do you want some coffee?"

He glanced at James. "Is it decaf?"

James grumbled. "Apparently, that's all we have in the house now. Better get used to it."

Jasper picked up the bread. "I'm good. Just water, please."

Kat shook her head and picked up her coffee cup. "I don't know why you two are making such a big deal about it. It's not that bad." She took a sip. "It tastes the same."

Jasper shook his head. "It's not the taste, it's the jolt of caffeine surging through your bloodstream."

"Which is exactly what you father doesn't need."

James grumbled again. "I'd almost rather be dead."

"Don't say that."

"Sorry."

Jasper took another bite, then glanced at James. "So, you wanted to talk to me?"

James pushed his cup away, then glanced at Kat. "Hon, can you excuse us for a few minutes?"

"Of course. I'm headed into the restaurant, anyway." She kissed James on the cheek, then Jasper on the forehead, and headed for the door. She picked up her purse and a jacket on her way out. "You call if you need anything, James."

"Will do." He waited until she left, then started to get to his feet. "There has to be a can of decent coffee around here somewhere."

Jasper put a hand on his shoulder. "Sit. Let me." He got up and began searching through the cupboards. In the back of one of them, he found a half-can of French Roast. He held it up. "Eureka!"

"Atta boy. Get a pot going."

Jasper started the coffeemaker, then poured out the coffee in James' mug. "Do you want another slice of bread?"

"Sure. One more. I'm sure she's keeping track."

Jasper cut two more slices, then leaned against the counter next to the coffeemaker.

James cleared his throat. "So. There are a couple of things I wanted to talk to you about. We'll get the business part out of the way first. I've been talking with Sheriff Benton."

"Okay."

"I put in my retirement papers."

Jasper pushed away from the counter. "You did what?"

"I'm done, Son. It's all yours."

"You're retiring?"

"Yes."

"You don't want to take some time to think about it?"

James shook his head. "I've been thinking about it. Long before the heart attack."

"You could cut back first and see how you feel in a couple of months?"

"Jasper. I'm done. If you think you're not ready, you're wrong."

"No. I'm ready. I'm just surprised, that's all."

"Poppie was right. You're the glue holding Gracie Island together. The town loves and respects you."

"Thank you. But isn't it ultimately up to Sheriff Benton?"

"I've already talked to him about that, too. He's sending the paperwork over in a few days."

The coffee finished brewing and Jasper poured two cups, then sat at the counter again. He took a sip, followed by a bite of the bread.

"Okay. I guess that's that, then. Does Mom know?"

"Of course. We've talked about it at length. I know you don't believe it yet, but I'm not the man I was fifteen years ago."

"I'm trying to get there."

"That's all I can ask, I guess." He drank from his cup again. "Now this is coffee."

Jasper didn't want to ask, because he already knew the answer, but he did anyway. "So, what's the other thing?"

"Let's go into the living room." James got to his feet and picked up his coffee cup.

Jasper did the same and followed his father, who sat on the couch with a groan. He sighed. "Take a seat, Son."

Wondering if his father was actually going to go through with it, Jasper set his cup on an end table, then sat in the chair next to it.

James took a moment before he spoke. "I know saying I'm sorry to you is like trying to empty the ocean one bucket at a time—inadequate and damn overoptimistic. So, I'm not going to do that. I know I failed you as a father. I tried to be a good boss, but maybe I was piss poor at that, too."

Jasper started to say something, but James raised a hand to stop him. "Let me finish." He took a breath, and then a sip of coffee. "Thank God you had your mother, because she raised a hell of a human being. I'm damn proud of you, Jasper. I always have been. But I could never quite find the words to tell you." He drank some more coffee. "I know I can't make up for the last thirty years, but I'd like to go from here, if you're willing. You don't really need a father anymore, but I'd like to be there for whatever you do need. If you'll let me, that is."

Jasper stared at the wood floor for a moment, then stood and took a turn around the room. He checked the photos on the mantle, and went to the window and watched a robin searching for something to eat, before turning to James. He walked back and sat in the chair again.

"I just have one problem with all of this."

"Okay. I figured you'd have several."

Jasper picked up his coffee cup. "What the hell kind of filing system were you using? I can't make heads or tails of it."

James laughed. "I'll come by tomorrow and run through it with you." He took another sip of coffee. "Or maybe the day after tomorrow. I'm retired now."

Jasper grinned. "I don't know what the hell you're going to do with yourself."

"Whatever the hell I want."

After Jasper left his father, he returned to the apartment and found Poppie in the shower.

"Hey, beautiful. It's just me."

She peeked around the shower curtain. "I'm glad you identified yourself. I was expecting someone else."

"Are you about done in there? I have something to tell you."

"I'll be right out."

Jasper left the bathroom and went onto the deck. *Chief Deputy Jasper Goodspeed.* It was sooner than he expected. But he was ready. He thought about what James had said about being there for him. "Time will tell, Chief. Time will tell."

Poppie opened the door. "So, what's this news you have for me?"

He looked at her wet hair. "Inside. You'll catch your death out here."

She held the door for him, then followed him to the couch. "You know that's an old wife's tale. You can't catch a cold from being outside with wet hair."

"You can on Gracie Island. Trust me. Just ask those guys who had to hold the lanterns on the point before they built the lighthouse."

She sat next to him. "They're all dead."

"Exactly. Making my point."

"Okay, come on. How'd it go with your father? I assume it's what you want to talk to me about."

Jasper leaned back. "You're looking at the new Chief Deputy."

"Like the actual chief?"

"James Goodspeed has retired."

"No way." She threw her arms around him. "That's fantastic. Congratulations."

"It won't really be much different. The job won't change much."

"But you'll be in charge. Will you have a deputy to boss around?"

"Yes. But hopefully, I won't be bossing him around."

Poppie laughed. "Of course not. You'll be a very good boss." She turned toward him. "Is that all he wanted to talk to you about?"

Jasper took a breath. "No. He got a little... He apologized, sort of, with a metaphor that didn't quite fit. He then asked if we could start fresh and have a relationship that resembles something a father and his grown son would have."

She put a hand on his thigh. "I'm so happy for you."

Jasper shrugged. "We'll see how it goes. I'm willing to give him the chance and see if he actually follows through."

"He will."

He kissed her, then got to his feet. "I need to get to the station."

"That's right. No more slacking off."

Jasper frowned. "I never slacked off." He thought for a moment. "Okay, I guess I've slacked off some. But it's hard to look busy when there's nothing going on."

"I hope that's always the case. Fender-benders and cats in trees is fine with me." She stood as well. "I thought firemen rescued cats from trees."

"Well, I'm also in the volunteer fire department, so..."

"Right. Another hat for you to wear."

He kissed her again. "I'll see you tonight."

"Come to the bar."

"I will."

"Have a good day, Chief Deputy Goodspeed."

"You too, Penelope."

When Jasper went into the station, Maisy greeted him with, "Good morning, sweetheart."

"That's Chief Deputy Sweetheart."

She smiled. "He told you."

Jasper folded his arms across his chest. "You knew?"

"Of course."

"For how long?"

"Since I talked to him while he was in the hospital."

"Wow. I can't believe you were in cahoots with the chief."

She handed him a cup of coffee. "So, how does it feel?"

Jasper checked his watch. "It's been less than an hour, but so far, not bad."

"You'll need to move your things into your father's office."

"Why can't I keep my office? What difference does it make?"

She nodded toward James' office. "The chief has always been in that office. The new deputy will be moving into yours."

"When's that going to happen?"

"Soon. Maybe as soon as next week."

Jasper frowned. "Wait a minute. You're in cahoots with Sheriff Benton, too?"

She patted his cheek. "I've been running this office for almost thirty years. Nothing goes on here that I don't know about."

"Maisy, you deserve a raise. I can do that, right? Give you a raise?"

"Of course. Right after you file the paperwork with the county."

"Paperwork?"

"I'd be glad to do it for you."

"Perfect. Give yourself a raise."

"Thank you, Chief. Now go clean out your office."

"That will entail moving the plant."

"Then get to it."

Chapter Thirty-Four

"I love rain when the sun's shining."

Jasper stood in the middle of the living room and studied the freshly spackled walls. He'd be happy with white, but Poppie had a more colorful vision of how the new house should look. He was half afraid of what she might come up with.

They were down to the interior details now. The outside was finished, including the wrap-around porch, complete with several chairs, a table, and a gas grill. The appliances were being delivered in a few days, along with the couch Poppie had picked out. The last step was painting the walls, then it'd be ready for the rest of the furniture. Jasper had left it all in Poppie's hands, and wanting to get the perfect pieces, she'd only settled on the couch so far. Last night, while snuggled into the bed at the apartment, Jasper had suggested she at least find a bed she liked. He didn't want to spend his first night in the house, sleeping on the floor.

318 THE BEST WOMAN

When the door opened, he continued looking at the walls. "Okay, I'm game for anything other than pink or purple. Or black, of course. Black would just be—" He glanced at her. Something was wrong. He turned and put his hands on her shoulders. "What's going on?"

Poppie put her arms around his waist and buried her face in his chest. When she started crying, he held her until her sobs subsided.

When she let go of him and stepped away, she wiped her eyes and said, "I'm sorry."

Jasper shook his head. "For what? What's wrong?"

She went to the wall and put her hand on it. "I can't help you pick out paint colors."

"Why?"

"My parents. I just got a call from my dad."

Jasper sat on a stepladder next to a bucket of spackle and a folded tarp. "Are they okay?"

Poppie shook her head. "They were in a car accident yesterday."

Jasper stood and went to her, then took her hands. *"Are they okay?"*

"My dad's pretty shook up. He has a broken leg and a concussion."

Jasper wiped the tears from her cheeks. "And your mom."

Poppie shook her head. "She got the worst of it."

"Is she—"

"No. But she's in the hospital in critical but stable condition." She sniffled. "Whatever that means."

Jasper pulled her in for a hug. "I'm so sorry."

Poppie stayed in his embrace for a moment, then stepped away again. "I have to go home, Jasper. They need me."

"Of course. I know." He sat on the stepladder again. "I could go with you, but..."

"No. I'd never ask you to do that. Besides, *Not Interim Chief Anymore*, Goodspeed, you have a town to serve and protect. The island needs you. Your family needs you. All three hundred of them."

He studied the plywood floor for a moment. "I have to ask." He looked at her. "You're coming back, right?"

Poppie nodded. "Yes. Of course. I just don't know when." She put her hands on her hips. "You're not going to get rid of me that easily."

Jasper stood and went to the wall. He ran his hand down it. "Then we'll paint when you get back."

Poppie took his hand and led him into the spare bedroom. "You need to quit calling this room the guest room."

"We're not going to have any guests?"

She walked around the room, then came to him and put her hands on his chest. "This room is going to be the nursery."

"Really?"

"Yes."

"And I don't suppose I have any say in the matter?"

Poppie shook her head. "You know how stubborn I can be."

"Yes. I do."

"You also need to think about adding on a room or two."

"I just finished building the house and you want me to do a remodel?"

She smiled. "When I come back, we're going to fill this house with babies."

Jasper took a step back. "How many babies?"

"We'll know when we hit the magic number."

He walked to the French doors and looked at the deck and the ocean. "So, the magic number could be one. Which means I wouldn't need to add on to the house."

Poppie came up behind him and put her arms around his waist. "I'm thinking it's going to be closer to three or four."

He turned and put his arms around her. "Hmm. How about one at a time?"

"That works for me." She kissed him, then took his hand. "I don't want you to come to the ferry with me. But can we take the dogs to the water before I go?"

"Sure."

They went out the door and Jasper whistled for the dogs. Penny was on the porch and came running around the corner of the house. Blackjack and Sam were exploring the tree line, but came at the sound of Jasper's call.

Poppie picked up Penny, and they headed for the beach. It was a lovely, calm day, warm for May, with only one cloud in the otherwise clear sky.

Poppie set Penny in the sand and looked at the cloud. "Is that a rain cloud?"

Jasper checked it out. "I hope so. I love rain when the sun's shining."

She took his arm. "I know you do." They started walking slowly down the beach. "I can come to visit. I'm sure I could work it out."

Jasper shook his head. "It'd be too hard. When you come back, I want you to stay. No more leaving."

"But you'll call me, right?"

"Of course. Every night. I'll call and talk to you until you fall asleep." He bent and picked up a seashell. "Take this with you."

"I don't need anything to remind me of you. You're pretty hard to forget."

He laughed. "Keep it. Bring it back. And we'll return it to where it belongs. It belongs here on the beach. And you belong here with me."

Penny ran to her and barked. "Along with Penny, and Blackjack, and Sam."

Jasper nodded. "And, apparently, a house full of kids."

Poppie kissed him, then looked up when she felt raindrops falling. "It's raining."

Jasper grinned. "It certainly is." He held out his arms and turned his face to the falling rain.

Poppie stepped away, and he looked at her. She put a hand out. "Stay. Just like that. I fell in love with you the last time it rained when the sun was shining. Stay here on the beach. Enjoy the rain. I'll see you soon."

"Penelope?"

"I love you Jasper." She held up the seashell. "We'll be back soon, where we belong."

More Books By Leigh Fenty

The Deputy
The Best Woman
The Chief
The Family Man
The Visitor

About the Author

Leigh spends her days with cute, sexy guys. Unfortunately, they're on paper. But still, not a bad way to spend your day. She also writes about strong, independent women, who can hold their own against these irresistible guys. She's not a pure romance writer, because she breaks the rules a bit. But that's the fun part. Leigh's stories have adventure, family relationships, and the struggles life throws at you sometimes. But boy always meets girl. They tussle a bit while they figure out what they really want. Then find their happily ever after. Even if it's not what they thought it was going to be.

Made in the USA
Middletown, DE
02 September 2024

60218385R00181